TAMING THE BAD BOY

JOLIE MOORE

MOORE DIGITAL
MEDIA INC

This edition published by
Moore Digital Media Inc
1125 N Fairfax Ave, Unit 46071
West Hollywood, California 90046

Cover: Najla Qamber Designs

eISBN: 978-1-944179-93-9
ISBN: 978-1-64414-010-9

for Kay Rogal/Brenda Longstreth (1966-2014)
Brenda was a fellow author and dear friend. She was the first
person to read this book and encouraged me to publish this story.
Her death was wholly unexpected. She will be missed.

ONE

DAISY

"THIS IS SO OUTSIDE MY WHEELHOUSE," Nari Yoon said. My best friend was nearly naked in her tiny bra and panties. Disgusted, she threw a heap of clothes on my living room floor. "Why, oh why do you think going to a gay bar is a good idea?"

"Can you please, please stop using 'wheelhouse'?" I held up my hand talk show style. "It's one of those damn words that's way overused." Then, as if talking to an impatient three-year-old, I explained it to her again, slowly. "I'm not making as much money on the straight stuff anymore. The old pros in the online forums, *fora*, whatever. They keep telling me I need to try a few male/male sites. I'm *not* a gay man. I just want to spend one night trying to put a finger on their tastes. The upside is that no one will hit on you. I promise." Nari hated going to bars. A Korean woman in a straight L.A. bar was the heat seeking a million penis shaped missiles.

"Fine," Nari said, stalking back to my room. She was in. Thank God. I would not have the courage to do that on my own. "So what do I wear to a gay bar?" she yelled. I didn't answer. She'd work it out fine. Nari did not need my help with fashion.

Twenty minutes later, Nari emerged from my bedroom, this time fully dressed in a body skimming, grey silk mini dress with a stand-up collar, and some kind of embroidered flower down the front.

"Um, that kind of screams Asian," I said. This was a woman who did not like to be boxed into a stereotype.

"I like the dress. My mom got it made for me in Singapore a few years ago. I never get to wear it. If no one is going to hit on us, I can be as Asian as I want, *capisce*?"

"That's Italian." I fished in my always full, Neverfull tote and pulled out the crumpled list I'd printed earlier. I looked at my watch. "So do you want to go to Big Fat Dick Friday or Fresh Meat Friday?"

Nari snatched the list from my hand. "Daisy Fletcher! Would you talk to your mother with that mouth?"

I shook my head, but the truth was that my mother would probably relish that kind of talk. She thought *I* was a prude. "Big dicks or fresh meat?" She put a red press-on nail to her matching ruby lips. "Are they both in Boystown?"

I shook my head. "Nope. One is right here. MJ's is on Hyperion."

"That settles it. A mile drive is doable. Plus there won't be any cruising on Rowena. Sunset is a bitch on weekends."

"We're already here?" Nari asked seventeen minutes later.

It had taken us longer to get down the elevator, into the car, and out of the garage of my condo complex than to drive to the club. I was lucky and found a spot on a residential street around the corner, squeezing my twenty-year-old Mercedes between two hulking SUVs.

How had I never noticed the club before? I'd been on that street a thousand times, buying shit wine at Trader Joe's, less shitty wine at Gelson's, or really expensive wine at Say Cheese next door.

Despite all those alcohol runs, the nondescript gray stucco building had never registered on my radar. I'd even been to that Burrito King across the street without noticing it. I looked around the streets of Los Feliz. Nothing about the upscale Los Angeles neighborhood screamed debauchery.

"Do you like this car? Seriously?" Nari liked her bling new and shiny. Any Mercedes older than a lease term was not on her approved list.

"It has airbags." It was a tank. Even with soccer mom SUVs and Hummers barreling down the road, I felt safe in the car.

"You will never pick up a guy in this thing."

"I don't want to pick up a guy." I'd seen the worst of men in my chosen profession. I did not need one in my life.

She looked up and down at my choice of clothes. "That's obvious."

I didn't think I'd done too badly. I was wearing a Ralph Lauren black silkish jumper with spaghetti straps and a matching faux-fur collar jacket. Modest pumps. My Connecticut born-and-bred mother would have been proud. "It's appropriate," I said.

"You dress like that Charlotte from *Sex and the City*, only with less, um, *sex* in this city," she laughed at her own joke. It was a high pitched cackle of a laugh. I started to think dragging Nari along was not a good idea. She would not be incognito at MJ's.

"Her character *was* from Connecticut," I said in my own defense. After living in Madison for my first eighteen years, and Olde Haven for four more, there was nothing I knew better than appropriate dress. Political fundraiser, baby shower, high school reunion, I knew exactly what to wear. After Nari, Ann Taylor was my second best friend.

"You haven't been in Connecticut in ten years."

"I'm thinking of going to our college reunion."

"And what are you going to tell them about your day job?"

"I'm a web designer."

She cackled then snorted. "Yeah, whatever. Let *me* talk to the bouncer. I'll get us in."

MJ's was, well, wow. In the last ten years I'd seen almost every sort of sexual display there was. But even this, men in full sexual display, was a lot to take in. I hoped I'd remembered my small leather notebook. I could probably make a lot of money in gay porn. Dozens of men loitered outside. Whether they were waiting to go in or waiting to go home with someone was anyone's guess.

Nari walked past the line of men and up to one with a clip-board and headset. A few hand gestures from her, and the bouncer sprung the latch and lifted the velvet rope. That was why I'd brought her. She could get into any place in L.A. Me, probably not. Without surgically enhanced tits or a skirt that stopped just below my ass, my appropriately dressed self wasn't getting in anywhere that opened after dark. Nari was always my ticket in.

Inside the club was a whole other story. The music was loud and the bass thumping. Men in the teeniest, tiniest underwear imaginable danced on boxes strategically placed around the club. How any man could ever have a conversation in such a place was a mystery. Truth-be-told, there didn't seem to be much talking going on.

Nari dragged me toward an open booth, and I followed her —knocking a few guys in the groin along the way with my poorly placed bag. My face tightened with embarrassment. Oops. I looked down at the tote hanging over my shoulder. Clearly this was a clutch kind of place. I mouthed 'sorry,' and shoved the purse as far into the booth as possible.

Nari volunteered to get us drinks. While she was gone, I watched. I itched to get that notebook out, but didn't want to look like a gawker at the zoo. I was as liberal as the next person in L.A., but didn't have any gay male friends. I hadn't even been to the infamous West Hollywood Halloween parade, even though I'd always secretly wanted to go. Except for various billboards along Santa Monica Boulevard promoting condom use, warning against meth use, or urging HIV testing, I didn't know a damn thing about the city's gay culture.

"What the heck took you so long?" I shouted, sipping the Manhattan she'd brought me.

"'Cute Asian Girl' does not work here," she shouted back. Nari put her glass of red wine on the table and we checked out the show. Not a single soul bothered us for at least an hour as the club filled to capacity. I kept trying to count heads, checking my numbers against the official limit on the fire marshal sign. I swore I'd leave, research or not, if the club looked like it exceeded capacity by too much.

A group of four or five guys pressed against the table, nearly upsetting the dregs of my drink.

"Can we share the booth?" the oldest looking one asked. His few gray hairs made me wonder what he was doing in this club.

Nari looked like she was going to shake her head. I intervened. This would be research gold.

"Sure." I pulled Nari's arm and scooted us to the top of the horseshoe shaped booth. The men piled in on both sides, except the asker, who went for drinks. I looked them over a little more closely.

"We're here for his bachelor party," one of the men said, jabbing a thumb toward another.

I wasn't the most savvy person in the world, but two gay men having their stag party in the same place seemed counterintuitive. So was one of them not gay? I smiled tentatively.

"So who's the groom?" Nari asked what I couldn't.

"I'm Scott, the straight guy," the blonde said, raising his

hand. Political correctness crisis averted. "My fiancé figured I couldn't get in trouble here. So she enlisted Rafe and Gabe to bring me out."

I studied the guys for the first time. They were your run-of-the-mill above average L.A. guys, except the guy next to me. His arm brushed against mine, and our eyes locked. He looked good enough to eat. Too bad he was gay, and too bad I didn't date. I pulled my right hand from my lap and extended it toward him. "I'm Daisy."

"Rafe," he said, grabbing the whisky or bourbon one of the guys had brought to the table. They'd got served a hell of a lot quicker than Nari. I put my outstretched hand back in my lap. Scott pointed, introducing each man in turn. They downed their drinks and left for the dance floor.

"Save our seats," the one called Arturo said.

"O-okay," I said. They disappeared into the gyrating mass of male flesh.

Half an hour later, they came back sweaty and far more tipsy than they'd been when we first met them. Drinks appeared again.

Nari looked at Gabriel and hot Rafe in turn.

"Are you Korean? Rafe?" She didn't keep the disdain from her voice when pronouncing his name. I shoved my right leg against hers.

They looked at each other. "It's Raphael, actually." Rafe/Raphael answered. "Our mom is from Incheon."

Nari said something in Korean. To my ears it sounded like "*An-yŏng-ha-se-yo*," which even I knew to be 'hello.' I watched a lot of Korean drama. It was quickly becoming a second language.

"Sorry," Rafe shook his head. "My Korean is shit."

Nari sat back. "Oh." Although she'd been born in New Jersey, her parents spoke strictly Korean in her house. Their only friends were from the small, tight-knit immigrant community in Riverside. To her, Raphael not speaking the language would make him one of those who dismissed their heritage like so much detritus. She hated those kinds of Koreans.

He looked at me. I'd been ignorable before. Now, in light of the evil looks shooting from Nari's eyes like laser beams, I was a likely refuge. "So, you're Daisy." Undeservedly elated, I nodded. "What are you gals doing here?"

"Just wanted a girls' night out without the guy pressure." I invoked our cover story.

"Guess that's not a problem in here. Do you live out this way?"

"Yep, I'm a Los Feliz girl." I did my gringo pronunciation, making it sound like Felix the cat. "You?"

"West Hollywood. Rent control. My brother lives in the same building." Well, that was expected.

"Is it crazy, living there?" My face flushed hot. I didn't want him to think I assumed every night in every apartment in West Hollywood a den of iniquity.

"No, it's a pretty quiet street, except for the tour buses." He accepted another drink, slammed it back, then looked at me again. More closely this time. That stare made me shiver. It was too bad he was gay, because we had a spark. I started wondering just how gay he was then shrugged it off.

People are born gay, it's not a 'lifestyle' choice, I admonished myself. My not so magic vajayjay wasn't going to turn him straight. I looked back into those chocolate brown eyes, trying not to get lost in their depths. He answered a question I hadn't asked. "F. Scott Fitzgerald died in my building. Huge tourist stop."

"He died in your building in West Hollywood. The *Great Gatsby* guy?"

"Yep. Keeled over of a heart attack." He turned away again.

I wanted to do anything to keep him talking. The warmth of his leather-clad leg against mine was what I'd been missing all night. I just hadn't known it.

"What do you do?" I asked. He hesitated for a bit. Hope burgeoned in my chest. Maybe he had a job like mine. Something you couldn't quite tell anyone about until you sussed them out. Radical feminists and religious zealots never got the straight dope.

"I'm a comic."

I could barely hear him above the latest song, louder than the last. Did he draw comics, like the funny papers?

"How does that work? I keep hearing newspapers are dead."

He squinched his very even black brows and gave me a funny look.

"Rafe, you have to do it!" Arturo yelled.

"C'mon, you're famous for it," one of the other guys chimed in.

"You know I've retired Rafe," he said.

Rafe or Raphael, which was it? Inside jokes were the hardest for those on the outside. I settled in to watch the back and forth. This was going to be good. I could tell.

Finally, the fiancé went for the kill. "It's my last day as a single man. You have to do this for me. All the fun is about to get sucked out of my life." He gave a little boy pout that seemed incongruous on a guy built like a linebacker.

Rafe acquiesced. "I need another drink for this." He snatched fiancé Scott's. "Lindsay will thank me for this." He downed it in one swallow like the others that preceded it. In the hot club, the swish of air turned my leg cold as he stepped from the booth and went to confer with the DJ. No matter how I craned my neck, I could no longer see Rafe.

Madonna's Vogue replaced Beyoncé on the turntable. The club suddenly went black. A single spotlight appeared on one of the dancing platforms and Rafe stood there in skin tight black leather pants and a black silk, button-down shirt. Clothes that had looked ordinary moments ago were sexy as hell under that light.

The din that had been constant, plummeted to a low murmur. I looked at the guys' expectant faces. Then shivered in anticipation. What the hell was going to happen? Then the music got loud again.

"Strike a pose," Madonna said.

And Rafe did. It was an incredibly sexy pose which I should have expected. I'd been in that damn club for nearly three hours. It had been nothing but posing from incredibly hot, incredibly unavailable men. With every beat of the music, she sang and Rafe undid one button after another.

The shirt sailed toward the table. I dreaded it touching the alcohol that had spilled on the wood. Real silk wouldn't survive it. So I stood and caught it in mid air. I was rewarded with a broad wink. I pulled the shirt to my chest, and I couldn't help noticing the heady scent that rose from it. Nari glared at me. After sending a brief apology to the dry cleaner who was going to have to fix it, I balled the shirt up and pushed it deep into my lap.

Lyrics got suggestive. The tight ribbed black tank Rafe was wearing close to his skin, came off as well. I didn't try to grab for it this time. I was already in for a stiff lecture.

Bumping and grinding, Rafe was butt down on the platform undulating to the beat, the tight leather pants obscuring nothing. The names of movie and sports stars blasted from the speakers. The top two buttons of his pants came undone. Hollywood's female icons thumped with the bass. The zipper came down.

I knew what was coming. How could I not? I couldn't look away. I could look all day. Looking was okay. Like the black and white video of the song, lights pulsed, throwing the club into black and white relief.

A quick black out, and the pants were gone. I must have missed the shoes and socks, because Rafe was gyrating on the platform almost as naked as the day he was born, save for some black boxer briefs shot through with silver threads.

Those threads were only on the front center, and back of the shorts, highlighting what was underneath. Before I knew it, he was letting his body go with the flow. It was a nice flow. His skin was golden, and bathed in a sheen of sweat. The lights cast blue, red, and ended in gold on him. Silence. A single beat. And it went dark again.

I didn't care if Nari thought I was crazy. I clapped and hooted as loudly as his friends and those around me. The lights and music started again, but Rafe was gone. Another of the inter-changeable hot go-go guys took to the platform. The replacement dancer's nearly naked form cooled me down right quick.

I pulled at Gabe's sleeve. "Wow, your brother was great out there."

He laughed. "It used to be part of his show. But he stopped doing it a couple of years ago."

His show? Did he draw cartoons while dancing? I didn't get to ask anything further. Rafe came back to the table dressed in his tank and pants. He looked around the table at everyone. "That is the absolute L-A-S-T time I do the 'Rafe' thing." He looked at the guys with a devilish squint. "Merry Christmas, *L'Shana Tova, Gung Hei Fat Choy*. I am officially retired."

He sat back and crossed his arms. The guys all laughed. "Lovely meeting you ladies," Scott said, and they all piled out of the booth. And just that quickly they were gone. If I hadn't been holding Raphael's shirt in my hands, I wouldn't have believed he'd ever been there.

After ten more minutes, music and lights that hadn't bothered me before, started driving me crazy.

"I've had enough. Let's go get something to eat." I shoved Rafe's shirt into my bag. I'd gotten some research done and landed a souvenir. Not a bad night all around.

"I'm all over that," Nari said. She had a hollow leg.

We pushed through the crowd and out the door. A heavy hand come down on my shoulder.

"Are you Daisy?" I nodded hesitantly at the bouncer. I wasn't moving until he was done. At least he didn't have a gun and a badge. I had a not-so-irrational fear of the police. I wondered what faux pas I could have committed in there, other than having a vagina.

Maybe they were going to ban me forever for the purse injuries? The bouncer slipped something from the spring loaded clip on his board and thrust it into my hands. It read Raphael Augustine and had a 323 number. "This guy wants his shirt back."

"I vote for Alcove," Nari said five minutes later, swinging her legs into the passenger seat of my car.

"C'mon. Let's go to K-Town," I whined. "*Bugeoguk* would be perfect right now."

"You're not hungover, Daisy. I don't think one drink in three hours is going to put you down. I want red velvet."

"Fine." I drove over to Hillhurst and parked on the street. We stood in line behind inebriated late night partygoers and ordered our food. Nari got enough to feed a family of four, and I got a plate of hummus and chips. The after-dark menu was designed to soak up the night's alcohol. The Alcove did not do late-night salad.

Nari rebuffed the advances of no less than four different men between the cash register and the table. Fortunately, we found a small unoccupied table on the patio, posted our number stands, and waited for our food.

"If we'd gone to Koreatown, maybe you wouldn't have been hit on."

Nari waved a hand. "Can't win. I don't want to date any of these men—white men with a fetish or Korean men whose families want me for my degree. Whatever." She eyed my bag, tucked halfway under the table. "*Do not* call Rafe."

"But he'll need his shirt back."

"You're attracted to him." How could she tell? I'd had two boyfriends and maybe three dates in the years we'd known each other. Not enough men for her to type me.

"He's gay. So I'll drop off the shirt, and that'll be it. I swear."

"Drop off?" Nari started fishing in my bag. Her muffled voice came up from under the table. "Have you heard of the U.S. Mail?"

"What are you doing in my purse?" I asked, poking my head under the table. We came back up when the server brought our food to the table.

"I want to see if this is even worth it." She pulled the seriously crumpled shirt out, shook it, and peered at the label in the dark. "Damn," she muttered. Nari picked up her phone off the table, hit a button, and used the light from the screen to read the label. This time her 'damn' was a drawn out, three syllable affair. "It's a Just Cavalli. Three hundred dollars easy at Neiman Marcus. He's gonna want this back."

"Just what? Why do you know that?"

"You know J. Crew. I know Rodeo Drive."

"Isn't Neiman on Wilshire and Roxbury?" I knew enough to know Neiman's hulking department store girth was *not* on Rodeo Drive.

"You get my point. Call him. Get his address. *Mail* the shirt. Lose his number."

"Why do you feel so strongly about this?"

"Because my gaydar is gyrating like there's a lightning storm."

"And you think I'm that hard up?"

"No, I think he's got your catnip triumvirate. He's cute, he's Korean, and he's unobtainable."

TWO

RAPHAEL

I NEEDED a few hairs of the big ol' mangy cur that bit me. And I needed my favorite Just Cavalli shirt back. But first things first. I looked at the address I'd logged into my phone weeks before. That looked about right. I pulled through the gates of some party facility in the Topanga National Forest. What had happened to Malibu beach weddings?

I walked across the gravel parking lot and stepped into a cavernous wood hall. Various people milled about arranging flowers and chairs and plates, doing all the pre-wedding jazz. I pulled one chick aside. Her blond hair was sleeked back in a ponytail. She wore a black bow tie. I could do things with that strip of silk. Maybe the wedding thing wasn't going to be so bad after all.

"Where can I get something to drink?"

She looked me up and down and gave me a half-smile. Not bad at all. "There's a lounge over there. The bartender is just getting set up."

I tugged at the tie. "Catch *you* later?"

Her smile was neither inviting or discouraging. I could turn her around later. That drink was my immediate concern for now.

Laid on the charm and persuaded the bartender to give me a double shot of Wild Turkey before the bar opened. Hope they didn't charge Lindsay's family extra for that. I pulled my sunglasses back down. Too many damn windows in the place. I couldn't wait for the sun to go down. I was not a daytime person. Could have been a vampire in another life—or the next life. I pulled the little notebook from my other pocket, searching for a pen. I could make a bit out of that.

I wandered around, rubbing the folded paper nestled deep in my pocket. Hated nights like these. Because my job was to be funny, people thought it okay to enlist me to entertain them at every damn occasion. Last night was case in point. I'd retired Rafe years ago. When my comedy got better, I needed to be naked less. Nudity was for baby comics. But that bit had gone down in infamy. Then there I was hugging the pole like a twink.

As soon as I learned to say no to that shit, the better. I followed the signs to the dressing room. My Arizona black sunglasses weren't enough. There had to be about a thousand high wattage bulbs on the wall. I turned off the make-up lights surrounding the mirrors, closed the heavy wood door, and propped my feet on the vanity. Got out a pen and polished up the act. I was on in an hour.

DOWNED MY THIRD DRINK, sidled up to the mike, ready to go.

"Fornication," I pretended to slur. A few titters of nervous laughter went through the crowd. That got their attention. 'Statlers' always did. "For an occasion such as this...." I started the real speech. Did the usual thing, thanked the hosts, and the band. "I'm honored to be Scott's best man. But I did ask him if

I'm the 'best man,' why isn't Lindsay marrying me?" Another laugh. Amateur joke.

The hangover of the night before faded away. I put down the champagne in my hand. Wouldn't need any more alcohol tonight. "When he first approached me about marriage, I thought he was asking for my hand. I tried to let him down easy because Proposition Eight hadn't been overturned yet." Easy liberal crowd. Easy laugh. People always assumed I was gay.

"Coming up with a best man speech is hard. Thank God for Google. Early yesterday morning, I started researching best man speeches on the Internet." I paused for a beat. "Five hours later, I started to look for speech ideas." That got a big laugh. I wonder if they'd think it was funny if they knew it was true.

"Seriously," I shook the paper in my hand. "Scott. I'm trying to read this speech, but your handwriting is awful." More laughter. I looked at Scott's parents. "I think I'm supposed tell everyone here about your most embarrassing moment." Stage whisper. "But I think the statute of limitations isn't up yet on that one. So we'll skip the criminal justice portion of this speech." Shit, that one fell flat. I hated doing new material before a crowd that expected a show. Moving on. I did the rest of the speech straight. I'm not a half-bad actor. There were a few tears. But weddings did that to people. They would have cried about almost anything. I could see the natives were getting restless. Time to end this thing.

"Even Stevie Wonder could see what a great couple Lindsay and Scott are. Wishing you many years of happiness." Cursing myself for not substituting the arguably more famous Ray Charles, I raised my untouched glass. "Let's toast the newlyweds."

I came off the dais to applause. That attention, that reaction was what I lived for. It was a high like nothing else. I sat restlessly in my seat as the wait staff started serving dinner. The cute blonde waitress came to our table carrying four salads. When she bent down next to me I put a hand on her back. "What's your name?"

She assessed me. I knew I was good looking. I didn't get to the ripe old age of thirty-three without an accurate assessment of my charms. But I was half-Asian, and looked nearly one hundred percent Korean. Gabriel looked way more white than me. It always took a little extra oomph in my game to get women past the tiny penis, Asian men aren't masculine stereotypes. "I'm Raphael," I said.

"Rose," she whispered. She looked around nervously. Rose probably was supposed to keep hustling.

"Do you have a break?"

"After dinner, between dancing and the cake."

"I'll look for you," I said with finality.

She scurried off. Rose was intrigued. I could tell. Adrenaline pumped through my veins. The chase was on.

The minute dinner was cleared, and the band started in on the dancing, I was out of there. The previous night's dancing was enough. It was the last I was going to do for a while. I went to the door nearest the kitchen and followed the scent of cigarette smoke.

The sea of white oxford shirts made it easy to spot the employees on break in the nascent moonlight. Rose was standing by herself, downing a shot of something. Tequila, mostly likely. She sucked a lime I hadn't seen and licked salt from the back of her hand. That was hot. I grabbed her wrist and pulled her around the side of the building.

"Hey—" Her protest was half-hearted.

"Hey, yourself." We walked back in another door, and I grabbed a candle from a ravaged appetizer display. I pulled her into the dressing room, shut the lights and closed the door.

I leaned against the rough plaster wall, and pulled her up

against me, hard. I laid one on her lips. Yep, it had been tequila and a good one from the taste of it.

"How old are you, Rose?"

"Twenty-one," she said, not blinking. As I watched her pupils dilate and obliterate the blue from her eyes, I knew I had her. And I did.

My timing was perfect. I was back just in time for the cake cutting. Scott and Lindsay stood there looking nervous, posing for pictures they'd have to live with for the rest of their lives. I felt, rather than saw my brother sidling up next to me. "Where have you been?"

"Around."

"You always do this shit, Raphael. Did you forget that you were supposed to dance with the matron of honor or Scott's mom? He picked you instead of me because you're good with people."

I was immediately pissed. "So I was runner up?" Gabriel and Scott were a year ahead of me in school. The groom had been friends with both of us since we'd moved from K-Town to La Crescenta when I was eleven and Gabriel twelve and a half.

"That's not what I meant."

"So why didn't he pick you, then?"

"Because Lindsay's family doesn't really do gay." Gabriel was as flaming as a torch. Had been for as long as I could remember.

Lindsay's family had settled in Pasadena well before the first Rose Bowl. Their attitudes hadn't evolved much since the early part of the twentieth century. "Then fuck 'em. Why should I try to make everything perfect for them? It's a big world out there."

"Because it's a wedding," Gabriel said with exasperation. I'd always found it ironic that he was the most traditional in our family. He'd been the biggest advocate of 'No on 8' because he'd been dreaming of going down the aisle since we were kids marrying off my G.I. Joes and his Ken dolls.

I didn't want to argue with him. I wanted to go home and relive that dressing room experience one or two more times. I apologized profusely then shucked and jived the best I could to make up for my absence. I did what I was supposed to do. And when the cake was done, I was done.

I popped Scott and Lindsay into their limo. Took Scott's tuxedo for drop off. And got into my car. As I was about to pull out, Rose ran across the gravel parking lot. For a moment, I thought about stopping her and getting her number. I rarely did a repeat, but maybe I could make an exception one time. Then she slid into the backseat of a Volvo SUV. The driver looked like somebody's mom. And there was a little boy in the passenger seat. For a moment, I got a queasy feeling in my gut, but I dismissed it as the ill effects of alcohol. Like so many of the others, I'd never have to see Rose again.

THREE
DAISY

"DID YOU CALL HIM?" The inquisition came after the hug. Nari took off her shoes, helped herself to a glass of water and wandered into the alcove off the living room—my 'office.' I lived in there. The living room, not so much.

I looked around the apartment, empty save for the two of us, and played dumb. "Who?"

"Cut the bullshit. Did you call that guy from the bar?"

I looked across the living area. I was sitting in my favorite office chair, and the freshly laundered shirt was hanging on the balcony door. I could barely see the subtle design on the shirt-front through the dry cleaner's plastic. I'd pinned the card with his number to the plastic and paper covering the garment.

"Not yet."

"Call him. Get it over with. Otherwise you'll build this up."

Nari would annoy me the entire night. And I wanted my Korean barbecue sooner, rather than later. "Fine." I walked from behind the desk, past the couch, and oh-so-deliberately plucked the card from the garment bag, picked up the phone and dialed. The phone rang a few times before I got voicemail. *Raphael Augustine, here. If you're interested in booking me, call my manager*. The disembodied voice recited a number. *If you need me, leave a message.*

Looking away from Nari's expectant face, I stuttered the beginning of my message. "Hello. Um, hi. This is Daisy Fletcher. I'm the girl, I mean woman who caught your shirt the other night at MJ's. I dry-cleaned it. I have it here. Let me know when you can get it. It looks expensive. Oh, my number is three-two-three..." I looked at the ceiling. Why did I forget the number I'd had for ten years at the oddest times? I hurriedly blurted the rest of the number before I had a second brain fart. "In case I didn't mention it, I'm Daisy Fletcher. Spelled the regular way." The computer cut me off before I could make a bigger fool of myself. When it asked if I wanted to rerecord, I itched to press '1' and try again, but just hit 'talk,' ending the call.

"Wow, that couldn't have gone any worse," Nari said. She folded her impossibly thin self into a more comfortable position on the couch. "Let me know when you're ready."

I went back behind the desk and shut down the computer in one click. "I'm ready."

Nari looked like she'd half dozed off while flicking through her phone. "Oh, wow. Okay."

Her surprise was warranted. I usually took forever to leave the apartment. It was the one hazard of working from home. Once I sat down in that damned chair, I always had the urge to tweak a website, or look at my stats. And if I opened my e-mail or the *GoFuckYourself.com* website, I was sucked down the rabbit hole, only to return hours later. But I was done for the night. I wanted food, I didn't have to cook.

"So my honorary Korean sister, where are we going?"

"You know how Soot Bul Gu Rim number 2 on Vermont closed?" Nari nodded. "Well the word on the street is that the owners opened a new place, Cho Dae Bak in the same place."

"Same owners, same location?" Nari asked. I nodded. "So how is it not the same restaurant?"

"I don't know. But I want innards and it had—has a special platter."

Nari faked going for her phone. "I'm going to call my mother and tell her we were switched at birth. You are so the daughter she would have loved."

"C'mon. You know how hard it is to get anyone to eat Korean food with me." I was whining but didn't care. "Everyone in L.A. has gone vegan or has some kind of soy allergy."

Nari came along. She always did. I knew she felt guilty about leading a super non-Korean life, save for the doctor job, and if she called her mom and told her about dinner, it would win her points. In what game, I don't know, but points were always good. Plus, I got the bonus of having a native speaker order food. As far as I was concerned, it was a win-win situation.

KOREATOWN WAS MORE crowded than usual. The parking was always bad in that part of the city, but not every restaurant was crowded to the gills like they were tonight. Even the valets were waving me away.

"What's going on tonight?" I asked Nari as I circled the block for the third time, looking for a space for my car.

While I waited with crossed fingers for someone to back out of a space, she looked at me like I hadn't graduated kindergarten. "It's Valentine's Day."

My head fell back against the tan leather headrest. I should have guessed that. Traffic had been down, way down today. My usual customers weren't sitting around surfing the internet, looking for 'love.' They'd been out with their real-life wives and girlfriends experiencing actual relationships.

I'd have to get hustling tomorrow morning. The letdown

from all that real world contact would lead to a boost in traffic. Maybe tonight I'd throw up a quick page targeted to all that Valentine's disappointment in time to be picked up by the ever crawling search engine bots.

Once we got into the restaurant, the wait wasn't too long for a seat at the counter. Unlike the endless couples holding hands and gazing into each other's eyes, we didn't need a booth for privacy. Before our order of various meat and innards came to the table, the smell of grilling meat made my mouth water.

Nothing I'd grown up with in Connecticut compared to the sights, smells, and tastes of Koreatown. I didn't think I'd be sorry if I woke up Korean one day. Coming from a homogeneous culture with a lauded food history seemed so much better than the crap beer and worse burgers that accounted for American fare. Once the waitress brought our order and started cooking meat on the grill, Nari started in on me.

"When are you gonna quit this and get a real job?" Sometimes she was worse than a nagging mother.

"I can't believe you're bringing this up." She hadn't bothered me about it in a couple of years. I thought we'd put it behind us for good. "You sound like someone's Korean mom." It was my best shot. I hoped it would keep her out of my hair for the night.

"Cheap shot." I guess it wasn't my best. I crossed my arms over my chest and leaned sideways, away from the verbal onslaught. "Answer my question."

"I make an honest living. I'm not hurting anyone. Why should I give up my job?"

Nari expertly flipped meat with chopsticks, gently resting cooked pieces in cups of lettuce on my plate and hers. "Um, because you can't tell anyone about it. Because you're not making what you used to. Morality aside, it's a dying business."

"Drying up, my ass. It's a hundred billion dollar industry. And that figure has more than doubled since I started."

"Would you get into newspapers, or magazines, or television? I'm sure all of those make a zillion dollars for Rupert Murdoch. He doesn't like to share."

I tried to stop my eyes from rolling. "Well no, obviously." Nari looked like she was going to cross her arms in triumph. "But if I had one of those jobs slaving for that Aussie come lately, I'd sure as hell hold onto it."

"You can't even tell your mother what you do."

I added *ssamjang* to some meat, wrapped it in a leaf and took a bite. Eating kept me from squirming in my seat. Her inquisition was having the desired effect. "If I told my mother, she'd want to help." Not one cackle at my attempt at levity. Damn, she was on a tear.

"If it's all so above board, why is it a secret? I think you're ashamed—"

"I'm not ashamed!" I wasn't exactly proud, either. "If I worked in corporate at Wal-Mart, I probably wouldn't tell anyone. Big tobacco, nope. Maybe not even big Pharma. You've been to a cocktail party in L.A. I'd be eaten alive by the morality police if I admitted to doing the big corporate thing. The same people who think nothing of exploiting folks on reality TV would be all over my ass about the activities of consenting adults."

"Bullshit, Daisy. I'm so tired of this. For the past ten years whenever we meet anyone new, you're this nebulous web developer or brand consultant. It's pretty sad that your friends and your family are too shallow to delve any further. But if you're not ashamed of pimping out tits and ass—then I think you need to just let it hang out."

This was the weirdest argument we'd ever had. "So you want me to tell everyone or quit? Why are you on me about this?"

"Because you're complaining more and more."

"It's what adults do. We work. We get off on Friday. Then we bitch about our bosses, hours, our crazy coworkers. Then we drink and start all over again on Monday." To emphasize, I snagged a passing waiter and asked for a bottle of *soju*. How many times had she complained about the wonky patient record system, or the registered nurse who'd somehow landed a job overseeing all the doctors in her clinic.

"Don't forget the gay bar."

"Why did that bother you so much?"

"I don't know. It's not like you were carrying a pro gay marriage banner. You're looking for ways to take money out of gay men's pockets."

"Um, every business owner is looking for ways to take money out of somebody's pocket. I wasn't discriminating." Nari poured me a shot glass of the rice wine liquor. I lifted the spirit with two hands and drank. The forty proof liquid burned fire in my mouth and throat. "If the waitress asks if we want *bokkeum bap* at the end of our meal, it's out of the kindness of her heart?"

"So, you're going to—what—build your master porn network until you're—what—fifty, sixty?"

"It's only temporary..."

"You've been singing this same song since day one."

"You're not—"

She steamrolled over me. "We graduated from college. You decided you weren't taking any crap New York jobs that would keep you living at your parent's house forever. Fine, I get that." She actually paused to take a bite. It was hell keeping that hollow leg filled. "Then you move out here with me. Decide you're not going to take any crap PA jobs, or live off my parent's largesse *even though* you could have lived for free."

"It's not like that..." But it was exactly like that. I didn't want to stay on the east coast. A million internships and jobs that paid barely more than minimum wage littered New York

City like Broadway after a ticker-tape parade. I would have to have lived with a zillion roommates in some bug-infested walk up or even worse, take some really shitty local job and live with my parents.

Then one month after graduation, it was as if the heavens had opened up and offered me a solution. Nari's parents had bought her a condo so she could focus only on medical school, not trying to eke out a student living. It had a second bedroom, she offered, and *poof* I became a Californian. Her parents loved it even more. I'd been giving off the chaperone vibe since middle school.

They were sure with me by her side there'd be no all night raves or live-in boyfriends. "I wish I'd never taken you to that party." Nari shook her head.

"But it changed my life for the better. Who was it, by the way? I should probably thank him."

"I don't know. Some guy from the law school, I think. Definitely someone who didn't have to study as much as I did."

"I didn't have any prospects when I came out here. You know that."

"Neither did Isabella Aconi, but now she's VP of some department at CBT."

As I had been taught as a child, I politely excused myself and found the one tiny coed bathroom that probably serviced both employees and patrons. I put the lid on the toilet seat and sat down. Trying to not let the tears pricking my lids come down, I buried my face in my hands. Nari wasn't being fair. Life had been so hard after college.

The country had been in another recession, and except for the weather, L.A. turned out not to be any better than New York. Whenever I'd surfed *Monster.com* or any of the job sites popular back then, I'd seen nothing but boatloads of unpaid, temporary, and shit jobs. Nari had always been generous, but I couldn't just live off her parents and mine for the rest of eternity.

Then at that party, my luck had turned. We'd been getting a lot drunk and a little bit high at some huge house in the Hollywood Hills. The twenty-something guy throwing the party boasted that the tri-level we were partying at was his. He'd bought it outright at the ripe old age of twenty-eight with proceeds from working in the porn industry.

Not the seedy, get your hands dirty porn of the San Fernando Valley, but the pristine world of coding and marketing at home from his computer. After I'd come down and sobered up, I shut myself into my corner of Nari's condo with my laptop, intrigued. I did a little exploration, a lot of research and my so-called career was born.

I went from sharing ramen noodles and *kimchi* with Nari, to buying us steaks. It was liberating to go from a phone call away from begging my parents for more money, to the life of a self-sustaining adult. At twenty-three, it had felt good, really good.

Throwing cold water on my bloodshot eyes, I flushed and left the single bathroom. I ignored the angry looking men and women in line for the lavatory and took my time getting back to the counter. She looked at me, then looked away, quiet for a spell.

"There's a new doctor at my practice," Nari said. My body slumped in relief. The serious talk was over. Gossip was our currency.

"Man, woman, young or old?"

"Man. Young." She poked her chopsticks in the *banchan* on the table. "He's from Vermont. Went to Dartmouth for both undergrad and med school."

"He must like the snow," I said.

"Not so much, I think. He did his residency in New York. He's been kicking around L.A. for a while."

Mr. Vermont sounded boring. I changed the topic. "What's new with Anita?" Nari's co-worker lived a more salacious life than anyone I knew in real life. "Is she going to keep the baby? Does she know who the father is?"

"So, his name is Lucas Tucker."

"The dad is some other guy? That name sounds totally white. I thought Anita was waffling between a Filipino and Mexican."

Nari filled my cup with *bori cha*. "Not Anita's guy. The new doctor."

Realization dawned on me in waves. I smelled fix-up. "What about Lucas Tucker?" I asked in the most saccharine voice I could muster.

"I was thinking of inviting him to brunch with us one Sunday."

"Why?" Although we occasionally had other friends from her job or from school at brunch, it was a meal we typically ate alone.

"I think you might like him."

"Ah Jesus, Nari. Are you serious?"

"As cancer."

"What's up with you tonight? First my job then my sex life."

"You're young, attractive, healthy. You should date."

"What about you?"

She silenced me with a single look that said it all: Andy Clarke. He'd been her college boyfriend. He'd been a secret from her parents. And he'd died unexpectedly. He was always off limits. Nervous, I tried to joke my way out of the maze.

"So, what? A nice guy can sweep me away from this life of debauchery a la *Pretty Woman*?"

"Maybe." She started blinking a lot then looked away from me. Unfortunately, some older guy who'd had far too much *soju* took her glance as an invitation to approach. I spent the next ten minutes watching as Nari politely declined the man's advances. He started with who knows who, trying to see if he knew anyone in her family. He talked about going to church, how he was single, how he was some successful commercial real estate agent.

With no help from the indifferent staff, Nari finally had to quietly but firmly put him in his place, after his hand brushed against her body. I don't know if he was grabbing for a boob or a butt, but thanks to Nari's maneuvering, he missed both.

The fatty meat resting on my rice was cold and unappealing when I finally had a minute to take a bite. "And that's why I don't date," I said.

We ate the rest of the meal in peace.

At least Nari smirked when the waitress asked us if we wanted *bokkeum bap*. I said yes. We always ordered the fried rice. Leftover meat, some *kimchi*, rice and eggs. It was heaven on a grill. We had a long-standing routine of eating a few bites and taking the rest home for breakfast.

We'd driven to the restaurant together out of habit. If parking was hell for one, it was only more hellish for two. But as we sat silent side by side for the ride north to my house, I suddenly wished I was in my car alone.

When we got to my place, Nari put the doggy bag on the butcher block breakfast bar.

"You can have the rice. I know how much you like it." It was her way of apologizing. We usually battled over that bag like two dogs fighting over a bone. When I didn't say anything, Nari shuffled to the door and slipped back into her shoes. "I have some lab results to go over. A lot of reports to dictate. Referrals to make..."

I knew she wanted me to let her off the hook, but I was still hurt. "See you later," was my curt reply.

Turning up the heat against the February night's chill, I

slipped into my oh-so-sexy Gap pajamas and sought refuge in my office.

First, I checked my statistics from the most profitable websites where I was an affiliate. Stats were already up after a day of low sales. I looked at the clock on the screen. Yep, after midnight on the east coast. The guys who hadn't gotten laid were horny and on line. Valentine's Day was a shitty night to troll bars, but the Internet was always open.

I was wavering between work and bills. Just one new page, I promised myself. I opened my website building software and Photoshop and got to work creating an ironic pink, heart-filled web page.

I looked through my huge multi-terabyte hard drive for something to hook the guys who would be visiting my page. But I didn't have anything they wouldn't have seen a thousand times. The hard core users were only swayed by new content. And I wasn't a content provider.

I'd always bought pictures from reputable photographers and used free content from the pay sites. But if you couldn't convince the guys that you had a line on the latest, just turned eighteen girls, or some kind of gonzo content they'd never seen before, they just clicked away from your page and on to another.

I looked at my surroundings with a critical eye. During the day, my apartment was sunny and warm toned. I'd probably be best off advertising for a few models and doing my own teaser pictures or putting up my own pay site. I rubbed my forehead. That was a future I wasn't ready to contemplate. Doing either one of those would solidify my place in this temporary world. I picked the best I could find, and hoped I could get at least ten signups for the evening. I could use that three hundred dollars right now.

Satisfied that things were humming along, I started in on the pile of bills on my desk. I surfed from bounteous breasts on display to the blue and white bank website. I entered the amounts I owed and clicked to pay my bills through my online banking system. I tried not to stare at my relatively paltry balance. Thank God I'd paid off the condo. I only had the ridiculously astronomical monthly home owners' association fees haunting me.

Then I slit open the next envelope. It was from the HOA. What now? I scanned the first few lines. Crap, it wasn't good. I read further. No, it was bad. They wanted to replace the roof on the fifty-year-old building and fix a bunch of water issues. And of course, they were going to issue a special assessment. I skipped all the rationalization and looked at the bottom line. Fifteen thousand dollars from every tenant before the end of the year.

I double clicked my accounting program looking for hope. It was not to be found. I knew how to work QuickBooks. Not all the bells, whistles, reports, and flow charts, but simple math I could do. The bottom line was my net worth wasn't growing.

Nari was right. I was in a dying career. I'd fallen into being a webmaster. And the heyday of little guys making big money in Internet porn had long passed. But there was money to be made if I could just figure out a way. Like every other industry, though, the big guys had consolidated and bought up the not-so-little guys. No doubt those mega corporations were making a mint, but I wasn't anymore.

What was I going to do? I had no appreciable skills. Ten years ago, it was hard to build a website. You needed to know HTML and Flash and even a little PHP script coding.

Now, even a novice could throw up a semi professional looking website in a matter of minutes. The only advantage I had over someone new entering the industry was that I had thousands of websites already up generating income. It had turned into a volume business, and I had more than five thousand sites. But the days of six figure incomes were over. Just like the newspaper business, web surfers expected free content, and could get it. They often got their rocks off long before getting to the pay wall.

Restless, I went to the bar and made myself a drink. After I downed the first martini, I reluctantly clicked the bookmark for the *sexychatpad.com* chat room. The empty bar at the bottom of the screen beckoned, the cursor blinking its come on. My hands moved as if from their own volition. Crossing my legs in anticipation, I typed in my online name, Lexi Quinn, and pressed Enter.

Chatrooms were sausage factories. This time, like every other, five or ten men instantly greeted me with a chorus of, 'hi,' 'you want to PM,' and 'hey sexy thing, tell us what you look like.'

Liars filled chatrooms. It was the one place I was honest. I dangled my particulars at the virtual party like bait. I let them know I was 5'4', with brown hair and blue eyes. My hands flew over the keys adding my measurements, 36-30-36. The men who really like boys, and the ones who liked fat chicks disappeared from the screen, onto greener pastures.

That left me with three or four possibilities. Now, I asked them for theirs. Of course, they all led with the size of their dick. Liars. Unless they were porn stars, they didn't have ten inches in their pants. And after seeing hundreds of girls gagged, I'd never want ten inches in my mouth.

But who was I to disabuse them of their fantasies? I watched the come-ons flicker up the screen, white letters scrolling over the black background. I picked the quietest guy, who called himself Peter. Yeah, not subtle. I signaled to him that I wanted to go private, and a new screen opened up on my window, where only Peter and I could see what was typed.

I knew what Peter wanted. He wanted what all men did.

Virtually, he'd open his pants, take out his penis, and I'd pretend to praise and worship it. But my day job was nothing but pleasing men, I was there to get a little something for myself.

I looked around my apartment, wary of peeping Toms. My windows were shaded by palm fronds and not much else. On the ninth floor, no one could see me. I was almost sure. The Los Feliz Towers were the tallest buildings around. The only light came from the monitor, no backlight to reveal my actions to the world. Easing the four buttons of my Henley tee open, I brushed my hand against one nipple. Pleasure twisted my belly.

I typed: I'm so hot for you, Peter, but I'm a girl who likes to come first. Is that okay? He agreed heartily. I'd chosen well, he was a woman pleaser. I typed: I'm wearing a button front shirt and low rise pants. Do you want to take them off me? His response was swift and sure. He said he would, telling me he'd love to slip the shirt off me and suck and bite my nipples. I crossed my legs tighter wanting to hold on to the feeling of anticipation as long as I could.

Peter told me that if I were there with him, he'd lick me all over, suck each nipple until I screamed his fake name, finger me until I came. I knew no real life man would ever do that for me, so I reveled in his attention. I sucked my fingers making them wet, dragging them all over my body, glancing on my nipples, brushing between my legs. The draft from my bedroom raised my gooseflesh, made my nipples harder than they already were.

When Peter prompted, I slipped my shirt over my head, popped the tiny buttons of my waffle pants. Peter wanted to go down on me. He told me he'd part my folds like a flower and suck the nectar. Words that would normally make me laugh in the light of day, made me wet at night. Tweaking one nipple, I slipped my fingers in and out, in and out, until I could no longer type. Before I lost it, I kicked away from the computer, needing the privacy of a darkened corner. I rolled back until I hit the wall. Waves of pleasure washed over me.

When I got my head back, it was me, in a cold empty room, with my clothes half off. When I looked down, my breasts and belly were bathed in the bluish light of the monitor. I rolled to the computer and clicked the browser shut, ignoring the pleas from Peter for his turn. My virtual date would have to find his pleasure elsewhere. Setting my pajamas to rights, I walked to the bar and helped myself to a second, stiffer martini. It was a three olive night.

The ringing phone jerked me from descending into my usual well of shame. I looked up at my apartment, totally black now except for the computer screen and the orange glow of the number pad on the phone.

I didn't need to look at the caller ID to know it was Nari. She hated to go to bed mad. "Hi."

"Is this Daisy Fletcher?" a deep voice asked. I pulled back the phone: *Raphael Augustin*. The last 'e' was missing. His full name was too long for the phone. How long had I paused?

"Yep, this is Daisy," I said finally. He couldn't see me. He didn't know what I'd done.

"Who's Bronwen?"

Other people had their nicknames on their caller ID. I'd had the same number forever and never thought to change it. "It's my full first name. I'm Bronwen Margaret Fletcher." Mortification caused me to over share. I took a deep breath, sloughed off Lexi, and reinhabited Daisy.

"That sounds very proper," he said like I was minor British royalty.

"It's not proper. It's just Welsh—a family name on my mother's side." I took a sip of martini, sinking into the desk chair. Gut churning, I wanted to chalk it up to overdoing it on soju, grilled tripe and *kimchi*, then pouring a martini over that stew, but I knew it was Raphael's voice. It had been a long time since a man had turned my stomach upside down.

"Can you bring my shirt over tomorrow?"

"What time?" He was gay. I didn't have to play hard to get.

Raphael must have been walking. He'd gone from somewhere relatively quiet to what sounded like a party. "Come over in the afternoon, I get up late." He gave me the address on North Hayworth. I typed it carefully into my contacts then added the event to iCalendar and ignored the excitement lodged in my chest.

FOUR

RAPHAEL

THE RINGING LANDLINE woke me up. Who could be calling? No one had my number. It stopped, and I turned over in my bed, trying to ignore the blinding sun peeking around the sides of the window shades. One day I was going to tape those damn things to the wall. Southern California was hell on night workers.

Then it started again. I pulled my phone from the table. It was ten after twelve. Then it hit me, that girl was probably ringing the buzzer. I jumped out of bed and ran to pick up the receiver in the hallway.

"Hi, um. It's Daisy? I have your shirt?"

I pressed the nine on the phone and heard the gate lock buzz then the creak of the rusting iron. I had just enough time to pull on sweats before the knock came at the door.

Wow. The chick was something in the light of day. I was glad I was pretty sober and could appreciate what I was seeing. She was like a bustier, brunette version of some actress I'd seen play a lot of retro parts. That actress—my fuddled brain couldn't put a name to her—had fueled a lot of fantasies on lonely nights. Her dark hair was cut short, falling in a curtain around her chin and even shorter in the back. She'd pushed her aviator sunglasses on top of her head, and her wide set eyes were the color of the southern California sky. If I'd known this version of Daisy was coming over, I'd have paid a little more attention to how I looked.

Daisy stood hesitantly by the door, toeing off her loafers. Who wore loafers? Why was she taking off her shoes? I looked her up and down. She was dressed like she'd walked out of a Banana Republic window display. I'd spent so much time looking at her, I didn't see the shirt she thrust at me until it almost hit my chest. Grasping the paper, plastic, and shirt in my hands, I had to admit I was happy to see this one come back. I had a few good shirts I liked to work in, and this was one of my lucky ones. Call me superstitious, but I always got laughs in this one.

"So, how did your friend's wedding go?"

Ah, the bachelor party. Right. "Scott and Lindsay's thing went fine. I'm sure they're bonking each other's brains out in Fiji or something."

"Were you in the wedding party?"

I sat on the couch. Her bare feet curled against the stone on the tiny slate entrance area. The poor thing was probably cold. "C'mon in. Sit for a moment." She did and sat on the far side of the sectional. "I was the best man. It was not cool, though. Lindsay's parents are not gay-friendly."

The blue eyes that had been steadily on me, skittered away. I'd seen enough bad treatment of my brother over the years. I did not talk to anti-gays. "Do you have a problem with gay people?" I asked pointblank.

Her eyes snapped up and gazed steadily at me again. "No. No. Not at all. I'm, uh. I'm sorry about that woman's parents. I hope you didn't feel uncomfortable."

"Nah, I'm used to it. I just did my thing and hustled out of there. My brother only told me about Lindsay's parents toward the end. Which is good. I'd have been really pissed otherwise."

I fell silent. Daisy looked down again. This girl was into me. I was so used to being the pursuer that I'd almost missed what this chick was practically throwing into my lap. "Hey, you eat breakfast?"

She looked out the window where the early afternoon sun was shining strong. "It's lunchtime."

"I'm thinking about hopping on over to the Griddle. The chili's good."

Nervous. I haven't seen a woman nervous in years. Barmaids and comedy nerd groupies were way more confident than this girl. I could see her making up her mind. If she liked me, I wondered what the hesitation was. Boyfriend, maybe. The Asian thing, probably. I was a lot of girls' first.

"Okay. But maybe you should get dressed."

Looking down at my bare chest and feet, I had to chuckle. Maybe it was because I was nearly naked. "You're right. I'll be back in a minute."

"Can I look around?"

"Knock yourself out."

In my room, I lifted my underarms. Passed the sniff test. No time to shower. I pulled open the closet. I had about twenty seconds to decide what would impress this girl. I pulled out clean underwear, fitted jeans and a cashmere sweater. Slipped into some Vans and came back out. Her empty loafers were still there, but Daisy wasn't. I found her standing in the dining room. She was staring out the window, absently running her hands along the deep windowsill.

"Ready to go?"

Startled, she looked up. "Yeah. We can walk from here, right?"

I nodded, grabbed my wallet from the table by the door and

gestured for her to go first. When we got to the diner, we were seated right away. It was late enough that the morning crush of brunchers had come and gone.

"I'll have the Mounds of Pleasure." I was in a chocolate, coconut and double entendre mood. "My new friend here wants to try the chili. What's on tap today?"

The waitress looked at me cockeyed. "So, the guy who made the Chili my Soul, he like, um died. So we don't have that on the menu anymore. Do you want more time to pick something else?"

Daisy spoke up. "No, no problem. I'll have the shrimp tacos."

Bonus points. She wasn't a salad eater. The food came fast. I'd ordered what the Griddle was known for, pancakes the size of Frisbees. Daisy didn't seem disappointed by the change in plans.

She pulled a passing bus boy aside. "Do you have El Yucateo or Tapatío at least?"

The man nodded and brought back two small bottles. Daisy applied the sauces liberally. She took a huge bite and didn't blink.

"I don't think I heard right at the club. What do you do?"

"I'm a comedian. You know, a stand-up comic."

"What does that entail, exactly?" Oh, shit. Entail? If I had to guess, this one was Ivy League all the way.

"Brown."

Perplexed was cute on her. "What?"

"You went to school in Providence. Am I right?"

"No."

"Damn, it was Owen." I shoulda gone with my gut. I always made mistakes reading people when I took a second guess.

"Did Nari…"

"Your Korean friend? Nope. You just scream New England

Ivy League. But you seem a little too down to earth for Dartmouth or Harvard."

"Um, okay. Do you go to clubs and work?"

That always reeled them in. Entertainment always seemed more glamorous on the outside than the inside. I sat back, arranging my body into my 'casually engaged' pose. "Oh sure. I do sets at the Improv and The Comedy Store all the time."

"Have you ever been on Conan?" She'd put her hot sauce drenched shrimp taco down and was resting her head in her cupped palms. I could see the little freckles that she probably hated dusting her nose and cheeks.

"You sided with Conan over Leno?"

"My friends and I watched Conan all through college. I've even been in the audience twice. He's so freaking funny. My parents used to let Jay Leno serenade them to bed." She cocked her head. "Okay, that probably sounded silly to someone in the industry. But it was cool being in the audience in New York City."

"Nah, I agree with you. Leno should have honored his retirement agreement. He has enough money and cars. But the old people liked him. Don't know if they're watching Jimmy Fallon now." I had her on the hook. Time to reel her in. "Haven't done Conan since the move to TNT, but I did Letterman a couple of times." And those were probably the last times. I'd worked like a dog to get in with the Late Show's booker, Eddie Brill. Then he'd been fired, and I was back to sending in tapes and doing showcases with nothing to show for it.

She asked the usual questions about Letterman. Everyone wanted to know if he was crazy, funny, or had a secret pacemaker. I laughed off the questions. I didn't tell her the truth: I'd never met David Letterman. The producers taped the stand-up segments after the show. The two times I'd done the show, I had waited in a green room all by myself for hours. Then I'd walked down that long deserted theater corridor, came out on stage, did my best and cleanest five minutes and went back to my hotel. I never met the great Oz, and I wasn't high enough on the food chain to warrant a seat on the stage.

She'd only eaten a half a taco. "You want that to go? I'll have enough here for breakfast for the next four days." That was the beauty of the Griddle. A bunch of people complained that they served too much food. I'd always maintained that they served breakfast plus leftovers.

"Thanks for this." Daisy pulled her wallet from her purse. "Sorry if I bent your ear about work." I pulled the check tray toward me before she could lay down her credit card.

"I got this." I put a stack of bills on the tray and gave it to our waitress, who happened to be passing by. "Keep the change."

Taco bag in hand, Daisy stood awkwardly. She was a tough cookie, but not entirely impervious to my charms. I could see that she was wavering.

"Let me walk you to your car at least."

"Okay." She pulled on that little sweater again. I usually went after the more obvious blondes, real or enhanced. But something about Daisy's subtlety enticed me. She did nothing to embellish her clear blue eyes. She kept that sweater tight across two of her best attributes. And her hair didn't look the least bit altered. In a town of blond highlights and low lights, she was an oddity. One I'd like to explore up close.

She pointed to an ancient Mercedes that was parked across the street from my house. Time for the last tug on the pole. "You wanna come in for a minute? Have another cup of coffee? I sure could use one that costs less than four dollars."

"Sure. Why not?" And I had her. I unlocked the door and she took off her shoes and resumed her place on the couch. I leaned down close and pulled the white paper bag from her fingers. It was the closest I'd ever been to her. She wore some light floral scent that lit up my insides like a Christmas tree. It was going to be a fun afternoon.

I took her bag and mine and put the food into the fridge. "What do you want? I've got beer, soda, or coffee."

She came into the kitchen and stood behind me. "What kind of soda?"

I pulled out something I'd picked up at Whole Foods or Bristol Farms. Daisy scrutinized the label on the clear glass bottle then twisted off the cap. "Thanks."

She eased herself onto the counter as I packed coffee into the Krups.

"This is a really nice apartment. How long have you lived here?"

I measured in the water. "Maybe five or six years."

"I miss the east coast, but sometimes I see a place like this in L.A. and it reminds me a little bit of home."

"Where's home?" I was wavering between South Shore Connecticut or North Shore Massachusetts. But I didn't make a guess. No need to make a fool of myself a second time.

"Madison, Connecticut. It's downstate, on the Sound," she said.

"How?" She quirked her head at my question, the straight dark hair hitting her shoulder. "How does it remind you of home?"

"The moldings, the paint. I don't know. I like it, though."

I leaned back against the counter. My right side brushed against her left. Steam hissed from the coffee pot. Boiling water dripped from the filter basket, filling the carafe with coffee. The aroma of Colombian Gold permeated the room.

"My brother did a lot of the work. He lived in this apartment before moving upstairs to a bigger place."

"Oh, is he a designer?"

"No, just gay."

She looked like she was hiding a smile. I tipped her chin up, turning it toward me. "It's okay to laugh. It was a joke."

My coffee breath be damned, I was going to kiss her. Then the phone rang, breaking the tension I'd worked to build up. Who was at the front door now? I went to the hall and picked up the phone and listened to the delivery man's spiel. "Yeah. Okay."

I poked my head back in the kitchen. "I have to get something from the mailman."

"Oh, alright. Maybe I should..."

"Stay where you are. I'll be right back."

Why did a package have to come now of all days? Daisy was a skittish one. I had to get back in there and close the deal. I signed some piece of paper and grabbed the box from the guy in a blue uniform. I was usually friendly with him. I think he'd even come to one or two of my shows, but I needed to get back to her before she changed her mind. Maybe I'd start a fire, ease that tiny sweater down, unbutton that dress....

Daisy had her loafers on and sweater pulled tight. She tucked her hair behind her ears. "I've got a lot of stuff to do. I should really go. Um, thanks again for breakfast." She pulled me in and kissed me on the cheek.

"Maybe we could do this again sometime." I was thinking sometime today or sometime later tonight after I got back from Comedy and Magic.

She ducked her head. "I'd like that, Rafe. I'd really like that." She gave my arm a brief squeeze, and she was out the door. "You may be my first gay friend."

Gay. She thought I was gay? No way was I getting laid today.

FIVE
DAISY

"OH, my God. You're going to be a fag hag." Nari laughed out loud. Nope, she cackled and hooted. I could feel the blood rushing to my face. I'm sure it was as crimson as a pollution tinged L.A. sunset.

I loved Nari, but she often carelessly brushed off my feelings. I'd just told her how much I liked Rafe. How we'd connected. How I thought he'd been going to kiss me. How I hoped he was bi.

"Shhh." I looked around, making sure no one was watching us. Not a single soul in the place knew me here, but I didn't want my gay man crush to get me any rude stares. We were a stone's throw away from West Hollywood. I pushed through the racks at Kitson and ushered her toward the dressing room.

We squeezed into the small room together. "I'm worried about the state of health care in America," I said.

She pulled her sweater over her head. I ducked to avoid her flying elbow. "What are you talking about?" Nari asked, tossing cashmere I knew to cost two hundred dollars down on the floor in a shimmering heap.

"I listen to NPR in the car. There's a huge shortage of

primary care physicians in this country. Yet you seem to have nothing but time to sit around nagging me, or making fun of me."

She pulled the new dress over her head. "Daisy, do you think Billabong is played out?" She spun around in an asymmetrical tie dyed dress. Like everything, except strapless gowns, it looked perfect on her. I tried not to let my envy take over. I just needed more salads and less of, well, less of everything else.

"Who or what is Billabong?" I examined the corners of the dressing room just in case some odd-looking animal from Australasia was about to hop out.

"It's the Australian brand that did this dress. They make beach and surf clothing."

"Like UGG?"

"UGG is so two thousand. But yes, like UGG."

I pulled the tag. "Ah, exploiting the people of China to make goods from down under. Just like UGG."

She pointed at me then at the dress. "Pot, meet kettle."

"Are you talking about me? I'm not exploiting anyone. The men and women who work in the industry are consenting adults. The people who view it are adults. Those girls in the videos work one or two hours a day, tops. I'm sure the people who make this are working about fifteen hours a day without so much as a pee break."

We were quiet as she switched one dress for another that looked just as good. I vowed to be model thin in my *next* life. This incarnation had too many cupcakes to sample. "Why do you need a new dress anyway?" The last thing Nari needed was clothing. The day I'd moved out of the second bedroom of her condo, she'd moved portable clothing racks in.

"It's for the medical conference in Hawaii."

"You're going to Hawaii?" I was kind of disappointed I hadn't received an invite. We'd been each other's dates and traveling companions for years. I wondered if she thought we'd outgrown all the BFF stuff.

"I always go away in March. You know that. I get some continuing education credits, and maybe this year, some sun. Last March in New York sucked except for the parade."

"So, seriously what should I do?" I turned the conversation back to Rafe. Being a fag hag was slightly less embarrassing than being left out. I didn't want her to feel like she *had* to drag me along.

"Do? About what? Raphael? Nothing. He's gay. You're not. End of story."

"But I like him. I swear we had, like, a certain chemistry." I couldn't quite articulate the tingle up my spine, or the quiver in my belly from last Saturday. I just hadn't had any kind of chemistry with a guy in years. "I told you I thought he was going to kiss me the other day."

"Maybe he's experimenting. Everyone's curious. Why am I even saying this to you? He's unobtainable. Let's see. You like dicks. He likes dicks. That's a lot of dicks."

"Is that how you talk to your patients?" Dick was not a clinical term.

"When are you seeing him again?"

I thought about lying. I wanted to say I wasn't going to see him again. But he'd called and left a message saying I was on the list for an eight o'clock show tonight. For some reason I couldn't fathom, I didn't want to disappoint him by being a no-show. "He's doing an appearance at this place called the UCB. He left a message saying I should come."

"When?"

"Tonight. You'll go with me, right?" She might not need me anymore, but I needed her as a buffer. I needed Nari to keep me from doing something stupid. Like trying to sleep with a gay guy.

"No can do."

"Why?" I must have screeched because two different sales-people knocked to make sure we were okay.

"My aunt and uncle are coming from Seoul, remember?" Nari's voice had lowered to a stage whisper.

"Oh, shit." Family was Nari's kryptonite.

"Yes, dear. How could you forget? You're coming out to Riverside next weekend, right? I need you to keep me from killing them all in cold blood. But tonight is family only. My mom's driving in. We're picking them up at LAX. Doing the Lawry's standing prime rib thing." Her relatives were impressed with the artfully displayed, hand carved beef every single time. At nearly one hundred dollars per person, I knew that adding me would stretch the budget too far. It was okay though, I'd probably had enough prime rib in my life to kill a cow.

"Well, that does sound like fun." Seriously. I liked her family. They sat on the floor, ate spicy food, and yelled at each other. It was way more interesting than gin and tonic in the drawing room with my family which often played out like a game of Clue, minus the murder.

"Sure, like tearing out my fingernails, fun. I'll have countless hours of my mother trying to impress them with her naturaliza-tion certificate, her money, her stature in the Korean church. Then I'll have more hours of disparagement from everyone as they try to figure out why I'm not, I don't know, running Cedars or something. Then they'll start in on my being single. On second thought, this UCB thing is starting to sound like fun compared to that." She looked at my straight leg jeans and French blue oxford shirt. "Do you think you should get some-thing new? We *are* at a store."

I was appropriate. Nothing at Kitson was appropriate for anyone over fifteen, or with more flesh than a stick figure. I stuck with my usual weekend attire. Maybe I'd tuck the shirt in.

After maneuvering the tank into a space on Franklin, I put The Club on the wheel and got out. I had lived in Los Angeles over ten years, but purposefully strode down Franklin trying to hide the fact that I couldn't find the address scribbled on the sticky note affixed to my index finger.

Nothing I could see on the street looked like a theater. Where was the marquee with its list of names? Squinting, I located it, a skinny building between Italian and sushi restaurants. If there hadn't been a small white sign announcing what was inside, I would have walked right by the black painted brick facade for the third time.

I gave my name to the guy sitting on a stool outside with the clipboard. He paused a super long time while scanning the list. "Wait, are you *Bronwen* Fletcher?"

Trust Rafe to give them my real name. "Yes, that's me." He scanned my ID like I was a potential terrorist, collected my ten bucks, and then let me in. The bulletin board in the tiny little foyer was crammed with headshots. Something in my belly fluttered when my eyes alighted on Rafe's picture. Despite the mantra running through my head, *I know he's gay, I know he's gay, I can't have him,* I still wanted to be near him.

Inside, it was not quite the Broadway type theater I was used to. Not a lot of red velvet there. Just bare floors, Spartan chairs, and a rough stage. I picked through the hundred or so seats and selected a seat three rows back. I was no longer the good girl who always sat in the front row.

Resisting the urge to fiddle with my phone, I closed my eyes, trying to give myself a small break from work. There wasn't anything work related I could fix or tweak now. People constantly stepped over me. Sometimes I truly wondered if I was invisible.

"Are these seats taken?" a man said, gesturing to the two

seats left empty on the aisle. I didn't look up from the hands in my lap.

"No," I answered, scrutinizing my nails. A screech sounded as someone did a sound check. I finally looked around and realized the little theater had filled up pretty quickly. Then I glanced at the people next to me. Wait. "Are you Gabriel?"

"Call me Gabe." Rafe's brother shook my hand. He pushed rose tinted lenses up on his head. "Aren't you the girl from the bachelor party?"

"Yep, that's me. Daisy." He introduced me to the friend with him. The friend promptly wandered off in search of a drink of some kind.

"Is this a coincidence?"

Now, I was a stalker. Great. "No. No. Rafe called and said I should stop by. I wasn't doing anything tonight so..."

"You stopped by."

"That's about the size of it."

Fortunately, the host came out on stage and everyone directed their attention forward. I couldn't put a finger on the last time I'd seen standup comedy. Maybe once at some club in Stamford, it was called the Comedy Star or something like that. It had been my twenty-first birthday. All I remembered was one comedian who told racist and sexist jokes, while claiming to be neither, and taking the drink minimum very seriously. I probably had my two cocktails and those of all my friends.

I immediately felt sorry for the host. He was a thin, geeky guy in a three-piece suit no less, who seemed new at stand-up or very uncomfortable on stage. I wondered if the sweat was from nervousness, lights, or the fact that he had three pieces of tan wool wrapped around his body. I think he was trying to be funny, but wasn't. After about five awkward minutes with scant laughter, he finally introduced a comedian and the theme for the night. Thank goodness.

This wasn't just straight standup comedy, but some kind of improvisation thing where the people on stage had to riff on topics projected on the screen behind them. I tried to listen as best I could, but my legs were bouncing on the balls of my feet. I just wanted to see Rafe.

He finally came out in a black shirt free from the confines of jeans and checked Vans. It seemed like the uniform for comedians, but he looked much better in it than all the other guys. He was slim and in shape. The other comedians all looked like they'd indulged a little too much. Maybe I was biased, though. His longish hair curled at the ends, and he kept brushing it back from his face. He took command of the stage like none of the others.

'WWJD: What would Jesus Drive?' posted on the wall.

"A fifteen-year-old Honda Civic. Have you ever seen a Jesus fish on a Bentley?" Rafe asked rhetorically. "Think about it. You see those little metal things stuck on Hondas, Toyotas, and a whole lot of pickup trucks. But on a Porsche, or Rolls Royce? No way. Next time an Italian sports car whizzes by you on Sunset, take a quick look. I promise you. Cristo is nowhere near that thing."

His on stage persona seemed a ninety-degree turn from the guy at brunch the week before. He had a clever one liner for everything. He was funny as hell. My gay crush went up two notches. Damn.

'Vampire Books' was up last. "Twilight is a girl's choice between necrophilia and bestiality." The crowd roared. Ending on at high note, Rafe disappeared into a side room where other performers seemed to be waiting—bottles of water in hand. I resisted the urge to crash that room and instead politely watched the two final performances. As soon as the host wrapped up, I was out of my seat, pulling on my jacket.

"Daisy," Gabe said grabbing my arm. "C'mon back and let Raphael know you were here."

And with that I was saved from embarrassing myself. I had a legitimate 'in.' I dutifully followed Gabe and his friend to the green room. Rafe was sitting in a director's chair, bottle of water casually dangling from his hand as he chatted with another good looking guy.

Something akin to jealousy skittered through me. When he saw us, he stood and the guy melted away. He gave his brother a one-armed hug. "Hey, bro, glad you could come." He gave Gabe's friend's the same half hug, half pat down that guys did. I hung back, unsure of what to do. Finally, he looked between the men, and our eyes met.

"Daisy!" He pulled me forward and kissed me full on the mouth. It was the kiss I'd wanted last Saturday in his kitchen. It was as good as I thought it would be. Abruptly, I pulled away, when I wanted nothing more than to press in harder. I'd made a few stupid mistakes in my life; I did not want to add kissing gay men to the list.

"Hi, um, hi." I tittered nervously, sounding girlishly stupid to my own ears. I cleared my throat and lowered my voice, pulling out all the sturdy Yankee I could muster. "You were really funny out there." God, I still sounded like a moron. Couldn't figure out who'd disown me first, my staunchly New England parents or my overpriced college. The next time I opened my mouth, I needed to channel William F. Buckley.

Gabriel and Rafe laughed. I wasn't sure what the joke was. Then in one heart stopping, soul-crushing moment I got it. Mortification warmed my neck, creeping up to my cheeks. Gay guy kisses straight girl. She gets hot and bothered. *Enter your favorite punch line here.*

"Let's get out of here." I must have looked like an unmoored ship, because Rafe grabbed my hand and led me from the club.

"Back to my place?" I nodded, embarrassment forgotten, loving the feel of that strong hand against mine.

We parted and I got into my car. I waited ten minutes before I started the engine. No way did I want to get to his house before he got there.

I would be the last to get to North Hayward I'd thought, but the only person in the living room was the guy who'd come to the club with Gabe. I stood there awkwardly for a moment. I reintroduced myself without leaving the tiled slate area by the door.

"Hey. Ted," he said. I stood there debating the shoe issue. Ted had his shoes firmly on his feet, but I didn't want to presume. Maybe he had bad foot odor, nail fungus, or holey socks. Gabe walked into the room, drink in hand and shoes on feet. I left on my loafers. Up until Rafe, every Korean household I'd visited had a shoe rack by the door and a naked foot/bare sock policy. Some even had spare slippers. I looked around; not a plastic shoe in sight.

"What do you drink?" Gabe was already on his way to comfortably tipsy.

"I'll take anything."

Rafe and his good-looking friend-slash-probable date walked in from the back of the apartment. "That's no challenge," Rafe said. "My brother is a mixologist of the highest order. Knock his socks off."

"Okay, I'll have a Brooklyn," I said, cringing inwardly. Why had I made it so damn difficult? This was a get-together, not the GREs. A long moment of silence hung between us. Then Gabe, Ted, and Rafe broke out in loud laughter. Now what straight girl *faux pas* had I made?

"Oh, snap!" Gabe exclaimed. I found myself lifted and spun in an unexpected hug. "You're a keeper. I'll be right back." Gabe disappeared through the front door, only to reappear moments later, red and yellow jar in one hand, straw covered bottle in the other.

"This is my friend Joel." I took a seat on a vintage wingback chair and tried parsing the intonation Rafe had given to the word friend. Boyfriend? Gay friend? Friend with benefits?

Black bar towel dramatically draped across his arm, Gabe presented the Brooklyn to me with a flourish. "Now I know a Brooklyn doesn't have a maraschino, but if you know about Luxardo, then you'll appreciate the real thing."

I took a sip. "You should be anointed." It was perfect. I hadn't had real maraschino cherries until my junior year abroad. Nari and I had done spring break in Italy, eating, drinking, and eating some more, and we'd fallen upon some farm that aged these cherries the right way. I pulled the frilled toothpick out and bit into the cherry. It was the real deal, not the candied plastic tasting thing Americans were saddled with. There had to be a straight brother somewhere in this Augustine mix. I was so ready to marry into this family.

When everyone was settled with drinks, I became the center of attention again. I hated being the new girl.

"Why do you call him Rafe?" Ted asked.

The room was silent, awaiting my response. "Um, you guys called him Rafe in MJ's. Before he did the, you know, dance." I hated the unsureness of my voice. I felt like an awkward thirteen-year-old who liked the popular boy who didn't like her back. I thought I'd left that feeling behind when I left Connecticut. I wanted everyone to think I was the cool girl in L.A. Heat rushed to my face as they all laughed at once. If I hadn't been inside, I'd have pulled out my sunglasses and hid behind them.

"I guess you could say that Rafe is my alterego," Raphael said.

"What do you like to be called?" I asked, perplexed by the alterego comment.

"Raphael works just fine, my sweet girl," he said, smoothing a hand over my hair. The warmth from his palm tickled against my scalp.

"What do you mean by alterego?"

Joel answered this time. "It's sort of like a stage name. It's the persona he adopts when he's on stage. Comedy is very personal, and he started using it to separate his act from his life. Did I get that right?"

"I think of it as the gay me."

How could he pretend to be gay if he was already gay? I was about to stick my foot deeply in my mouth and ask the twenty-five thousand dollar question, when loud pounding rattled the front door, practically shaking it from its hinges.

Joel dug something from his pocket and ran from the room. Frantic toilet flushing joined the door pounding.

"County Sherriff!" A voice boomed on the other side of the door. "Open up!" The locks and chain rattled as the pounding continued.

"What the fuck?" Gabe shot off the couch and pulled the door open. No one had locked it behind me. Six Los Angeles county sheriffs spilled into the room. Was this a raid? In my entire life, I'd never seen so much police muscle up close. Nor that much firepower. They looked ready to kill us dead.

"Which one of you is Raphael Augustine?"

I looked up at Raphael who stood stock still by my chair. I rose out of my chair, inching away from the group. I wanted to be well out of the path of bullets should someone start firing.

Joel came in from the hall, looking around nervously. Heavy silence blanked the room for several heartbeats before all hell broke loose. "Who's Raphael?" one burly cop shouted. He had his elbow cocked, hand resting on the grip of his weapon.

Raphael moved forward. "It's me. What's going on?" he

asked too casually. Did cops bust into his place all the time? I was scared shitless and no one had asked for Daisy Fletcher.

"What's going on, son, is that you're under arrest."

"For what?" Gabe asked.

Another cop pulled handcuffs from his belt. He slipped first one then another on. "Raphael Augustine. You are under arrest for violation of California Penal Code section two sixty one point five."

"What is that?" Joel asked. "Unpaid parking tickets or something?"

"No, sir. It's unlawful sex with a minor." He shook crumpled paper. "Victimized a young girl."

My usually agile brain had turned to mush. But my mouth continued to work of its own volition. I looked at Raphael who was being backpedaled out of the apartment.

"Wait," I cried.

The cop paused for a moment.

"You're not gay?"

Raphael looked at me oddly. "You thought I was gay?" The sheriff deputies led him out to a waiting car, its lights casting blue and red shadows across the driveway.

Gabriel glanced my way. "You thought he was gay?"

Ted pulled Gabe's hand. "We're going to have to bail him out. Let's *go!*"

SIX

RAPHAEL

AS THE DEPUTY rolled my fingers through the invisible ink, I was wavering between humiliation and speculation. I was one hundred percent sure I'd never slept with an underage girl. I mainly stuck to cocktail waitresses and barflies, and they all had to be well over the age of consent. That's what bouncers were for. But embarrassment gave way to me contemplating how I could turn this into something I could use on stage. Asian guy gets arrested for statutory rape. Cue jokes. It could work.

I looked at the deputy who was rolling my fingers across the computerized screen first then the white index card next. "Who's the girl?"

"What?" he asked, looking at me with what I think was disgust.

"The girl who made the underage sex charge." I couldn't quite get my mouth around the words statutory rape. I did nothing without consent. A little seduction and a tiny bit of coercion were not rape.

"You don't know?"

"I'm maintaining my innocence here," I said, not completely exercising my right to remain silent.

He let go of my wrists and fumbled through some papers. "Rose McIntosh. That ring a bell?"

Fuck. I usually hooked up after a few drinks. I could remember a face and a few other choice body parts. Names weren't my thing. Rose wasn't ringing any bells at all.

"Do you have a date there?"

"February eighth." I shook my head. "Two weeks ago," he said, leading me. The date seemed familiar for some reason. Then it hit me. That save the date magnet had been on my fridge for about two years. Scott's wedding. The waitress. Rose.

"She told me she was twenty-one."

"Save it for the judge." He shoved some papers at me. "You're released O.R."

On my own recognizance. I could walk out without posting bail. At the front of the station, Gabe and Ted were there browbeating some tall beanpole of a deputy who looked well under eighteen. And he had to be of age to work there. My radar couldn't have been that off. Filters. I'd always trusted the filters.

"They said we wouldn't have to post bail. It's only a misdemeanor."

"We were so worried," Ted said, all ten fingers pressed to his mouth. I wasn't in the mood for gay drama. I just wanted to get home. The prospect of jail time was not sitting well on top of the cocktails.

"Look I just want to get home, go to bed, and forget this shitty night ever happened." I'd done that millions of times after a bad set. I had some rum and overpriced health food store brand cola that would go down very smoothly right about now.

AFTER THEY DROPPED me at my place, I couldn't do anything but sit on my couch and fidget. Rose couldn't be underage. She just couldn't have been. I had a foolproof system.

Another comic had told me when I was starting out that to work in a bar or club that served alcohol, and that was every comedy club, the servers always had to be of age.

The darkness of the living room felt oppressive. I got my laptop computer from the bedroom and pressed the power button. Nothing happened. I'd gotten the MacBook a few months ago, hoping that I would spend more time writing during the day. I'd always been a guy who composed my jokes on stage, or scribbled ideas on pieces of paper. But as I was getting older, thinking about putting together a solid sixty minutes so I could maybe open for some of the bigger guys, or even headline myself. I'd realized my best ideas were often lost in the laundry. Hence, this damn brick of broken metal.

It suddenly clicked that the battery may be dead. It had been at least a solid month since I'd turned it on. I dug through the shit on my closet floor and found the power cord. In the moonlight, I found an outlet next to the couch, pulled out the lamp cord and put in the computer cord. It powered on this time. Thank goodness. I'd never gotten around to setting up Internet, but fortunately all my neighbors had wireless. I clicked around until I found Gabe's signal. His password was easy to figure out. It was our childhood dog's name. I typed in UltraMagnus and was rewarded with five green bars, an instant connection.

Typing, 'How old do you have to be to work in a bar?' I clicked through a few sites until I found one that listed every state. And in every state the minimum age was eighteen. I leaned back with my hands behind my head. All was well. The computer clock said it was only midnight. I got my keys and strode out.

TIMMY MILLER HADN'T PASSED me on to a paid regular

yet, but I was sure I could get a fifteen minute spot in the belly room tonight. I walked through the dark, soul sucking hallways of the Comedy Store. It wasn't the same without Mitzi's craziness, but she had Parkinson's and probably would never return. I pushed my way into Timmy's office.

"Got anything tonight?"

"And you're Kevin Jeong?"

"No, Raphael Augustine." We did not all look alike.

"Oh, wait. You used to do the gay Madonna striptease, right?"

"Yep." I'd never live that shit down.

"That was funny. A little hacky, but funny."

"So, tonight?"

"You're in luck. That half-Japanese guy from Showtime's MVP bailed tonight. You can have his spot."

I took what was offered. At about one o'clock in the morning, it was finally my turn.

"You know, I could tell you my usual jokes, and you would laugh." I could see the crowd getting uncomfortable, but I didn't give a shit. "But tonight I got arrested for statutory rape, so I'm not in the mood for laughter." That got a big laugh. They thought I was kidding.

"I'm not kidding." Silence. Dead silence. And I had them. It turned out to be the best set I'd done in a very long time. No jokes about pop culture or gay West Hollywood, and they still laughed.

After my set I sat in the back, watching the few remaining comics do theirs. A guy I'd known on the road circuit for years, Ellis Armstrong, pulled up one of the old wooden chairs and sat leaning over the back of it. He plopped his drink on the table sloppily. "You didn't Google the loopholes."

"What loopholes?"

"If you're not bartending, just serving at a place that happens to have alcohol, the servers don't have to be of age."

Though I'd vowed just a couple of hours ago not to rely on anecdotal evidence, this somehow had the ring of truth to it. "Seriously?"

"Look man, my much more successful brother is a lawyer." His voice got so low, I could barely hear it. I had to lean in real close to hear over the noise of waitresses collecting their tips. "I shouldn't be telling you this, but you know Travis Williams, right?" I nodded. Everyone had heard of Travis. He was the biggest cocksman out there. "He had this problem last year. And the girl was a sixteen-year-old waitress. You know Dr. Grins?" I'd played there not six months ago. "Well, technically it's not a bar, but a theater/restaurant with a liquor license. So the girls there...some are sixteen."

"And their parents let them work there?"

"You asking about raising kids, or staying out of jail?"

"You haven't exactly given me the get out of jail free card, here."

"There is no card. There's no defense to this crime. You're going to have to hope this Topanga girl drops the charges or something. But in the future..."

"I'm done with club hookups."

"Yeah, okay. Whatever you say, man." Armstrong gave me a broad ass wink. "I'm just trying to help." Downing his drink, he left the empty glass on the table, and up and walked away.

SEVEN
DAISY

NARI SUFFERED from the little girl, big car syndrome—a veritable plague in L.A. She was no more than a hundred and change, but drove a Land Rover that outweighed her by five thousand pounds, easily.

We hadn't talked much during the nearly hour long drive. Nari got tense when it came to time with the family. She'd already emptied her bowels twice before we got in the car. Every mile we drove into the desert, her knuckles got whiter, vocal cords standing in sharp relief.

In all the years I'd known her and her family, I could never figure out why she hated the visits from her aunt, uncle, and assorted cousins so damned much. I'd known them for nearly as many years as we'd been friends and loved them like my own, less colorful, family.

Her mom had already done the Beverly Hills Lawry's thing with the family last week. The second to last weekend before the other Yoons left, her mom was doing something at home. I loved her parents' mid-century house. It wasn't new or modern or showy. It was big, airy, and homey—just right. Nari and I stopped inside the front door, taking off our shoes and leaving them on the rack. I always made sure my feet were manicured when I went to her house.

Even in ugly slippers, Nari floated in like a cool breeze. She was flawless as always, every hair in a bun. Her ruched top would have hidden a myriad of body flaws, if she had any. The tailored white pants showed nary a wrinkle even after being stuffed in a car for the last hour.

I marveled at my best friend because I could never wear white. *Kimchi* would fly from my chopsticks to those pants like iron filings to a magnet. Nari, on the other hand, would leave there as cool, collected, and clean as when she'd walked in. I would have been jealous of my best friend had she been a happier person.

Her mom, who called herself Sunny, was in the kitchen taking the plastic wrap from dishes she'd likely been preparing for days. I hinged at the waist, bowing in greeting. She was swishing her plastic gloved hand through some kind of flavored soybean sprouts when I finally zoned in on the backyard. Through the window, I spied her dad grilling what looked like baseball-sized rocks.

"What *are* those?" I asked her mom.

Her parents had oodles of patience with me. I asked a lot of questions about food and culture. They always answered patiently because I ate whatever I was given without question.

"Oysters."

"They're huge." I'd never seen anything like these mollusks on steroids.

"We'll eat them with *gochujang* or *gireumjang*." She looked at Nari for translation, but my friend shook her head. Nari knew I needed no translation. My mouth watered.

Her dad's sister shuffled in from somewhere else in the

house. Her greeting for Nari was filled with effusive Korean. Nari bent down to hug her aunt, her arms stiff. The aunt stepped back and looked at Nari with what I saw as pride. Nari's younger cousin, Eunji came in, phone in hand.

"*Unni*, did anyone tell you?" Eunji asked, a smile drifting around her lips. Nari shook her head. "I've been accepted at Cornell. I'll start the first year in August."

Nari's congratulations was cool, detached. I piped in. "That's great! You'll need to bundle up. It's cold in Ithaca."

Nari's cousin looked at me. "Thanks Daisy," she said. "I've always wanted to study abroad."

The aunt lapsed into Korean, no doubt singing Eunji's praises. Landing a coveted Ivy League spot in the U.S. was as big a deal abroad as in the states.

Nari's dad came in, placed a pan of oysters on the tile countertop. He extended a hand toward me. I bowed slightly then shook his hand. "Good to see you," I said.

"Daisy." Her dad wasn't a big talker, but he'd always treated Nari like a precious flower. I'd always thought she got her cool reserve from him.

I dug in my purse, pulling out a handful of DVDs. "Where can I put these?"

Nari's aunt took the cardboard boxes, shuffling through them. "You still watch these?"

"Faithfully. Love triangles, tragedy, death," I said, pointing to a different DVD with each adjective.

"*Boys over Flowers*, that was too young for me. *Coffee Prince* was popular as well with the young crowd." She pulled the bottom one from the stack. "*Foxy Lady*? You watched that? What did you think?"

We launched into a long discussion about the merits of a drama that featured an older woman, younger man romance. If

Korean dramas followed a certain formula, this one was a little bit different. Sunny and Nari left to set the table as her aunt, cousins and I started reminiscing about some of the classic dramas like *Winter Sonata* and *Autumn in my Heart*.

In spite of the language barrier, their limited English and my very limited Korean, our feelings about these series transcended international borders. I was laying out my theory that a Korean drama wasn't complete without at least one dramatic scene where the main character presented a letter of resignation to his or her boss, when Sunny ushered us into the dining room.

Today the extra leaf had been added and the dining room table was set with countless palm sized stainless steel bowls brimming with *banchan*, along with plates and bowls for everyone. Usually Nari's family ate around a low table in the family room, and I liked that intimate setting best. But for the relatives, Sunny did the formal thing. We were still gasping with laughter when we surrounded the table.

I sat first, urging the others to follow, trying to get everyone out of Sunny's way, so we could eat. She squeezed my shoulder gratefully and brought a stone pot full of bubbling soup, red with *gochugaru*, and the half-shell oysters to the dining room. I shivered in the chilly room. I would have loved to eat outside on their patio and look at the lush garden full of persimmons, Asian pears, lychee, and other fruit I couldn't identify. It was an unseasonably warm day outside, though, so air conditioning it was.

Nari and her cousin were fluent in English, her parents were somewhat conversant, but it tapered off after that among her aunt, uncle, and younger cousins. They started out trying to speak in English to include me as they all caught up on family gossip, but quickly reverted to Korean. I didn't mind. I could follow some of it, but eating kept me busy enough.

After the oysters and soup, we were eating bits of fried fish and barbecued meat when Nari's aunt addressed me.

"What is it you do again, Daisy?"

No matter how many times someone asked me the question, I hesitated, always a beat too long. I'd told the half-truth so many times, you'd think it would have rolled off my tongue by now. "Affiliate marketing."

"What is that exactly?" her uncle probed.

"I place ads for different things on websites and drive traffic to larger companies. If they buy, I get a percentage of the sales."

"So that is how you make money? You have no products yourself, no warehouses?"

"Nope. I rise or fall based on my own marketing efforts," I said.

He turned to his younger three children. "See, that's how you do it in America. Use your own initiative to make money."

Nari's dad interjected. "She's done quite well. Her car is paid for. Her apartment too. She has no debt. Isn't that right, Daisy?"

I nodded and smiled. I may not be proud of the way I'd gotten the money, but my success had been hard earned.

Uncle and dad nodded, each murmuring their version of "good for you."

The aunt looked at Nari, who was eating her rice, practically one grain at a time. "Have you got a boyfriend yet?"

"*Ajumma*," Nari whined.

"What? You're not young anymore. Now that you have your job security, isn't it time to have a family?"

Neither Nari nor I really dated. I knew why I didn't date, having seen the worst from men, but I'd never put a finger on Nari's reasons. Mourning the loss of her boyfriend from a decade ago wasn't enough justification.

It wasn't like there was a shortage of men asking her out. If she wanted, she could have had her pick of every eligible man in a four county radius. She was the kind of woman who didn't need a wingman. Everywhere we went, men offered to pay for her parking meters, her gas, her drinks, her dinner. She could live for free in that city. Nari never accepted a single offer.

"Your younger cousins will get married before you, if you don't hurry."

"There is no hurry, Ajumma. I have my career."

Her uncle put down his chopsticks. "What are you doing again?"

"I'm an internist, *Jakeunahbuhjee*," she said.

"Will you be promoted? Run your medical group? Maybe go higher up at the hospital?"

Nari put down her own chopsticks and sighed. My bowls and plates were clean, of course. Nari looked like she hadn't taken a single bite. Though I was sated, I looked at her plate with envy. Maybe I'd get to take home her leftovers.

"I see patients every day. The job doesn't change. In ten years, I'll be doing the same thing."

"Do they pay you more? How can you be as secure as your friend Daisy?"

She looked at me sideways. "By selling sex," she mumbled. Fortunately, that was lost in translation.

I looked balefully at the second helping Sunny offered me, but turned it down politely. It was time for me to do what I'd done for nearly a decade; play buffer.

"I met someone," I found myself saying. All eyes turned to me. "He's Korean," I said.

All attention left Nari and turned to me with the force of a police interrogation. I dutifully told them his name and that he was a successful comedian. That he'd been on TV. What I didn't know, I filled in. I'd learned to stretch the truth with thirty-year old women doubling as MILFs one day and barely legal teens the next. Fibbing about Raphael was easy. They'd never meet him.

As we left that night, piled high with Tupperware bowls full of *kimchi*, I promised to bring Raphael the next time I came to see them.

Her mom ushered us to the door. "Nari, I do hope you meet a nice man like this Raphael one day."

We held our tongues until we got to the truck. Easing down her parent's street, Nari waited until we were out of sight of the house and her family's watchful eyes.

"Good thing you left out that arrest for statutory rape," she said, giggling behind her hand.

"That...wouldn't have gone over as well," I said.

"Nope. Nope. Too bad they'll never get to meet him," she said. That he would have been a great buffer didn't need to be said.

LATER THAT NIGHT, a phrase my father had repeated thousands of times echoed in my head: Go big or go home. I needed to move to the next step in my career. I wasn't quite ready to give up on my little fiefdom. Nor did I want to slink home to Madison, tail between my legs.

I scribbled out plans on what would be involved in setting up my own pay site. I'd need to hire out the coding and design. I could do a lot of stuff on my own, but usernames, passwords, taking credit card payments... I knew my limitations. But I also knew enough people, at least virtually, who could help with that. The other part, content, I'd have to do myself.

Original content. That was the only way I could see to drive up sales. Everyone was reselling what was already out there. But the girls who set up their own sites were pulling it in. I wasn't porn star material, so I wasn't going to masturbate in front of a webcam. But I was in L.A., the porn capital of the world. There had to be hundreds of people willing to earn a few hundred bucks. If I monetized it just right, I could make thousands.

I pushed through the papers on my desk looking for my last bank statement. I had fifteen thousand dollars in my savings account. This could go either way. I could pay the condo's special assessment and not have to worry about that, or I could start hiring girls, guys, and a sound engineer. I would do the camera. I crumpled the assessment. If this hit just right, I'd have enough for that assessment, future car repairs, and much more.

But first, it was going to kill my bank account.

FIVE DAYS of posting internet ads and sifting through the responses, and everything was perfect except the location. I'd looked into renting some big old tacky mansion in Woodland Hills but it was out of my budget. That left my apartment—which seemed—gross. Then it hit me. Nari was back in Riverside for the final weekend party with all her parents' church friends. Her apartment was fully furnished, completely empty and I had a key.

I drove over to Nari's condo. She'd never moved from the one her parents bought her for medical school. It was right around the corner from nothing. A no man's land south of Hollywood. Kind of near Paramount, kind of near Koreatown, kind of near Larchmont. In L.A. real estate speak, it would be Thai Town adjacent. I was hopeful that her neighbors wouldn't notice a little commotion in her place. I'd known some of the neighbors when I'd lived there, but with the kind of turnover we got in that city, you never knew who'd be there now.

I took one of those huge leather satchels out of her closet and filled it with all of the valuables I could find. All her jewelry, old iPhones—damned if she didn't have one for every release—and her iPad. It wasn't that I didn't trust the crew that I'd hired, but I didn't want to have to replace anything. I definitely couldn't afford that.

She had leather furniture that would wipe clean, and I'd change the sheets on the huge bed. I looked at the phone in her bedroom. Should I call Nari? I was about fifty percent sure she'd say yes. But then I remembered her recent harangue to try to get me out of the business. When she talked about being honest about my profession, I didn't imagine using her place to create new content was what she had in mind. I stood up and smoothed out the duvet cover. What she didn't know wouldn't hurt her. I'd never tell.

Slipping five amateur porn stars and three crew members into the apartment wasn't too hard. It took two elevator trips to get them and all their stuff up to the apartment. I pushed aside the clothes on Nari's portable rack and offered it as a place to hang up the girls' stuff.

"So did you bring enemas?" one of the girls, the blonde asked.

I shook my head. "No. I don't plan to do any anal today." It was probably a mistake, but I didn't want them to do anything I wouldn't want to do.

They all looked surprised. Who was I to limit what could happen between consensual adults? "You know what? I think we may do it. Did you bring your own?"

The young girl I'd hired because of her Goth girl looks, fished around in her bag. She pulled out bottles and packages. "I've got three."

"Oh, okay. Why don't you guys take turns with the bathroom? Then we'll decide about the order."

The sound guy had his boot clad feet up on Nari's leather couch.

"Can you please not do that? This is my friend's apartment. I promised to leave it like I found it."

He threw up his hands and promptly spilled the coffee from the cup he had in one of them. "Sorry, again I guess." I ran to the kitchen to get towels to sop up the mess. Had this guy ordered the largest coffee ever? I shook my head, happy that he hadn't spilled anything on her white flokati rug. Nari loved that round rug and would kill me if the wool was brown instead of its pure off-white.

When the girls came back in, I gathered the crew and actors in the big living area.

"Okay, here's how I saw the day. I think we should be able to do a number of scenes." I dispassionately outlined the girl/girl, girl/guy, and gang bang scenes I'd envisioned. If I played my cards just right, I would end up with about three hours of video. It didn't sound like a lot, but cut several ways, I could get a bunch of short and longer videos. Not to mention all the still shots. Between that original content and some purchased, I could have a small pay site up in no time.

The director, Bob "The Bandit" Whiskey rolled the camera, and the Goth girl who called herself Jinx stood before the lens in the spotlight.

"Jinx? This is for the twenty-two fifty-seven notice. Please hold up your license and state your name and birth date."

"I'm Ashley Padgett. I was born on February twenty-one nineteen ninety-six."

"Wait, what?" I couldn't believe what I was hearing.

"Cut!" the Whiskey Bob yelled. "It's gonna take a very long time to get through this if you interrupt. What's wrong?"

I pulled my hair back, giving my face some air. "I'm sorry. It's just that I remember nineteen ninety-six."

The crew burst out laughing. It didn't stop for a full five

minutes. "Oh honey, if you think nineteen ninety six is young, just imagine what it's like at my age." I looked at him closely for the first time. He was probably around fifty. "They get younger every year. They're always eighteen. Let's get going. Action!"

All five performers gave their real names, addresses and dates of birth on camera. I had them hold up their driver's licenses and state that their performances were consensual. If I was a stickler about one thing, it was staying away from any hint of child porn. I needed a Traci Lords scandal like I needed an STD.

Whiskey Bob looked at me. "Shooting script?"

I handed over the 'script.' With gonzo porn there was no pretext of dialogue. Thank goodness my writing skills weren't going to be tested. I'd never taken the prerequisite screenplay class at UCLA.

"Girl with the dragon tattoo?" Bob chuckled to himself. "Sorry, bad joke there. Girl with the lizard tattoo, what's your name again?"

"Jinx."

"Jinx and Indigo, this is your scene. Have either of you done a girl/girl scene before?" Indigo nodded, while Jinx shook her head. I thought I heard Whiskey Bob mutter something about amateurs under his breath. "Okay, here we go. Jinx, you're the young innocent. You lay back on the pillows, gaze out the window like you're thinking. Indigo, you come in, confront Jinx on thinking about you. Indigo, you'll be the lead. You'll kiss her. Jinx, you're enjoying it, but you keep saying no, because you have boyfriends or whatever. Indigo, I want you to really push it, holding her hands over her head, pushing your hands down her panties, fingering her cunt, biting her nipples. And whatever you do, go slow. We're aiming for about forty five minutes of tape here. Got it? Okay. Action."

I wandered out of Nari's bedroom and into the living room. In the last few years, I'd seen enough sex to last me a lifetime. The guys were eating all the food I brought and flicking through their phones. Thank God I was paying by the scene and not the hour. I'd thought about scheduling them later, but couldn't afford any kind of flake factor with a one day shoot.

"Cut!" Whiskey Bob yelled. "Daisy, come in here." Bob turned to the camera guy "Set up the cunt cam."

I hadn't heard of the 'cunt cam' before, but it didn't take a degree from Owen for me to figure it out. "What's up?"

"Just wanted to know if you want to spice this up with some fake squirting or something? Squirt videos are all the rage right now."

I put all ten fingers on my forehead and massaged away the tension headache forming. I'd only wanted some unique video to bring the jaded web surfers in the door. I did not want to be making decisions like this. "No, no squirting. Just the usual."

Whiskey Bob shrugged like I was the stupidest person ever. "Whatever. Your money to waste."

I turned away, ready to get back to the living room. Maybe I should pull out my laptop and get some work done. Fuck, he was probably right. Maybe I wasn't making money because I wasn't taking chances. The web had gotten more raunchy in the last ten years. Who was I to judge?

"Jinx, Indigo—you okay with that?" They looked nonplussed. Nodded. Didn't anyone ever ask them what they wanted? "Fine," I said to Bob, "you're the expert. I'll trust you."

I didn't go back in there. I'd see the video soon enough. No doubt I'd see the video a thousand more times than I wanted.

After that, Whiskey Bob and friends didn't call me back in. The combinations changed and a couple of the girls went home, their scenes done.

At three o'clock, I looked at my watch. Whiskey Bob saw

me. "This will be the last one. We'll do the last MMF threesome here on the couch. Turn off your computer. I don't want that in the shot." The lighting guy gave me a couple of memory cards. "The two hundred fifty-six gig cards are the video, the sixteen gigabyte cards are the pictures. You should back them up to your hard drive as soon as you can."

I bundled up my computer and got out of the way. I'd back up the cards later on my desktop. I didn't even know if I had enough memory for that on my three-year-old hard drive. While they were setting up and filming, my mind wandered to what I'd need from Fry's and whether more electronic equipment fit into my quickly dwindling budget. I went into the bedroom to clean up then took a load of laundry downstairs. Damn Nari for her all-white bedding.

When I got off the elevator, blue plastic laundry basket in hand, something that sounded like a scream came from the other side of the apartment door. I looked up and down the hallway frantically, glad that none of the neighbors were around. I ran as quietly as I could, jammed my key in the lock and came in, trying not to slam the door behind. I didn't need anyone calling the cops today.

"Oh, fuck," I whispered as what was happening seared into my brain. Nari, her parents, her relatives, and a few others stood by the door while two men undeterred by the commotion double penetrated Jinx. With the glare from the five hundred watt spot and a penis in each orifice, no sane person could be in doubt as to what was going on.

"*Oma, appa, emo, sam-chon...*" Mom, Dad, aunt, cousin. Those were the only words I understood from my limited knowledge of Korean. The rest registered as gibberish, though I could glean about ninety-eight percent from the tone.

"Daisy?" Nari's mother looked at me, her eyes wide as saucers. "What..."

My bow was second nature. It was what I always did with her parents. "Mr. Yoon, Mrs. Chang." To Whiskey Bob. "Can you?"

"We'll cut out the sound and replace it with music. Don't worry."

That wasn't what I meant. I meant could he somehow turn back time. Stop me from making the worst mistake of my life. Stop the three people on the couch from having sex. But none of that happened. I looked from Nari's mother to her father to her aunt. The cousins had already been shepherded from the room by her uncle. I hoped to hell they didn't see anything. I knew how hard it was to un-ring the bell of hardcore porn. Once you'd seen it, nothing could wipe it from your mind.

"I'm sorry. So sorry," was all I could get past the lump in my throat. My heart beat so fast in my ears, I couldn't hear anything Nari said to her family. But her look of horror, of shame, of disappointment in me would haunt me for many nights to come.

From the way Nari hustled them out of there, I knew she'd have to do a lot of explaining on her end. It was clear that it would take a nuclear bomb to get the action to stop, so I let it run its course. The damage was already done.

Peeling apart the stiff one hundred dollar bills, I paid everyone in cash, shooed them out without so much as a thank you, collected my things, and ran from Nari's apartment as fast as my loafers would take me.

It was only when I got home, that I realized I'd forgotten Nari's stuff in the building's laundry room. Hopefully, someone would kindly set it aside for her. I just couldn't go back there now. I had no words for my friend.

FOR THE NEXT TWO WEEKS, I only did two things. I edited, reedited, and packaged my videos, and supervised the development of my new paysite. I also picked up and put down the phone so many times, my thumb could dial by muscle memory. I knew with all my heart and soul that I owed an apology to Nari and her family as well. But what could I say? My best friend's family had taken me in like one of their own. I was so deeply humiliated. I couldn't imagine ever showing my face in front of them again.

Glad that Nari hadn't invited me to Hawaii, I dialed her cell. For the hundredth time, I put down the phone before I got to the last number and got up from my desk chair. I had a graphic artist working on the tits and ass pay wall for my latest dot com. I could never understand why every paysite looked like carbon copies of each other, but they must sell, so I was doing the exact same thing.

The sex business didn't have a shred of innovation. I had a technical guy working on the back end. He promised me I'd be able to monitor lost passwords, process credit card payments, and even do my own affiliate service where I paid other webmasters to lead folks to my own pyramid scheme.

I was looking in the fridge and debating which of my unused web domains I should use when the phone rang. I picked it up without thinking, and then I looked at the caller ID on the phone, its orange LED screen beckoning. "Yoon, Nari" it read. My stomach plummeted from its usual place down to my toes.

Shit, shit, shit. She was home from Hawaii. I didn't do confrontation. I'd never done it, no matter what happened in my relationships. I hit the mute button, and the ringing on the kitchen phone stopped, even though the extensions in my office and bedroom kept bleating out their pleading tone. Finally it ceased. I waited. Nothing from the little light that flickered when a message was waiting.

Knowing Nari was trying to reach me made me fidgety. I

tried to do a few stretches and ran in place for a minute. I picked up the big floppy stuffed frog from my couch and alternatively punched it and kissed it. Much to my disappointment, it didn't turn into a prince or Raphael either. I needed someone to come save this damsel in distress.

EIGHT

RAPHAEL

I NEVER, ever expected to hear from sweet little Daisy again. One solid arrest for statutory rape put a crimp on most hookups. Especially one in which the girl thought you were gay and only found out you were straight by hearing all about your exploits with a supposedly underage girl from a county sheriff. But there it was: Bronwen Fletcher's name on my Caller ID as clear as day.

"What's up Bronwen?" I loved that name.

"Everyone calls me Daisy," she said huffily.

"But Bronwen is so much classier."

"Whatever. Look, I'm having a shitty day. Would you like to get a drink?" The bravado had gone from her voice. Left was nothing but weariness. Despite that world-weary sigh, I couldn't help needling her just a little more. It was kind of a tick I'd picked up hanging with comedians.

"Lilly Pulitzer swears?"

"Seriously?" She sounded exasperated. "You're the only person I can think of who's having as bad a time as me right now. I just need to drown my sorrows. But drinking alone smacks of alcoholism."

"Being acceptable is important to you?" Why was I still talking to her and not figuring out how to get us together in a place with a soft horizontal surface? I knew that's what she really wanted—the kind of succor and solace men specialized in. Her answer broke into my thoughts.

"Far less than you think. Do you want to get a drink or play word games?" She was right, I was having too much fun. If I wanted to actually fuck her, rather than fuck with her, we needed to be in the same room together for a start.

"I don't think, in my current circumstances, I need to add a DUI to my record."

"So come to my place," she said, rattling off an address in Los Feliz. "I don't have as extensive a bar as you and your brother, but I've got the basics covered."

Just like that, I was back in the game. A girl invited you to her place for only one of two reasons, sex or seduction. Daisy seemed like the seduction type. But sex was sure to follow.

When Daisy opened the door to her apartment, I knew I had judged it right. I'd yanked ripped jeans and a classic white pocket Gap tee from my closet. Dressing the part was half the battle. Gone was the cover model for the Preppy Handbook, and in its place was a very rumpled woman who looked like she needed a hug.

Except when I gave her that squeeze she so surely needed, Daisy almost slipped through my fingers. The woman was wearing honest-to-goodness silk. She moped in silk? Now that was class. My dick jumped to half-mast at the thought of slipping her out of that crinkled white top and striped pants. You could take the girl out of Connecticut....

"That was fast," she said, closing the door and motioning me in.

Like I'd let her change her mind. "No traffic on Franklin."

The apartment looked like it had never aged past 1962. It

reminded me of all those early Technicolor TV shows I'd flipped past on Nick at Night when I came home from a club, ready to wind down. I don't know what I'd expected from Bronwen, but the modern vibe threw me off.

Of course, Los Angeles didn't boast many center hall brick colonials. She had a mid-century apartment with grass green furniture right out of Mad Men. The bar didn't looked like Don Draper stocked it, though. Only one half-empty martini glass rested on its smooth surface. The furniture kept the alcohol well hidden.

"What are you drinking?"

"Martini. What's your drink? I can't remember what you were having the last time I was at your house. The police raid clouded my memory."

So that was how it was going to play out? "I don't have a 'drink.'"

"C'mon, you're in bars all the time. What do you usually get?"

I wasn't in bars, exactly. But every club had a full bar of course, because the two-drink minimum was the money maker. And as the entertainment for the night, my drinks were always on the house. I rarely drank before a set, but after, I'd been known to close down the place, usually taking a waitress along with me.

"Screwdriver," I said. After years of ribbing, I knew I was supposed to only like manly drinks, shitty beer, tequila with a worm, scotch neat; but I liked some sweet to help the bitter go down.

She swished into the kitchen, coming back with orange juice. I didn't quite catch how the bar worked. One moment it was nothing but smooth wood staring at me, and the next, a whole set of bottles appeared. The full complement of a bartender's recipe guide staring back at me. She must drink like a WASP. A legal WASP.

Vodka and ice cubes appeared, and in less than a minute, I had a drink in my hand. I helped myself to the couch. Minimalist Scandinavian furniture was as uncomfortable as it looked. Daisy pressed buttons on a slim remote control, filling the room with classic Frank Sinatra. She and her refreshed martini took up residence on a puke green chair. She tucked her bare feet under her. I looked between her and the door behind her, meaningfully. Daisy didn't take the hint.

"Bathroom?"

She gestured to the door I'd just glanced at. I put down my drink and walked to the back of the apartment. There was one bathroom on the left and a bedroom on the right. I only had to get her to move about twenty feet from that chair to the neatly made up queen size. I flushed the toilet and ran the water to make it look like something had happened in there.

Daisy was still perched in the chair so I scooted to the end of the couch nearest her. She had no curtains. The lowering sun filtered through the palm trees outside her huge picture windows.

"Where's your sidekick?" I wanted to make sure this stayed a party for two.

"You mean Nari?"

I nodded. That Korean girl had shot daggers my way at MJ's. She was a cock blocker if I ever saw one.

"She's not speaking to me right now."

Women always seemed to be fighting about something. Trying to figure out which of my mother's friends was in or out at any given moment was like playing chess. "It that the reason you're drinking?"

"Kind of." She focused her blue eyes on me like lasers. "Was that girl really underage?"

I drained my glass, hoping the alcohol would ease the churning in my gut. I'd put lawyers and trials and jails out of my mind for the time being. Learning to compartmentalize made it easier to get up on stage and entertain a crowd. Bob from Des Moines did not drive to Chuckles or Funny Bone to hear my problems—he wanted me to relieve him from his. "She was serving alcohol. If she's underage, she was lying to more than one person."

"Oh, okay." Daisy visibly relaxed.

Did she think I trolled schoolyards? Maybe she was letting me off easy. Either way, I didn't want to talk about it. "Back to you feeling shitty."

"So, Nari is probably really mad at me."

"Probably?" From my experience, women didn't operate in a gray space. They loved you or wanted to kill you.

"You want a refill?" She took my glass before I could answer, and it was again full of orange juice and vodka. Daisy made a new drink for herself. Her walk back to her chair wasn't the steadiest and I wondered how many drinks she'd had before she'd called me. I liked to ease my way into girls with alcohol, but I didn't want them passed out under me in bed.

Daisy took a long, deep breath, followed by a long, deep gulp. "I used her house to film porno and she came home unexpectedly," whooshed out in one beat. "I think she's pissed." I watched her looking at my mouth which was opening and closing like a dying carnival goldfish.

Nothing about the girl or her demeanor said pornography. Nothing. Los Feliz wasn't in the infamous San Fernando Valley. I looked down at the orange juice pulp clinging to the ice cubes. There must have been a lot of vodka because I'd surely heard her wrong. Daisy drained her third or fifth martini. "Oh, close your mouth. Everything *I* was doing was legal. I just skipped the permit process. You cannot say the same."

Nope, I couldn't. The room had just tilted off its axis, and it wasn't because of the three, no two, just two screwdrivers I'd had. Every little thing I'd assumed had just been upended.

"So you...do what exactly?" My gaze wheeled around her apartment like the arms of a first time skydiver. I looked in vain for DVDs splashed with half naked women with outsized breasts, or whips and chains, but it looked the same as when I'd entered—conservative and green.

"I usually tell people I'm a consultant," she said, watching me.

"You just gave truth to that lie."

"So...I'm not a consultant." I could see her weighing the idea of telling me the truth. I wanted to say I wasn't judgmental. But that wasn't true. At some point we all judge. We all have a line we don't cross. I was about to find out if she'd crossed mine—wherever that was.

"So you don't work for McKinsey," I said, even though I knew that was a little snarky.

"You've heard of McKinsey?" Daisy asked like I'd fallen off a turnip truck. Was she just an east coast snob, or did she think comedians were a bunch of rubes?

"I'm a comedian, not a groundhog," I replied. McKinsey was only the most prestigious consulting firm in the world. I knew tons of pushy Asian parents who would've died and gone to heaven if their kids landed a spot there.

She cocked her head to the right, just a little too jerkily. Daisy was going to be one of those drinkers who tried to hold it together at all costs. "Did you go to college?"

"I did three years and change at Pomona," I said. Pomona wasn't Owen, but it had a respectable pedigree.

"So you didn't graduate?" she asked, her voice going all New England patrician on me. Well, that was kind of judgey of her. I wanted to say something about Jesus and casting stones, but she didn't look like an expert on the Book of John.

"Much to the horror of my mother, I am a college dropout," I said for probably the hundredth time in my life. I think white people see me, Asian guy, and assume model minority student. My answers are always a disappointment. "But enough deflecting. You still haven't told me what you do for a living."

Daisy sighed. The shadows darkened, the thick palm fronds throwing the room into an unnatural dusk. She squeezed her eyes shut. "I have a network of websites where I sell subscriptions to pornographic pay sites," she blurted out in one breath.

And the plot thickened. "You're a porn webmaster?" The girl had more layers than an onion. I tried to meld the two images in my head. Conservative Connecticut Bronwen selling tits and ass to horny guys all across the world. I knew those guys. A lot of them—personally. Despite what they claimed, comedians didn't take laptops on the road to write jokes.

"Yes," Daisy revealed through clenched teeth. "You're the first person I've ever told...other than Nari...who's always known."

"But that's working behind a computer at home, right?" I said, gesturing toward the huge screen sitting atop her desk in the small segregated den area she'd set up at the far end of the living room.

"Pretty much."

I drained the watery concoction left in the glass. Daisy shifted like she was ready to refill my drink. I placed my hand over the top. I needed to sober up. Things were getting interesting.

"How did you end up filming porn in your friend's house?"

"Long story short, I need to start using my own content. And I didn't want to do it here, so...."

"You borrowed your friend's apartment." Even I was grossed out by the thought of strangers having sex on my couch, without a really thick antibacterial shower curtain thrown over the cushions. But I'd never seen a plastic cover in a porn flick. "I thought you guys were good friends. How long have you known each other?"

"Since college." Daisy counted on her fingers, even though they weren't enough. She winced. "Like, fourteen years."

"Holy shit. That's not cool."

"She wasn't supposed to find out. Okay. When her family comes to town, she's usually in Riverside for days on end entertaining them; helping her mom and stuff. I usually go out there for a meal or two to act as a buffer. They never come back to town, ever. I couldn't do it here. I only have the one bedroom and the one bathroom. There was nowhere for the girls to change or wash up. I didn't think...."

"That's obvious," I said. L.A. was full of cool, laid-back people. But I couldn't see how that would be cool with any of them—no matter how laid back—without their express permission.

"I'm already beating up on myself enough as it is. I thought you of all people wouldn't judge."

She was up, ready for a refill. I didn't want to watch her get drunk. Not tonight. I plucked the empty glass from her hand and pulled her down on the couch next to me.

I pulled her blue velvet headband from her hair. I wasn't thinking about her bad behavior. I was thinking how much I wanted her. She'd been on my mind since the day I'd met her. I loved conservative girls. But I adored naughty, blue-eyed ones even more. The fact that I knew she was over eighteen took the cake.

Bronwen didn't expect me to kiss her. Girls never did. It was like having a super power. As I leaned in, her eyes widened and her lips parted in anticipation. A whiff of pine from her gin-sweetened breath came with her exhalation of surprise. I covered her mouth with mine and my gut untwisted for the first time in days. Women were the best medicine. Daisy leaned back, but I closed in. I wrapped one hand around the base of her skull and laid the other against her back. Though the silk was cool to the touch, I could feel the warmth radiating from her skin.

Soccer. I tried to flood my brain with my version of hell. The mind-numbing idea of watching a soccer game, or worse ice hockey—soccer on ice—always kept my cock under control. I wanted nothing more than to drag her into that bedroom, pull off her lounging clothes, and get my freak on. But her slight hesitation and her molasses-slow pace told me that she wanted to be seduced.

She'd need the words and low lights and probably a candle or two. When she slid her hands under my shirt, along the bumps of my spine, I remembered where I was: at the home of a woman who sold fantasies for a living.

If Daisy was any good at her job, then she already knew what men wanted. She had a good idea what we liked on the menu and how to serve it up to us. I banished sports from my mind. I needed to let my inner freak out. This was going to be the next best thing to bedding a porn star. All the freak, none of the disease.

NINE
DAISY

"HE ISN'T GAY," rang out in my head. No guy could kiss me like this and like men better than women. He grabbed me with both hands and urged my mouth open for his kiss. I thanked God he was a take-charge kind of guy, because I wasn't a take-charge kind of girl. The whole new millennium, aggressive female sexuality thing just wasn't me.

Raphael broke the kiss just as I was getting a little tingly from the feeling of his lips on mine. He grabbed my hand and stood up. I was relieved that he didn't want to stop kissing me. Trepidation that he would want more than I could give, slowed my movements.

He walked me back to my own bedroom, turning on one of the bedside lamps. My navy shade muted the harshness of incandescence, and the cream colored room remained dim. He stood before me, his breathing getting heavy. His arm came around my sides and Raphael pulled the camisole over my head.

Before I could get used to the early evening air swirling around my nearly bare chest, he'd found the side button of my pants. They pooled around my bare feet and I carefully stepped one foot then the other out of them. I rubbed at the gooseflesh on my arms. This felt so very technical, like blocking out a play. I wanted to get back to the kissing part. I wanted to feel warm and tingly again.

"Do you watch a lot of videos?" he asked as he pulled his shirt over his head. From the tone of his voice, I knew he wasn't talking about Hollywood movies.

"It's my job," I answered offhandedly as I stared at his golden-hued skin. He was my fantasy come to life. As much as I hated to admit, I had a type. Nari was right about Korean men being my catnip.

Since her mom had started lending me Korean dramas on VHS all those years ago, men who looked a lot like Raphael had starred in all my fantasies. Almost every Korean soap starred a ridiculously handsome, self-assured, sensitive guy with unshakable loyalty to a woman. I wanted him to be that man. I wanted to be that woman.

I closed my eyes to clear my head, to focus on the here and now. Raphael pulled me close, his bare skin warming me. I ran my hands through his thick hair, reveling in its springiness, so different from mine, as he kissed my ear then sucked at my neck. He kissed his way down my shoulder, sliding my bra strap down. He pushed the other down and fumbled with the catch a bit before the bit of elastic and lace gave way and fell to the floor.

He shucked his jeans in one fell swoop and pushed me down on my bed. I wished right then, I'd stopped at one or two martinis. My head swam a little as my body tried to find equilibrium. "I'm so glad I don't have to pretend with you," Raphael said as he hooked his index fingers in the lace at my hips and pulled my white bikinis down my legs. I held my breath as he ogled my body, worrying that I wasn't enough for him. My job had taught me that men liked their women with big fake boobs, taut asses, and willing lips.

He kneeled between my legs. "God, I want to suck your little pink nipples so bad, feel them bead up against my tongue." My stomach tensed, waiting for him to make good. He kissed one nipple then the other in rapid succession. But his touch was too brief. Before I could revel in any pleasure from his full-lipped mouth, he'd moved on. He spread my legs further apart, as he moved toward the end of the bed. "I gotta see if this pussy of yours is as pink and pretty as your nipples."

Obviously, I knew a lot about human sexuality, but Raphael's frankness discomfited me. I squirmed, and I think Raphael took my discomfort for lust. Without preamble, he poked a finger inside me and fastened his mouth down there. It was too much, too soon. But I couldn't get my slow-moving brain to make my mouth say it out loud. I tried wiggling back from the onslaught, but Raphael's mouth was relentless. My body got there before my brain could. My womb tightened, and my thighs wanted to squeeze. Waves of an unexpected orgasm ripped through my body. Cries I didn't initiate escaped my lips. I covered my mouth with my hand, embarrassed by my reaction.

Raphael was propping pillows behind my head and holding his erect penis in his hand when I finally opened my eyes. "You don't have to hold back for me, babe. I love a screamer," he said. "My cock is so hard right now. I'd love you to put me in your mouth." I opened my mouth to protest, to say something about this not being what I imagined. He took my gasp as an invitation, and his hard, throbbing penis pushed past my lips making a beeline for my tonsils. "Oh, baby. Suck me dry," he ground out. My pussy tightened again, and I silently cursed myself for my reaction. The smell, feel, taste of him made all my synapses fire.

I wrapped my right hand around him like I'd seen so many women do in the videos and did my best imitation of a porn star.

I sucked and licked as hard as I could, squeezing his balls with my free hand. This was just technical now. Gone were my notions of hours of kissing overlaid with the gauzy haze I'd seen in films. This was just about two people getting each other off, nothing more.

"Oh, shit, babe," Raphael said before he pulled from my mouth. He leaned across the bed, pulled a condom from his jeans and skimmed it over his penis. He urged me to turn over, so that I was on my hands and knees. I obliged and he thrust into me. He held my thighs tight and pushed into me again and again. "Damn, this is the best ride I've had in a long time." Just when I started to get another tingle of pleasure and was on the verge of coming again, he came with a couple of jerks and pulled out.

I collapsed on the bed, hoping for an earthquake. Anything to bury me so deep in rubble I didn't have to think about what had just happened. I guess that was what hooking up amounted to these days. When he went to the bathroom to shed the condom, I turned out the light and turned on my side, feigning sleep. Raphael came back to bed, gave me a perfunctory kiss on the cheek and made himself comfortable. In less than ten minutes, he was snoring softly.

My faced flushed hot. Tears stung my eyes. I grabbed my throat when I started feeling the martinis come back up. I closed the bathroom door softly and turned the taps on full force before I prayed to the porcelain god. It seemed like a long time before I could pull back, sure another wave of vomit was coming on. I flushed, wiped my mouth as best I could with a wad of tissues.

The damp wad of paper stuck to my hand, I glanced at the brown wicker wastepaper basket for a second. The condom was just laying there all exposed, limp and wet—evidence of my mistake. I dropped the tissues on top, obliterating it from my vision, but the thought of what had happened just minutes before brought on a new wave. I brushed my teeth and washed up as best as I could, but I was dog tired.

I looked at my red-rimmed eyes in the mirror and hated the woman reflected there. I came back into the bedroom and looked at Raphael in the muted light. He was sleeping like a baby. I hoped and prayed he'd be gone by daybreak. I lay as close to the edge of the bed as I could without falling off and closed my eyes. My mother always said everything looked better in the morning.

The harsh winter sunlight assaulted my eyelids. I pried open one sticky eye, looked at the clock and groaned. I was not a late sleeper. By now, I usually would have showered, pretended to consider going to the gym, had too much bacon, and started working. Then I remembered. I wasn't alone. For the last ten plus years, most of my sex life was solitary. My friends thought I was picky, snotty, or frigid. But my job had nearly obliterated my desire for men.

I heard Raphael let out a breath, and now I remembered why I'd stopped dating. Men were animals. They were no more than beasts, slaves to their desires. They were only after one thing and the more depraved, the better. I lifted my pounding head and looked over at Raphael. The creamy, high thread count, percale sheet I'd so lovingly smoothed on the bed yesterday morning, slanted across his smooth chest and ripped abs. I cursed as my belly twanged.

How could I still be attracted to someone who didn't give a shit about mutual pleasure? My dad Hugh always said men wanted one thing. So I guess last night shouldn't have been a surprise. But when do men ask what women want? It wasn't Victorian England. I didn't want to lie there and think of the Queen. I wanted kissing, and touching, and consideration.

I closed my eyes against the ache in my head. Maybe that's

why he liked his women, no, girls, so young. From watching reality TV, I think for girls twenty and under, everything was on the menu. After watching years of talk shows, I knew they started doling out blow jobs at rainbow parties in middle school. For me, the menu was as boring as an ice cream shop that only served vanilla.

Despite the persistent nausea and cottonmouth, I stood on shaking legs and made my way to the bathroom. I took a long shower and wrapped my thick green terry cloth robe around me. Pushing open the bathroom door a crack, I peeked around the jamb. Damn it. I was sincerely hoping Raphael would have heard the shower, woke up, and snuck out quietly. He didn't seem like a morning after guy, and I couldn't wait to see the back of him.

I debated between trying to get my underwear out of the dresser without making a sound and getting some much needed coffee into my body. Coffee won out. I was downing a large glass of tap water and shaking two aspirin from the bottle, contemplating my susceptibility to Reye's syndrome when the intercom buzzed.

My heart beat a rapid tattoo of irrational fear. Who would be coming over for a visit? In an instant, I knew. Nari. I ignored the insistent buzzing for what seemed like forever before it stopped. Maybe she'd give up. I'd been avoiding her calls for days. No way I could ever make it up to her. I'd have to adapt to a life without my best friend. War widows had done it. I could soldier on.

I turned to give getting dressed a try when a key jiggled in my lock and the door to my apartment flew open. My heart leapt to my throat, as my mind went through all the women-in-jeopardy scenarios I'd ever seen on Lifetime.

But it was Nari, which meant only my friendship was in jeopardy, not my body. Of course, she'd been holding my spare key for years. But, I don't think she'd ever used it until now. Nari owned every inch of her five-foot nine-inch height, and before I could say anything, she was towering over me, her face full of thunder.

"Hello," I said so softly that I could barely hear my own voice. Me: stalwart New England woman reduced to jelly within seconds. My ancestors would so not be proud.

"Fourteen fucking years, and I don't even rate an apology?" she bellowed. I'd never heard her raise her voice. Never. It was a point of pride. Everyone in her family yelled, screamed, and railed, but never her.

"I'm sorry, Nari." It wasn't nearly enough, but sorry was all I could think to say. I scooted back toward the stove, but she didn't let up. She advanced until she was screaming near the top of my head again.

"Sorry for which part? Using my apartment to shoot porn?"

"I'm really sorry."

"For possibly getting me a huge fine from the city?"

"I'm so sorry."

"For making me hire a professional steam cleaner to disinfect my apartment?"

"You have no idea how sorry," I whispered.

She continued like I'd never said a word in apology, but she did lower her voice. "Oh, are you 'sorry' for humiliating me in front of my parents and family? You know how prideful my mother is. This fucking thing is reverberating all across Korea. If my condo board had discovered it, they would have loved it. They would have probably figured out some way of throwing me out. Or are you sorry for losing five hundred dollars worth of designer bedding? What happened to my sheets and duvet? Did you just burn them for me as a favor?"

What the fuck else could I say? I'd totally written off the friendship. I just knew that she would freeze me out after this.

Nari was not good to people who betrayed her. I hated confrontation. I never, ever expected to have to deal with what I'd done. It had been a shit move. But I figured she'd never speak to me again, and they would be my demons to overcome alone. But there were my demons, staring me right in the face.

"So, that's it? You weren't going to call me, were you? I love you too much to let you get away with this, Daisy."

Raphael chose that moment to come into the kitchen in the tiniest European style briefs ever made. I didn't remember those from last night. "What's all the commotion? You guys are making it hard to sleep off this vodka." He looked at the aspirin bottle still gripped tight in my fist. "Can I have a few of those and some water?"

Nari looked at me, understanding dawning. "You slept with him? The guy who was arrested for statutory rape? Has your judgment completely gone out of the fucking—"

"That charge is totally bogus," Raphael broke in.

He wasn't helping. Nari looked about one step away from calling the county and having me taken away for a little involuntary mental health treatment. I looked at Raphael and shook my head, willing him to disappear. I just wanted him to go—forever. Nari was one hundred percent right about my utter lapse of judgment.

"Raphael, can you please leave?" I asked. When he didn't move, I added, "Now?"

The message finally pierced his hungover brain, and he took the hint. In minutes he was back, dressed in yesterday's clothes. In the light of day, doubt filled my head. How could I have thought this guy liked me? I must have been blind, or half drunk last night. Ripped jeans, a t-shirt. He hadn't thought I needed much impressing, I guess. Raphael hesitated. "So, I'll call you."

I wanted him to lose my number. No doubt an endless line of high school girls and cocktail waitresses wound around his block in a long line waiting to fulfill his base needs. My breeding won out over my anger at both him and myself for him not turning out to be what I wanted. "Sure, I'll talk to you later." He leaned in to kiss me, and I turned my head abruptly.

"So.... Okay then," he said, shoving his hands deep in his pockets and walking out the door. Nari took the liberty of slamming it behind him. I didn't want to face Nari or the rest of the world in my bathrobe. I turned my back on her and walked to my bedroom. I slid open the closet and was comforted by the neat rack of utterly presentable clothes lined up in color order.

I armored myself in a gray glen plaid dress and black velvet ballet flats. I slipped a matching black velvet headband on and felt much better. Maybe the headband was like a good acupressure band. I was debating on jewelry when Nari called out. "I'm not going anywhere. You can't hide out in there forever. There is no back door."

Shit. I put down the gold Tiffany locket my parents had given me for my sweet sixteen and walked back to the living room as slowly as a contrite toddler.

"Come here and sit with me," Nari said.

I joined her on the couch, propping my stuffed frog between us. I'd seen her mom and aunts throw a hand out to smack an unsuspecting relative. I wanted to steer clear of her hands in case they got any ideas. We sat there in silence for a long time. I smoothed my fingers against the lines of my dress, flattening out any bumps in the fabric. Nari's breathing evened out. It looked like she was meditating.

Reaching across the chasm, she took my hands in hers. This wasn't going to be good. I blinked back the tears I could feel coming on. I was about to lose my best friend in the world. "You have to quit your job." I blinked again, this time in misunderstanding.

"Um, I like to eat, Nari. You know that. You eat with me a

lot. I have to pay for all this somehow," I said, gesturing around the apartment. It was furnished. I had heat and air conditioning, indoor plumbing. I liked first world living.

"That's my ultimatum."

"So if I don't quit my job, you're going to stop being my friend. Okay, how juvenile is that?" I was angry now. Who in the hell was Nari to come in and dictate how I should live my life? It had been a long time since she'd helped me pay my bills. How I made my money was my business. "Do I have to write mean notes to the fat girl and sit at your lunch table too?" I was not ten years old.

Nari wasn't smiling. "I'm dead serious, Daisy. From where I'm sitting it looks like your life is spiraling around the drain."

"Gee, thanks. Now paying my bills on time and voting in municipal elections is spiraling down the drain. I'd hate to hear what you think of the president."

"You know what I think of the president and his policies. But this is not about him. He and his wife can deal with his conscience. I'm here to be yours." I searched the room for a trap door. I wanted nothing more than to find an escape route so I could go somewhere to lick my wounds and sleep off my hangover. When I was silent, she tipped up my chin so my eyes met hers. "You slept with a guy after he was arrested for rape? What's wrong?"

The screaming, yelling, and railing I could ignore. But when Nari's brown eyes bore into me and her voice went all soft with sympathy, I couldn't take it anymore. Tears I couldn't stop leaked from my eyes. I fucking hated crying. I never did it. My mother Doris said crying was useless and I totally agreed with her. I'd never seen her do it, and I don't remember crying past the age of three.

"Nari, don't make me do this. I have bills. Lots of them. The HOA wants fifteen thou."

"You can swing that with your savings."

"I don't have anything in the bank. I just used it..." I cringed at bringing up the shoot again.

Understanding dawned on her. "Oh, I see."

"So, that's your only expense? I know your car is paid for. That tank will last forever. Your condo is paid off. So you need to keep this job to what, pay DWP and SoCal Gas?"

"I don't have any skills. A degree in Film Studies is not a resume maker."

"I'm hungry. Can you pick up something from Square One? You know what I like."

"Do you want to go—?"

"I think this is the least you could do." She was right about that. I got my jacket and scurried out the door.

The Sunday brunch crowds in L.A. are hell. Nari knew that. I could only hope that having my hungover self stand in a long line under the white hot sun was my only punishment. Well, this and scraping the bottom of my bank account to replace her priceless bedding. It took me over an hour, but I brought back a cardboard box of Portobello eggs Benedict for her and brioche French toast to soak up the alcohol I didn't throw up last night.

As cool and calm as could be, Nari was sitting at the table, hands folded primly in front of her when I got back. She didn't lift a finger when I, sweaty and agitated from driving and parking, tried to wield the bags without ruining the food. She didn't bat an eyelash while I went to the kitchen, got plates and utensils, poured her the last of the orange juice and set the table. After I sat and spread my napkin across my lap and caught my breath, she slid a piece of paper from the kitchen note pad I kept for grocery lists across the table.

It had a name and a 323 number scrawled across it. Despite

her best efforts to be different, Nari fit into more than one stereotype—her handwriting was atrocious.

"What is this?" I turned the paper over, seeking guidance.

"You have an interview with Isabella Aconi tomorrow at eleven a.m. I suggest you drink a lot of water and get a good night's sleep."

TEN

RAPHAEL

WHERE THE FUCK was my lawyer? I looked around the room, and I didn't see the prick I'd paid seventy five hundred of Gabriel's hard-earned dollars to. I was going to have to work very hard to repay my brother and Ted. I closed my eyes to block out the images of all the shitty backwater gigs I'd have to do to pay them back. *Tennessee, here I come.*

A clerk or bailiff, someone in a uniform started calling names. A lot of bald black men and tattooed Hispanic guys stood up around me in the back of the room. We were separated from the front of the courtroom by floor to ceiling bulletproof glass. So the security, pat down, and endless scanners were a scam? I popped up, poised halfway between standing and sitting in my seat. I thought I saw my lawyer's gray head among the clusterfuck of pinstripes and three pieced suits in the front of the room.

The courtroom quieted down when the judge came in. Case after case was called. I kept trying to figure out what's going on, but my mind wandered to jail and shanks and ass raping. Most of the guys around me had at least a hundred pounds on me, and at one hundred and seventy, I wasn't exactly a lightweight. All the sodomy jokes I'd heard for years suddenly weren't so funny. But the dick jokes...the dick jokes would still crack me up even if I was locked in a cell.

"The People against Raphael Augustine," the clerk called before she recited an endless series of numbers interspersed with the words 'case number' and 'Penal Code.' The guy next to me goosed me and I jerked to attention, standing reluctantly. All the people of California against me. Seemed like overkill. Before I could get my feet comfortable under me, it was over. My lawyer pleaded not guilty, the judge set bail, and I had to sit and wait.

"That's another couple thousand I'm never going to get back," Gabriel said to me when I met him outside the courtroom a few hours later.

"I thought the whole idea of bail was that you get the money back when I show up for my trial."

Normally non-violent, Gabriel smacked me upside my head. It was a classic move of my mother's that I'd never seen from him. "And this is not eighth grade civics. You—no, I pay ten percent, the bondsman puts up the real amount, and he gets it back when you show up. And if you don't..."

I scoured my brain. "Bounty hunters?" My life was about to turn into a very bad reality show.

"That's right." Gabriel put an arm around me and folded me into his car. "You're not going anywhere if I have any say about it."

ELEVEN

DAISY

WHEN DID television studios turn into Fort Knox? What did they have in there on Fairfax and Beverly, nuclear secrets, gold, what? Maybe they were protecting the prizes from *The Price is Right*. But armed sentries seemed excessive for tacky jewelry, dining room sets, and tin can cars. After a protracted conversation with the guard offering my identification and at least two whispered phone calls, I was let into the studio. The Bronwen/Daisy thing appeared to be the source of the confusion. I couldn't be the only person on earth with a nickname. Never had I had this much trouble boarding a plane. TSA could learn something from CBT.

After snaking past blaring sixty-inch screens, posters full of airbrushed actors, and employees in skinny jeans and flip-flops, I was finally led to Isabella's huge—"I've excelled in my career"—vice president's office.

While some nebulous assistant went to find water, I eyed the seating situation. More couches, another big TV. I pulled a spindly wood chair from the corner and tried to gracefully arrange my overdressed body. I looked down at my navy dress with white piping around the sleeves, neck and faux pockets. I'd thought this was casual, but these California twenty-somethings redefined casual. I leaned back, almost toppling the seat as I tried to hide my superfluous blazer by draping it on the nearby couch.

Of course that's the moment Isabella breezed in looking like a mannequin for the business woman display at Neiman Marcus. Her black pencil skirt was so thin I assumed she must have a negative size. Coupled with four-inch heels, it was a wonder she could walk.

I rose and air kissed her in true superficial L.A. fashion as Isabella wasn't European by any stretch of the imagination.

"How are you and Nari? I hardly ever see you guys, and here we are in the same city."

I smiled sweetly, hoping my lips didn't slide their way to syrupy. "We're all just so busy. Especially you. Congrats on your promotion, by the way."

"Oh, it's just a title. Director one day, Vice President, the next. Still the same job. So do you know what we do here?"

"Programs practices," I said, phlegmatic. That was the name of the department displayed in bold on the business cards on her desk.

"The great part about working here is that we watch TV all day." I think I was supposed to laugh. "I'm only half kidding. We vet scripts, attend the table reads and go to tapings or watch the tapes. Does that sound like something you could do?"

"What would I be looking for, exactly?"

"Well, we have to avoid George Carlin's seven dirty words, of course. Then there's violence, sex, bad messages."

"It sounds like you're America's kindergarten teacher." Hadn't we got beyond worrying about penises on national television? I looked around to make sure I hadn't been sucked back into the 1950s.

"You'll learn that the rest of the country isn't L.A. or New

York, or even Connecticut for that matter. They don't want sex or violence on their television."

I took a deep breath. Didn't the company that owned HBO or Showtime own these people? Had she never heard of the Internet? Flyover folks had more virtual sex in their lives than the rest of us, Los Angeles and New York, combined. I kept my mouth shut and played along. I nodded and tried to look thoughtful, pretending I cared about sex on television and wayward rockers who spoke out of turn during award shows.

For the next hour and a half, Isabella schooled me on television and the importance it played in the lives of ordinary Americans. She was likening crass entertainment to something like a cross between Jane Austen and air traffic control. It was somehow precious and had to be protected from disaster at all costs.

I tried not to roll my eyes or contradict her out loud. Honestly? She couldn't possibly believe one nipple and two swear words were the worst thing that ever happened in this country. I'd seen this girl take off her bra and dance on a bar. Even that had not made the Ivy walls of Owen come crashing down around our ears.

"So," she said. I tuned back in. It sounded like Isabella was wrapping up. "I'm going to send you over some scripts. Have a look at them. Why don't we meet again?" She moved to the huge leather chair behind her desk and clicked on her keyboard imperiously. "How about Friday afternoon? Maybe we'll get a drink after?"

I nodded agreement. It wasn't like I was busy on Friday.

A MESSENGER WAS LAYING a thick packet at my door when I walked up to my apartment, juggling my navy blazer, purse, and much-needed groceries. That was fast.

"Hi."

The way he jumped up, I think I startled him. The man in gray shirt, pants, and hat pulled an ear bud from his ear. "You're Daisy?" When I nodded he replaced the ear bud and walked toward the elevator, whistling to himself. I called after him asking about signatures, but he never turned back. I picked up the grocery sack and the packet.

The landline was ringing when I finally managed to get the key in the lock and jiggled the door open. I dropped everything again and answered the phone before it stopped ringing.

"Did you meet with Aconi?" Nari.

"You didn't think I'd show up?"

"Your judgment hasn't been the best."

"Apparently, I have to go read some scripts," I said then hung up before I said something I regretted.

The script thing was an excuse. I put my food away and tossed the scripts in a corner. I didn't have time to play Hollywood. It was time to go live with sultrynewcummers.com and make some money. I needed to fill up my depleted account. The videos were cut, the back end was done, and the infrastructure was in place. My payment processing guy assured me that I'd get payment for signups at the end of every day. I needed that cash. I opened my XHTML coder, checked the files one last time, and hit publish. I had just moved out of the business of selling access to a bunch of other sites, to selling access to my own.

BY FRIDAY MORNING I was pretty sure I was going to cancel my appointment with Isabella. My bank account looked like the heyday of the internet had returned. If things kept up like this, I'd be able to pay my assessment in no time. In the excitement of counting my new, shiny pennies, I forgot to call and cancel.

By noon, guilt started wearing on me. I rolled back in my own leather executive chair and toed at the pile of stuff on the floor, looking for the thick envelope I'd tossed five days before. I picked up the scripts that spilled from the torn folder. I spun the little brass paper fasteners joining the pages. Had they found those in a time machine? I scoured my desk, found a red pen and got to work. If I'd learned one thing in the Ivy League, it was how to cram.

"I hope you didn't spend too long working on these," Isabella said as I walked into her office, clutching scripts and red marker against my chest like a middle-schooler with a Trapper Keeper. This time my short khaki skirt and ice blue twinset was a better fit for the über casual atmosphere of the network.

We sat at the conference table in her vast office. I felt like we were back in college, getting ready to pull an all-nighter. All we needed was Domino's Pizza and NoDoz. Isabella didn't look like she wanted to take a walk down memory lane so I picked up my pen, poised to take notes.

First, we tackled a script for a Saturday morning cartoon. It was terribly violent, and I pointed that out. "So, we're not overly concerned about violence. Wile E Coyote has been trying to kill Bugs Bunny for years. The first issue you wouldn't be able to figure out. We have to vet these scripts to make sure they meet the government's educational requirements."

Maybe the job had more to it than met the eye. "Oh, okay. Well, the kids are in a car without a car seat or seat belts."

"Yup, that's one issue. This is a pretty clean script, so there's only one other thing: one kid calling the other a scumbag."

"That's not one of the seven words." Scumbag wasn't nice, but didn't seem that bad.

Isabella pulled some tome from the shelf under the flat

screen television and flipped it open to 'S,' and pointed a manicured finger. "A scumbag is a used condom. So we can't let this
fly." I guess you learn something every day. I didn't see too many
condoms in my business, used or otherwise. We went over a
sitcom script and one for a late night sketch comedy/variety
show. That show could get away with a lot more, but the
network still reigned in on how many times you could say words
like 'penis.' I had to laugh inwardly. I wondered how many
times a day I thought of cocks. It was probably a lot more than
the average Midwestern television viewer.

The good girl inside me wished I'd looked at the scripts a lot
more closely. It might have been interesting to learn more about
job. But, I'd done my good deed. I hope this was enough to
redeem me in Nari's eyes. I looked down, ready to grab my
purse.

"So, I have to put out some fires on a show tonight and can't
join you for that drink. But the job's yours if you want it."

"Oh, but I missed scumbag and the penis count. I just
assumed...."

"It's not rocket science. You'll pick it up. After all, you went
to Owen." Isabella's voice lowered. Her door was wide open.
"We've got a couple of ex-lawyers who think they know everything and actually know nothing. But the rest went to UC
schools, after the budget cuts, and even they don't mess up too
often." Her voice returned to a normal level. "I mean, whatever
kind of consulting you're doing, you've been able to keep your
head above water. I can't say the same for half the people who
wash out of here."

I was being offered a job. A real one in an office away from
my house.

Isabella paged her assistant. "The girl you'd be replacing is
going on maternity leave next week. Can you start Monday so
you can shadow Emily?"

"Sure," I said, shaking her hand formally. I'd have liked to have had a minute to think about it. But if I turned this down an it got back to Nari, there'd be no excuse good enough.

Yet another girl who looked like she was fifteen escorted me across the lot to a low squat building that housed Human Resources where I soon found myself filling out a job application and handing over my social security card and driver's license.

"Do you have a resume?" The HR rep asked.

"No, I wasn't planning on meeting with you today," I said. I didn't say that I hadn't had a resume in ten years and even if I did—what would I put on there? Consultant could only take me so far.

"No problem," she said. "A lot of people don't, in this town. Everyone's more out of work than in." She paused to tick boxes on the application. "Looks fine. Did your new boss tell you your start date?" I nodded. "Good. Welcome to CBT."

Dazedly, I walked from the building to my car. The sweat on the back of my legs sizzled like eggs on a griddle as they made contact with the hot leather. I was too surprised to really notice more than the initial pain. Opening all the windows, I started the car. I only had two days of freedom left. I had a job I didn't want and it started Monday.

TWELVE
RAPHAEL

I PULLED my bag from the spinning metal carousel in the base-
ment of—I looked around for any indication of where I was—oh,
the Cleveland Hopkins International Airport. I assumed that
'International' meant I could get flights to as far away and exotic
places like—Canada. I turned my phone back on and the screen
lit up with indicators for missed calls, e-mails, voicemails—and
what looked like increasingly frantic text messages.

Before I could reposition my suitcase in my hand and finish
scrolling through the messages, looking for one from Daisy, the
device vibrated in my palm.

"Hello, Gabriel."

I pulled my ear away from his yelling. He was full tilt mad. I
pushed 'end.' I'd give him another twenty minutes. Once in my
hotel downtown, I'd try him again when I could sit down. I
switched off my phone and took the empty train to Tower City.

I'd forgotten that it was still like winter, even in April.
Seventy degrees and sunny can make a man soft. I pulled my
leather coat tight around my throat and leaned against the wind
for the three-block walk to the Sheraton. I had the hotel routine

down cold. Hung up black shirt, shook out my jeans, and made sure my Vans were sparkling clean.

Turning on the Wi-Fi on my phone, I tweeted my followers —hoping to draw some fans to the show tonight in this shitty weather and also looking for dinner companionship. I hated eating alone in a city, and room service universally sucked. A nice looking girl tweeted me back, promising to show me the town. Well as nice looking as you could get from a fifty square pixel Twitter profile picture.

Flicking my finger over the tiny button, I turned the cell service back on. I didn't have a chance to put it in my back pocket before it vibrated.

How did he do that? Was he in his apartment constantly hitting redial? Maybe Ted had designed some kind of program that dialed his phone in a continuous loop. "Hello, Gabriel," I said, putting the phone to my ear.

"I can't fucking believe you jumped bail." Gabriel didn't often swear. If he'd been a comic, he would have been a late night TV show, college tour dream.

I opened my hands dramatically then cupped my other hand to my free ear, though I had no audience. "And yet, I don't hear any bounty hunters pounding down the door."

"You're a son of a bitch," Gabriel said, but I could hear his breathing easing.

"Don't talk about my mother that way."

"Where were you?"

"On an airplane. Mr. Three Piece Pinstripe said I didn't have to be there."

"But," he sputtered.

"But, what? Why don't you tell me what happened?"

"I get to your preliminary hearing, and the courtroom is packed and crazy. I don't see you or your lawyer. Finally, your case is called, and some sheriff all badged and gunned up sits on the stand." I didn't point out that in other contexts Gabriel liked badged and gunned up men in uniform. "He says that the victim said that you had sex with her. And I was so pissed because your lawyer didn't object. I thought the whole point of our legal system was that the victim actually had to be there to point the accusing finger."

"I think that only happens on TV."

"Anyway, he says you had sex with her in a dressing room during a wedding. He made it sound sordid."

"I don't do sordid. She wasn't the bride."

Gabriel snorted, not even acknowledging the good thing that I did, not fucking the bride. "The prosecutor finishes up questioning the cop. Both of them smile smugly, like you were Charles Manson or something and they'd just saved Los Angeles County from your wrath."

"And then..."

"Then your lawyer stands up and asks for the victim's birth-date. He says something about it being necessary to establish the crime. The cop looks at his lawyer. And that guy starts flipping through all the files piled high on his table, but he can't find it." Gabriel's voice takes on an excited tone, his earlier anger gone. "So your lawyer snaps open his briefcase, and all of a sudden you can hear a pin drop in the room.

"He brings up a certified copy of the girl's birth certificate. And hands it to the cop. The cop reads out her birth date and it's eighteen years to the day of the wedding. Then the judge, who I thought was asleep, asks for the paper. He looks at it, shows it to the prosecutor. Then they all go up there and there's a lot of whispering. The lawyers walk back, and the judge announces that the case is dismissed. Just like that."

"It all worked out perfectly, then."

"How could you not be here? Why didn't you tell me you

were going? Ted and I were there. He even took off work. We were worried sick about you."

"I told the lawyer that I'd gotten a last minute booking, and he told me that nothing in the law says the defendant has to be present. I was innocent, so I took this Cleveland gig featuring for Earthquake. I have to pay you back somehow."

"You motherfucker," he said. Gabriel was winding down. He'd be lovable gay guy again by the time I got back.

"Can you please stop talking about Oma that way. I gotta go, I'm working in a few, gotta eat. See you on Monday night." I hung up on him again.

The food at Fat Cats was easy on the stomach, and my dinner companion was easy on the eye. Gotta love the Internet. It didn't lie this time. I'd had some bad luck with ambitiously Photoshopped profile pictures and over-filtered glamour shots, but Jude was the real thing. She was like Daisy Fletcher with blonde hair and not as cute.

I fiddled with the phone on the table. All the messages were from Gabriel, Ted, and Mr. Pin Stripe Lawyer. Nothing from Bronwen. I'd tried texting Daisy, but she straight up ignored me. It was too bad. She was the first girl I'd liked in a while. I liked talking to her and the sex had been hot. I'd have loved to have done it again sober and maybe would've gotten the chance if her BFF hadn't shown up in full banshee mode.

"Hey...Rafe." I'd pulled Rafe out of retirement. Raphael was having a tough go of it these days. My date's shiny pink glossed lips pouted at my inattention. I'm sure she thought the arrangement of her lips was cute. I found it kind of sad. But I put the phone aside and refocused on the girl in front of me, not the girl I wanted.

"Hey, Jude." Not even a small smile. She'd probably heard that one too many times. "Can I see your license?"

"Why?" She said with another whiny pout. So not cute. "I look shitty in that picture."

"I like to compare states," I lied. She reluctantly pulled the laminated card from her wallet and I grabbed it before she could change her mind. I gave her mine just to keep her occupied while I did an age check. I held it up to the dim light. Her birthday was January 11, 1992. After a quick calculation in my head, I figured she was twenty-two and legal. I squinted at the small card more closely. Ah, now I could see why she hadn't wanted me holding this little thing in my hands. She was a brunette. Genetics hadn't produced that gorgeous hair color. The cute celebrity copycat style was all salon, all the way. I handed it back.

She smiled sheepishly. "You're not mad about the hair?"

I laughed. A genuinely deep belly laugh. "Honey, I live in L.A. Most California blondes are really Iowa brunettes in disguise." The girl visibly relaxed, the laughter that bubbled from her mouth a little hysterical. I ordered her another appletini, which Jude downed in one gulp. "Do you want to come back to my room and raid the mini bar?"

I let her settle the bill—I was broke after all—and wrapped myself tightly, preparing for the onslaught of wind and cold. I'm sure there was a reason these five lakes were so 'great' but wind-chill and lake effect snow weren't high on my list of greatness. The short walk back to the hotel was brutal.

The girl peeled off several layers of down coat, scarf, hat and boots. The earlier bravado of a girl who'd agreed to a date over Twitter was flailing. I pulled two locally brewed beers from the minibar, twisted off the caps and offered her one. She hesitated just a moment before accepting and taking a healthy swig.

"Have you done any TV?"

I relaxed. She knew the game. Another starfucker. I was the quasi-celebrity in town for a long weekend. I gave her my standard spiel about being on David Letterman and Jimmy Kimmel. She was in their target demographic and said she caught the shows when she could. I also laid it on thick with my 'inside knowledge' of television. I dramatized what it was like slogging through Los Angeles rush hour traffic to make tapings of so-called 'live' shows at four and five in the afternoon.

"Jimmy Kimmel Live isn't live?"

I laughed, my industry insider laugh. "No, it's taped, just like The Tonight Show. They call it 'live-to-tape' which means they leave in most mistakes. But taping gives them control to delete or fix anything that's too much of a problem."

"Wow, L.A. sounds like so much fun. I've always wanted to live there, you know."

"So why don't you come on out?"

"I've got a good job here with Key Bank." She turned away, embarrassed. Getting up from the bed, she started fiddling with the ice bucket and toiletries on the counter. "Plus my mom says acting is a pipe dream."

I wanted to tell her the L.A. basin was filled to the brim with beautiful, talented girls who wanted to act. But I also planned to sleep with her, so I equivocated. "Do you do any acting here?" For the next ten minutes she talked about some dinner theater productions she'd done in some place with 'Heights' in the name.

I pried the now empty beer bottle from her hand and steered her toward the bed. When I kissed her, I sensed her bravado was all gone. Shit, I'd assumed anybody who agreed to a hook up on Twitter knew the score. I took a deep breath, getting the little head under control, pulled back and looked at her. "You're so beautiful, honey." I pulled her newly manicured nails along my erection. "I want you so bad."

Her dark lashes swept closed over her ice blue eyes. I could practically see her debating whether she wanted to go through with it. I kissed her again, trying to tilt her my way. Her response was hesitant, but she didn't protest when my tongue swept her mouth, or my hand slid under her sweater and undid the single hook on her bra's front clasp.

Her skin was cold to the touch, her nipples pulled to tight pebbles. I laid my warm hand over one breast, rasping my palm against that nipple. I pushed her down on the bed and used my other hand to pull the teal mohair sweater over her head. I pulled that other little pink nipple in my mouth and next thing I heard from her was a moan tinged with surprise. Clearly none of these big old Midwestern guys had done their job right when taking this girl.

I pushed my own desires aside and stripped her naked, kissing and licking her everywhere. She never opened those blue eyes to look at me, but I didn't care. She was probably shy, but my dick didn't need eye to eye contact. I pulled a condom from my shaving kit next to the bed, slid it on, pushed her legs apart, and took her in one stroke. At least I tried. Her knees closed against my naked hips like a vice.

"Hey there. You okay?" I said, stroking her dampened hair away from her face. I tried pushing into her again. I only slipped in a millimeter farther. I squeezed her breasts and licked at her lips, trying to maintain my erection. I pushed again and finally gained entry.

She gasped.

"I didn't hurt you, did I?" She didn't answer, but I wanted to move. Thoughts of Daisy flashed across my mind, and I couldn't not move. I started pumping and didn't stop until I came. I pulled out and went to the bathroom to clean up. She was under the covers when I got back, her back turned toward the windows.

I slipped into bed behind her and snapped off the bedside lamp. The glow of the Browns stadium and other faint lights twinkled before going black over the expanse of Lake Erie. I scooted behind her, touching her breasts again. Her breath hitched. I slipped a hand between her legs and stroked her until she came quietly, drenching my fingers.

I'd forgotten to close the curtains and a surprisingly sunny morning greeted me. I looked in the bed, but it was empty. Aww, that was too bad. I was looking forward to a repeat performance of last night. I'd have even sprung for breakfast. I tried tweeting her again, but Jude ignored me. I showered, but didn't let the disappearing date get me down.

Relieved of pending criminal charges, I was on fire. I did two performances that night and killed it each time. Even Earthquake had to hand it to me. That weekend, I'd delivered him six audiences who were primed and ready for his show.

That first morning sun didn't last long, and I was a happy camper when the deiced plane rose above the clouds and I could see the sun again. I'd barely made it from the LAX short-term airport parking and onto Sepulveda Boulevard before my phone rang.

"Raphael? Joel. We have a problem."

"This had better not be about the money." I'd told the club manager in Cleveland to call Joel because somehow the talents' checks had gone missing last night. And of course, no bank was open on a Sunday. But the Improv was a big club, and I figured they'd make it right. Every comedian I knew was on social media—and a club owner that didn't pay was blacklisted by any comedian who was in it for the money within a matter of days.

"This is not about the money. That's been straightened out by corporate already." Joel didn't sound as mellow as normal. This was a guy who was a pretty good booker despite his nearly daily smoke out.

"So, what's up? I'm about to get on the four-oh-five—"

"What happened with Judith Roberson?"

My car crawled onto the freeway and I wondered for the thousandth time how could there be so many people on the road. "What are you talking about? Who again?"

He repeated the name. "Did you have sex with a girl while you were in Cleveland?"

That sweet girl from Thursday had already slipped my mind. Bad, bad hound dog comedian, I mock-chastised myself. "Sweet little Jude? She was a tight—"

"I do not want to hear any details about that night. You need to get over to my place right now. She found me through the club manager and she's threatening to call the cops on you for rape if you don't pay up."

My car swerved, and the phone hit the floor board with a crack. Horns blared at me from all sides. Several cars did their best to escape my orbit. My heart thudded and my limbs got all loose and shaky as adrenaline coursed through my veins. Forget arrest, I'd almost killed myself back there. Me and the freeway weren't compatible right now. I pulled onto Santa Monica Boulevard and wound my way to Joel's Studio City pad on surface streets.

He was in his little yard, pacing behind the picket fence.

"How much do you have saved?"

"Saved? Shit, nothing. I'm in the hole about ten grand over that last little incident."

"Ten grand?"

"I owe Gabriel. Lawyers charge flat fees, and the bondsman doesn't give money back either."

"What happened in Cleveland? I got you booked there so you could make some money, not fuck a virgin."

"How was I supposed to know she was a virgin? I assumed that she knew the score. I hit her up on Twitter, for God's sake. She was twenty-two. Trust me, I checked ID this time."

"Did she say no?"

I couldn't help a little smile from creeping onto my face. "She didn't say much of anything. We were horizontal most of the time and she wasn't chatty."

"Her family's saying they've gone to the hospital and she had abrasions."

My butt hit his flagstone entryway with a heavy thud. For once, I didn't care that I'd probably gotten a year's worth of grime on my white True Religion jeans. "This is bullshit. Abrasions, where? I wasn't exactly pinning her down." I looked around as the neighbor watered his lawn with a hose, one blade of grass at a time. "Can we go in?"

"Lisa's in there with the kid," he said like I was a threat.

"Let's go to your office." I marched through the front door to his office above the garage. It was where he smoked, so I knew he had to have a lock on the door or some good insulation. Their little toddler wouldn't hear a damn thing.

I stood with my back to the door, watching the neighbor, waiting for Joel. "So what kind of abrasions are we talking about?"

"Vaginal."

"Fucking A. She was really tight. It took a little, um—coaxing—to get the deed done. You know what, whatever. What's it going to take to make this go away?"

"I think somewhere between ten and fifteen grand."

"I'm a fucking road comic. I'm lucky if I clear sixty thousand a year. And that doesn't even take into account taxes or your cut. Unless I get some development money or a hand comes down and anoints me with a Comedy Central special, it ain't happening."

"What about your brother?"

"That fucking well is dry, man. D-R-Y."

"This is about your freedom. You'd better figure out a way to get the money."

I looked at Joel in his nice house, with his nice yard, brand new BMW, part-time nanny, and ten percent of my money. "You."

"Me, what?"

"You lend me the money."

"I'm barely keeping my head above water here. I can't just pull money out of our checking account."

"Yes, you can. And you will. You so fucking owe me this." He did owe me. I'd turned a bunch of my friends onto him. We were all the reason he was sitting pretty. If we all got different management, there would be no Joel Besser or Rogue Talent. "Lisa must get fat fucking residuals." His eyes darted to the side. I'd hit on truth. His wife Lisa had been a child star on a long running show. I saw that saccharine shit on every channel, every day between five o'clock and midnight. "Just do it, man." I walked out. I'd played my cards. If he didn't do it, I was fucked ten ways to Sunday. The last thing I needed was some kind of arrest warrant hanging over my head. I had to go through airline security at least four or five times a month, both ways. I'd never know when the ax was going to fall.

THIRTEEN

DAISY

I SAT on a couch in a lobby for two hours before I saw a single soul aside from the security guard. Somebody should have told me television wasn't an early morning gig. I could have been updating my websites or doing something productive. I considered checking my stats on my phone, but decided against it. No cell signal penetrated the thick walled building, and who knew if they were spying on the free Wi-Fi network. I know that Nari expected me to fold up my porn tent as soon as I got this job, but I wasn't ready to quit, just yet. Hollywood jobs weren't known for their longevity.

Someone finally noticed me and directed me back to HR. There, I dutifully filled out my W4 and I9 forms. The corporation that owned the television network had a large stack of documents. At the bottom of the stack was an employment contract. The salary was forty five thousand dollars a year. In all my posturing on Friday, I'd never thought to ask how much the job paid.

I'd never really had a job after high school. A red flush of mortification came over my face. Is this how much people got paid here? Should I have negotiated more? Did Isabella low-ball me and hire me on the cheap so that she could pay herself more —maybe get an even bigger television in her office?

Nari earned three times that. I'd never be able to afford to hang out with her anymore, not that I wanted to shop at Kitson or Fred Segal. Banana Republic was just fine. But I liked the idea that I could.

When the HR woman left to photocopy my identification documents, my thumbs flicked across my phone finding a website that calculated net paychecks. As a single person, I'd take home about twenty seven hundred a month. I could live on that, I guessed. My HOA fees would definitely be covered. I didn't know what would happen if my car died, or how I could save for later. I had no idea how other people worked all this out. But this, combined with the money pouring out of my sultrynewcummers.com spigot... well now, that would be great.

It was already eleven thirty by the time I got back to the offices. But people were finally there. Taped up on the fake wooden door of a small office, overlooking a parking lot, my name was written in blue marker. From walking down the hall and looking in other offices the size of broom closets and about as appealing, I was just grateful to have a window.

Sitting down at the computer, I set up my password, e-mail, and stuff. I tried for a peek at sultrynewcummers.com, to see how it looked on a low-resolution monitor, but was met with a blood red screen with a big black X across it. I quickly backed out to web neutral Yahoo News and vowed not to do that again.

Isabella and a pale, thin but carefully dressed man appeared at my door. Did everyone there look not like a department store mannequin? Isabella was as perfect as before in an ivory dress so fitted, I wondered how she could breathe. This was a far cry from the girl who only wore sweats in college.

"I always take newbies out to lunch on the first day. Let me introduce you to Connor."

I stood, ready to shake his hand, then fell sideways, twisting my ankle and knee. They rushed to my side, helping me up.

"I'm okay," I said. I'd forgotten that I always took off my shoes when sitting at a desk. I'd only had my feet in the toes when they'd come in. It was a habit I'd formed when working at home. "Let's just go." I noticed that Isabella didn't trip on the worn carpet, even in her three inch beige heels.

When my former classmate and now boss offered me a choice between the commissary or the Farmer's Market a block away, I knew that she'd totally lowballed me. Isabella was keeping the money she'd saved hiring me in her pocket. I picked the commissary.

Armed with three salads, we snagged an empty table.

"Connor, you should know that Daisy and I met each other in college. Don't worry though, I promise not to show any favoritism. I mean none past hiring a total newbie for the job." She laughed, my inexperience a joke.

"What did you do before this?" Connor asked innocently.

Shit, shit, shit. Why hadn't I spent the weekend thinking of some plausible answer to what had happened with the last decade of my life? "I, uh, did some consulting work," I answered, my voice getting quieter by the word.

"Well that's a broad term that could cover just about anything," Connor said shrewdly. "What kind of stuff? Entertainment?"

"You could look at it that way." It was the most honest statement I'd made in ages. "I did a lot of web development and affiliate advertising. I created a network using SEO optimization to drive customers to various product and content providers." Connor nodded like I wasn't a complete idiot or smut peddler. Even I was proud of my explanation. It totally sounded like some businessy thing my dad Hugh would have said.

"Oh, sort of like the MySpace guys did before it became MySpace."

"Exactly," I said. "Unfortunately my little business didn't come with a twenty million dollar pay day. It was a lot easier to make money in the early going before consumers got more savvy and click through rates fell through the floor."

"What is your business called?"

"Images of Harmony," I answered automatically. That was the unfortunate truth as well. I'd always considered my business name an ironic twist, of sorts. I put down my fork and surreptitiously wiped my palms on my favorite dress pants. I was doing so good at telling mostly-truths. I just hoped IoH slipped his mind and he didn't try to Google me back at his desk. My websites were on a well known, not safe for work, porn host, which was why it had come up blocked on the corporate network.

"Daisy will be giving up all that, of course. Working in this job is a full time commitment," Isabella piped in. I didn't think working there meant I'd have to give up my other source of income. But I would certainly pretend I had for her and Nari as well.

"What was Isabella like at Owen?" Connor's eyes danced mischievously.

Weekend bingeing, naked table dancing Isabella would have to stay in the past if I wanted to keep this job longer than four hours. I punted. "What happened in Olde Haven, should stay in Olde Haven."

"Although I think," Isabella rolled her eyes heavenward like she was digging into the far reaches of her memory, "at that time our little Daisy was Bronwen from Greenwich or Darien or some wealthy town."

"My name is Bronwen, but I've always been called Daisy," I said, trying to build my own picture of a middle class girl from a boring old town. "I lived in a little town called Madison. Nothing nearly as fancy as Greenwich."

"Isabella, I've never asked where you're from." Connor turned toward her, his brown eyes showing genuine interest.

In sharp contrast, I got eyes like daggers from Isabella. I couldn't quite remember where she was from. "New Jersey," she said. Her tone put an end to the getting to know you conversation. "Connor will be training you over the next few weeks," Isabella was all business now.

"What happened to the person I was replacing?" I asked, a little perplexed.

"Oh, Emily Meyer? She called on Friday, which was why I didn't have time for a drink. Of course, she had to leave earlier than expected. Emily's on bed rest right now," she said. Nothing in her tone suggested she was worried about Emily or her baby. Pregnancy and bed rest had clearly put a crimp in her department.

"I'm taking over all Emily's shows right now," Connor interjected. "You'll work on those with me, and hopefully you'll be handling them on your own in a few weeks."

"So if Emily's on maternity leave, when is she coming back?" I was sure I'd signed up for something more than a temporary position. I know the employment contract said 'at will' about a thousand times, but who expected to be laid off after only a few months?

"This is Emily's third. She wasn't able to work out something part-time with HR. I don't do part-time in my department. We all need to be available at a moment's notice. Coupled with emergencies, there are Grammys, Tonys, People's Choice—that all go late into the night." Isabella shrugged one slim shoulder. "I assume she'll come back in a less demanding department, or she won't come back at all." She flicked her hand like the Emily problem was easily dismissed. "Not to worry, you're in for the long haul," Isabella said breezily. I guess if she wasn't worried about my position, I shouldn't be. Isabella and I hadn't been that tight in college. I knew I'd have to keep my day job, now my night job.

Alumni relations got me a job, not job security. I'd have to tell Nari, I couldn't quite give up porn just yet. I guess my biggest worry now would be fucking up the job and hoping they'd keep me on. First, I had a job I didn't want. Now I had a business I wasn't sure I was going to be able to keep. Fucking life. I tuned them back in, picking up bits from their conversations about different producers. I was going to have to learn—from scratch—what was acceptable and what wasn't.

I chewed through my lettuce, dried fruit, and sunflower seeds thoughtfully. My hands were getting clammy, and sweat prickled against my newly shaved underarms. I was going to be responsible for keeping violence and sex off television. Me. The irony hit me just then and I started laughing.

"What's so funny?" Isabella asked.

"Share the joke," Connor said.

I couldn't share. I just shook my head, feeling my face get hotter and hotter, and tears rolling down my cheeks in my second unprofessional move of the day. "Sorry, it all just hit me," I started, truthfully. They looked at me strangely. Neither one of them lifted a fork to their mouths, nor put a straw to their lips. I scrambled for something to say. "I, uh, just had a thought about a comedian I once saw and a joke about the Janet Jackson, um, 'wardrobe malfunction.'"

I could tell neither one of them thought that was funny in the slightest. I stuffed more roughage into my mouth. Wow. They took this job seriously.

Connor broke the awkward silence. "So Emily was covering

four shows, and she'd just started a new reality show." He laid out my typical workweek. I'd have to review scripts from two dramas and watch the dailies sent from production. I'd do one game show. And I'd be assigned one three-camera sit-com. Each staff member only had one, because they were all taped live on Friday night and a staffer could attend only one at a time.

There went my Friday nights. Not that I'd ever done anything on Friday night, but I could have had a life to give up. And also, I'd start from scratch on a reality show featuring stand-up comedians. I laughed, inwardly this time. Damned comedians wouldn't leave my life. I shook my head. I still thought about Raphael. I'd itched to answer his text. Only the thinnest layer of pride kept my thumbs from the phone's virtual keyboard.

"Sorry." Connor stopped speaking for a moment. "Do you have anything you don't understand?" How long I'd been quietly shaking my head, I didn't know. Unless I started stepping up my game, Connor and the rest of the staff would think Isabella had hired an idiot crony.

"Nope, just taking it in," I said. Right then I vowed to stop laughing, crying, falling, and shaking my head at inappropriate moments.

AFTER LUNCH, Connor dumped a banker's box on my desk. I lifted the foot-high stack of papers from it and plopped them on my desk while he looked on.

"I'm guessing, this will be keeping me busy."

"Isabella doesn't hire us for our looks."

"What is all this?"

Connor explained that the comedian based reality show I'd been assigned was called *Heir to the Throne*—as in the winner would be crowned the so-called King of Comedy.

"Again, Hollywood loses the originality contest."

Connor laughed behind his hand, but quickly caught himself. No dissing our paymasters, was obviously rule number one.

JOEL TURNED to a cabinet in the back of the room. He pulled a door and took out a leather binder. He sat down and scribbled out a check for fifteen thousand dollars, tearing it from the book violently.

I reached over to take it, but he pulled it back, writing VOID in huge block letters across the front.

"What the fuck?"

"I'm not going to let you give her a check. It doesn't work this way. I'll handle the negotiations, have her sign a release, and pay whatever is necessary." He handed the bum check to me. I took it reluctantly.

"What am I supposed to do with this?" I asked, letting the paper flop between my fingers like a limp dick.

"I'm handing this over symbolically."

"What the fuck?"

"Your vocabulary astounds me."

I gave him the stink eye.

Then Joel adopted 'the tone.' I was the small child and he was going to teach me a lesson. "I will do this for you because I'm your manager and your friend. But I have one condition."

"What's that, Dad?"

He gave me the side eye. "You have to get off the road."

"So you want me to give up my livelihood?" I let the check flutter to the floor. "That's a deal I just won't make. I guess I'm going to have to take my chances." He was still talking to my back.

"You'll never pay me back if you're not working. I want you to audition for *Heir to the Throne*."

I whipped around, knowing I must have misheard. "My God, you want me to do reality television. You might as well put the nail in the coffin of my career."

"Look, you won't have to sit in an audition room for six hours. The producers have arranged auditions for the top agents and managers. It would be a showcase just like SNL or Toronto."

"If I can get past the cringe-worthy reality show part, please tell me how I'm going to get paid."

"If you get picked, you'll live in a joint 'house' and you'll get a stipend of twenty five hundred a week."

I had to admit that twenty five hundred a week wasn't too shabby. I was lucky to get half that in a good week. I'd love to have the cash and avoid the middle airplane seat, crappy comedy condos and fried food. I'd grown to hate molded and formed 'chicken.' I could pay Gabriel and Joel back and still bank cash. I took a deep sigh and did the sign of the cross for the possible end of my ten-year career.

"What would I have to do?"

He took his phone from his pocket and scribbled some information down. "The audition is Tuesday night at the Ice House. That gives you a couple of days to work out your best five minutes."

"Clean?" I asked. Television, for obvious reasons, required a comic to work clean—no swearing, no sodomy, no bestiality—the main tools of the comic's trade.

"No. They just want to see if you're funny."

I ALMOST MISSED the one story burgundy painted building on my first pass down Mentor Avenue. A line of people stretched down the street and around the corner. Some people were eating from camp stoves, others hovered in tents, trying to keep themselves dry from the rain. I made a second pass to confirm what I'd seen. I gave up parking close by on the street, finally found a space in a nearby public parking structure, and called Joel.

"I have an audition spot, right?"

From the cursing through the car's mike, I assumed he was looking at the crowd too. "I don't know what the fuck that's about, Raphael. I'm going to call the producers now. I heard nothing, nothing about this being an open call. Where are you?" I told him. "Wait right there. Let me confirm with the network."

I watched the rain dripping from the cement openings in the parking structure. It rarely rained in California, and I'd always liked it as a child. My mom would make some kind of spicy soup like *gamjatang* or *kimchi chigae* and she'd put on a classic movie and snuggle up with my brother and me. I banged my dashboard when I felt a thickening in my throat. Gabriel and I had to cut ties with our parents. It was the right thing to do. I missed Oma sometimes, but not seeing her or Dad was for the best. The bleating phone distracted me from my thoughts.

Joel started speaking without prompts. "What you saw is supposed to look like an open casting call, but it's all for the cameras. You guys will audition first inside the club. Then they'll do some extra shots with those guys and audition some of them for the bad comic outtakes. No worries."

I parked and fished my umbrella out of the trunk. A spider fell out when I shook off the dust. I walked the block to the club, past the long line of hopefuls. They smiled at me and were generally cheerful. But the crowd took a bad turn when someone pushed open the door and let me inside. I heard a lot of yelling about cutting in line, and 'let us audition.' A producer shook my hand and showed me to a seat in the club before he yelled at his assistant to calm the hordes by handing out releases and Bic pens.

The noise subsided when the door closed. I sat at one of the tiny wood tables, only big enough for a two drink minimum, and tried not to get my sleeve gummed up with whatever sticky residue remained.

A line of producers sat in the back, and we were given the order of auditions. Ten comics would go on stage. We'd get five minutes each. I was third from last. I tried to focus on my act and not think of all the famous names permanently inscribed on the outside of the building. They all had to start somewhere. Although that somewhere wasn't reality show hell. Not for the first time, I wished I'd come up in a different era. Then I thought about Gabriel coming out in that different era and felt chagrinned.

The producers were a tough crowd. They didn't laugh at much. Some scribbled notes while others lit their faces blue with their smartphones.

Though I knew it was a risk, I did new material.

"Do you ever wonder why some people live down to their stereotypes?" Well, I had the attention of at least two of them. "Think about it. Is there any reason you should know someone is gay from looking at them? Sex is private, right? So why can you tell a dyke from a hundred paces? When she cuts her hair short, puts on a hundred pounds and tucks in that flannel, what message is she trying to send? And gay men, you're no better.

All those shirts three sizes too small and the hand gestures. What's up with the hand gestures? If we need to know you're gay, then we'll meet you in a club or something. But does everything in your life have to make you so excitable?" I was getting laughs, if 'you've just lost the PC war chuckles' counted. "And why do black guys all walk with that limp? You know the noticeable dip every time the right leg goes down? Is there a school that teaches that? Dorsey High, maybe?" I threw in some of the stuff I'd started at the beginning of the year including the Jesus fish jokes. They weren't howling, but no one was looking at their phone by the time I wound up my set.

I STAYED to watch the last three comedians perform, all of whom I knew. It looked like the line up for Mo' Betta Mondays, the weekly black and minority night at the Hollywood Improv. Producers were filling up the affirmative action spots. Twenty-five hundred dollars a week kept me from being too insulted.

The rest of the comics did okay, because who couldn't do a five minute spot? I had a good thirty minutes and was working up to a full hour so I could headline on the road. I walked out with Joel, past the comedian wannabes who were still lined up outside. I almost felt sorry for them. Clearly these were people who had no idea how Hollywood worked. They'd probably be filmed for silly outtakes, a la American Idol. I'm sure the next William Hung was just around the corner.

Joel stood by my car. He'd parked just a few slots away. "So when will we know something?"

"Very soon. It's going to tape now to be aired this summer."

"What's the so-called prize?" All reality shows had some prize, even if it had to be donated to charity, as was the case with B list celebrities on up.

"Quarter million dollar development deal with one of the

network's channels or they'll fund an hour special on their comedy network. None of that has been finalized. But for sure you'll get headliner bookings at the Improv with full pay."

Money may not be the root of happiness, but it would certainly solve a lot of my problems. It could even do something for my career. I figured I'd move from featured act to headliner in the next three years, but if I could jump ahead, like a kid skips second grade, I'd do it.

I WASN'T EVEN home when Joel called again.

"You got it."

I hooted and hollered in my car. When people stared at me, I realized I'd left the window down when I'd opened it to keep the car from steaming up. I was still mad as hell at the Cleveland girl for throwing around false accusations, but maybe she was the best thing that ever happened to me.

FIFTEEN

DAISY

DURING THE FIRST two weeks on the job, I never had time to look at the papers from *Heir to the Throne*. Every day the stack sat there, threatening to topple. I wished it back in the box Bewitched-style, but magic wasn't my strong suit. Connor hadn't so much taken over Emily's work, as much as dumped Emily's work in my lap and made sure I didn't fuck up too badly.

I honestly alternated between the belief that the job was important or a complete sham to appease right wing Christians and those endless family values councils who'd initiated post-card campaigns that killed innocent shows. I'd learned a lot about those so-called letter-writing campaigns during my first few days. Those were to be avoided at all costs. Isabella feared a single three by five card more than she worried about the FCC.

Connor pushed open my door without knocking. Note to self: don't pick nose or adjust underwear in your office, not that I'd ever do either. He thrust more papers at me. Despite the so-called electronic revolution, television was still paper driven with endless piles of scripts, memos, and 'notes.'

"Here are the dossiers from the remaining contestants for Heir."

"Just pile them here, I haven't even had a chance to look at the rest." I gestured for Connor to sit down. I knew he was busy, but someone had to give me the scoop. And bothering ice-queen Isabella didn't seem like an option. "C'mon, Connor. Give me the quick and dirty. What am I supposed to do with all this, exactly?"

He glanced at his watch, sighed. "Let me break it down. There are the contestant questionnaires, psychological profiles, and background checks. These guys, and maybe a woman or two, will have to live in a house together for about six weeks. You need to make sure they don't kill, maim, or in any way harm each other on our watch."

"Don't you have them all sign releases for that? What about that entire floor of in-house Legal?"

"Releases don't make us immune from all liability. And Legal? Those skinflints? They'll maybe assign one lawyer to the show. They should be checking too, but they have other issues. So this falls on us. Just read through it all, flag anything that seems like it needs a second look, and discuss it with me tomorrow morning. Okay?" He was up and out before I could do more than nod.

Tomorrow? I glanced at the computer. It was already past three, and I had two more hours of television to watch. I looked around for a bag or box to put all this stuff in. The job hadn't seemed the type to require a briefcase. I guess I was now one of those people who brought work home. Not to mention all the work I already had at home. I popped the DVDs into my purse, found a box in the copy room, and left a Post-it on my door that I'd be working from home.

.   .   .

WHILE HALF WATCHING the decades-old police drama with actors who all looked like grandparents, I started in on the stack. I was pretty sure they'd assigned this show to me because nothing happened, ever. Someone died, old people drank sherry, talked a lot, and somehow solved a murder. I didn't think anything interesting or objectionable would ever come from the gray hairs, so I figured I was pretty safe keeping it on in the background.

The premise of the reality show was simple enough. Ten comedians would compete for the King of Comedy title. They would have to write new jokes every week and compete in some silly challenges to keep from being voted off. The winner got a deal that would pay them a lot of money to develop a TV show for the network. I hated cheesy reality shows, but the prizes looked good. For a brief few seconds, I wondered if I could write a few jokes, be the diversity candidate. Surely there weren't too many like me trying to compete. After I fantasized a few more minutes, I got to work.

The full-length pictures of the contestants could have been duplicates of one another. Was there a cabbage patch that created nothing but soon-to-be-middle-aged, balding white guys with a paunch? Throw in a flannel shirt and Vans, and I think they should have called the show, Pod People. I looked at my stack again, but counted only eight people. I looked around and finally found the papers Connor had brought into my office this afternoon. Ah, the final two applicants. Connor had attached a sticky note to the top that said, 'diversity' applicants.

I took a quick glance at the pictures. A black woman graced the top and an Asian guy below. My brain hit a snag and I looked at the second picture again. Fucking A. It was Raphael. He was a possible contestant for *Heir to the Throne*.

. . .

NOW FAMILIAR WITH the background check reports, applications and psychological profiles, I looked at Raphael's application again. He'd checked the no box next to the question about felony convictions. The investigator's report was similarly blank under the convictions heading. The report had no 'arrest record' heading. This was the first glaring error I'd come across. I couldn't believe they had not thought to list arrests.

I could totally see a scenario on some stupid dating show where the guy had been arrested for domestic violence a zillion times but never convicted because the victim always backed down at the last minute. Would I want to work with a guy like that? Would the network want a guy like that around others in isolated conditions?

I plucked the picture of Raphael from its stapled moorings, wanting to kick myself for the jolt I felt in my belly just looking at him. How could I still be attracted to some guy who'd been arrested for statutory rape right before my eyes and treated me like shit in bed? It was perplexing. If I believed in therapy, I'd probably get some.

While I was dialing the number on the contact sheet, I couldn't decide if my nice girl was winning or if I was turning into one of those idiot girls who chased bad boys. When no one answered the phone, I almost hung up. Almost.

"Hi, Raphael. This is Daisy Fletcher, you know, Bronwen. Anyway, I'm calling in an official capacity. I'm counsel for CBT' Program Practices. I'm calling about your application for *Heir to the Throne*. Give me a call back at your earliest convenience." I looked at the phone. I was such a fucking liar. Who would call in an 'official' capacity from their home phone? I jotted some thoughts on sticky notes and put them on the stack. I needed a dinner break.

I slurped at thin, prepackaged miso broth as I watched the dramas I'd brought home. Neither one of these productions pushed any boundaries, so I'd probably be safe not sending notes back. The intercom buzzed, and I almost spilled the thin brown soup on my pale green couch. Fortunately, the napkin in my hand saved the day.

"Who is it?"

"Raphael," the disembodied voice said. I pushed the buzzer without replying. In less than two minutes he was at my door, knocking. I hesitated a long moment then unfolded myself from the couch and opened the door.

He came toward me like he was going to hug me. I had to pull myself back from the lure of his perfect hair, apologetic brown eyes, and taut body—obvious under his heather gray t-shirt and fitted pants.

"So that's how it's going to be." Raphael said.

For one moment, I wished I'd grown up as anything but a repressed New England WASP. If I were Italian, or Irish, or Puerto Rican, or Korean or black, I could have told him off in a million different colorful ways. But I couldn't get my British Isles descended lips to form the words this man needed to hear. "Your application says you've never been arrested or convicted of a felony."

"Is that a question?" He stood awkwardly between my door and the kitchen table. "Can I come in?" I stepped back a few feet and he shut the door behind him. I went to the living room, picked up a stack of papers and came back, thrusting them at his chest. Raphael gestured toward the white tulip chairs. I nodded and pulled up another chair. He placed the stack on the round tabletop, nearly toppling the four tiny cactuses I kept in the middle of the table. "Why do you have my application for *Heir to the Throne*?"

"Didn't you get my message?"

"Excuse me if I can't quite follow how one minute you're shooting porn and the next minute you're working for CBT.

One Janet Jackson nipple did not change it into the Playboy Channel."

I wanted to say that I shouldn't have to explain myself. Instead I gave him the rundown about making things up to Nari and getting the job at Program Practices. "So what are you going to do?"

"My manager filled out the application. Anyway, there's nothing to worry about. The case was dismissed."

"Just like that?"

"The girl was eighteen."

I didn't need to glance down at the application to check his date of birth. I'd memorized it. "I guess you like them young."

He leaned back in the chair, owning it. "I liked you, Bronwen."

I unconsciously massaged the little wrinkles that were already developing at the corners of my eyes. "Really? I'm not in your target age range."

He pulled my hands from the side of my head and held them in his. "You never called me back." I snatched my hands away. Touching Raphael was like playing with fire. I couldn't believe he had come. I should have shit canned him from the show and called it a day. No one would have ever batted an eye and they could have filled his slot with some other 'diversity' candidate. No doubt that line was long in L.A., where the streets were paved with the shattered remains of dreams. "Can I take you to dinner – to make up for whatever I've done wrong?"

"I drive, and I pick the restaurant."

SIXTEEN

RAPHAEL

I LOOKED over at the woman who treated me like I had leprosy and my heart beat a little faster. Bronwen was still doing it for me. She made me think about things other than getting laid, writing jokes, or drinking. That was a lie. She didn't make me forget about getting laid.

Bronwen made me forget about getting into anyone else's pants but hers. In retrospect, the cocktail waitress from the wedding and the Cleveland Twitter hookup paled in comparison to this fully formed woman who sat next to me. She pulled into a restaurant on Kingsley, a Korean chain that specialized in soondubu chigae.

At early bird time, the usual line wasn't snaking through the vestibule and out the door. We were seated immediately.

"You didn't have to bring me here," I said. "I'm only half Korean."

The look she gave me told me I'd stepped in it again. "It's chilly outside and I was in a soup mood. If your non-Korean half can't take it, I'm more than happy to eat alone."

I held up my hands in supplication and ordered my *soon-*

dubu, medium, after I explained to the waitress that I didn't speak Korean. It was the one Korean phrase I'd perfected.

I shouldn't have been surprised that Bronwen took a huge bite of the whole fried yellow corvina when it arrived. She sunk her teeth into a fried flank and chewed fin and everything without reservation.

"I thought we were getting along great," I said by way of an opener. Being a guy meant facing rejection about fifty percent of the time you put yourself out there. I don't know why potential rejection from this woman bothered me so much, but it did. I gave myself a quick pep talk. I'd scored before her and would again.

"Do you mean after your arrest for rape or after...," she faltered a moment, "...that night?" Then deftly picked up her fried fish with her chopsticks, bit the head clear off, swallowing it whole. For the first time in nearly two decades I'd been dating girls, I was unmoored. It was like the chair had been pulled out from under me, and any minute, I was going to fall to the floor. The precarious balance between being grounded and being on the ground was hard to maintain.

"I thought we had a good time together that night," I said, all bravado and confidence gone from my voice.

"I was drunk," she said.

The clang of the chopsticks on the tile floor reverberated in my head. Oh, shit. Was I walking into yet another rape charge? I picked up new chopsticks from a cup on the table and pushed the bones of my fish aside. The starchy rice and bubbling soup in front of me, the kind that had comforted me so much in my childhood, suddenly turned into a cauldron from hell.

"I wasn't exactly sober either," I said defensively. "I didn't do anything you didn't want to do." She ate very carefully for a quiet few minutes. I could hear the yelling of the waitresses to each other, the bustling of the patrons, the sound of metal chopsticks and spoons scraping against stoneware, but the silent bubble between us grew and grew. "Bronwen? We clicked. We understood each other. We had wall banger sex, right?" I hated the plaintive note in my voice. Why did I need confirmation of something I knew to be true?

When she finally put her chopsticks down and looked up, the blue eyes that penetrated mine were red rimmed. She shook her head slowly. "You really thought that what happened between us was good?" Her eyes searching mine and her tone told me she probably didn't think so.

"I didn't have to pretend around you. Your job," I faltered a little. "You know what a man wants. That was incredibly sexy."

"So what does a woman want?" she asked pointblank. I hoped that none of the elderly patrons who surrounded our table spoke English. Eighteen years of experience with the opposite sex and my mind emptied. Bronwen jabbed a chopstick in my direction. "What? You're thirty-three and don't know the answer to that?"

I shifted uncomfortably in my seat. I was always the one doing the seducing and the convincing. But I always had words, and my mouth, and my hands at my disposal. Without those tools, I was defenseless. "I thought you...wasn't it good for you?"

"Sometimes an orgasm is a reaction as uncontrollable as spontaneous laughter, or as reflexive as passing gas."

I guessed there wasn't going to be any sexy talk tonight. "I give up, Bronwen. What did I do wrong?" I sat back and crossed my arms. My posture wasn't receptive, but I'd gone down on her, for pity's sake. I thought most men didn't do that. I had and she'd come. What was I missing?

"You treated me like I was some object, there for your pleasure. You wanted the light on. You wanted a blow job. You wanted to do it doggy style." Each sentenced was punctuated by a jab of her chopsticks. A few grains of rice flew across the table at me like little white missiles.

"It's not like you were a virgin."

"What, a woman only engenders consideration her first time around? After that it's open season?"

"But you knew the score. It's your job to know the score." The sands were shifting under my feet. Daisy and I were not on solid ground.

"Just because I sell access to pornography does not make me a whore."

"You're judging women who sell sex for a living?"

"I'm not judging. If women didn't sell sex for a living, I'd be homeless. The women in videos or whatever are paid to be treated that way. My point is, they know what they're signing up for. I wanted..." Her eyes flickered away. "Well, I know what I didn't want."

I leaned forward, my most charming smile played on my lips. "Can we go back to your place? Try again?"

She was not charmed. "Do you want to be on the show?"

I didn't see what one had to do with the other. "Sure, yeah. My career could use a kick in the pants."

"Then I think this newly minted CBT employee can't take you home."

My penis was as deflated as my career. I flagged down the waitress and pulled my credit card from my wallet before Bronwen could pick up her purse. It was the least I could do, apparently.

Daisy pulled up to my car and hit the emergency lights. The blinking of the little orange light in the dashboard matched the beating of my heart. I wanted to come up to her place, to show her that I was more than some oversexed mass of testosterone. But, I didn't know how to get from point A to B with her because I'd never done it before. I'd never wanted to—

"So, I'll just approve your application." I couldn't read her. "I guess I'll see you around. Goodnight, Rafe."

I pulled her hand from the gear shift and held it loosely in mine. I kissed it gently. "For you, Bronwen, I'll always be Raphael."

She snatched her hand back like I'd given her the kiss of death.

SITTING around my apartment waiting for a call that wasn't going to come, wasn't getting me anywhere. I drove over to the Hollywood Improv and talked my way onto the Underground show. The booker liked so-called up and comers. I dangled the catnip in front of him, telling the booker that I was going to be on the next big reality show though it was hush, hush. He went for it like a cat. Skipped the line and got on stage before the crowd was too drunk. While the host introduced me, I gave Rafe last rites and buried him but good.

Before I lost my nerve, I adjusted the microphone. "So my girlfriend was in my bedroom last night. Let's just say, she's eighteen." The crowd reacted like expected. We all liked looking at the Olsen twins and Britney before their magic birth-day, but weren't supposed to acknowledge it. "What? I don't have a bouncer outside my front door checking ID. Anyway... when I drove her home, I had to park around the corner. And when I was giving her a boost to get into her bedroom at her parent's house, I realized something. I can't sleep with any more girls with pink canopy beds."

SEVENTEEN

DAISY

"HOLY SHIT," I said then covered my mouth. All these years past adolescence, and I still felt awkward swearing. My mother and a few bars of Ivory soap made sure of that.

"No worries, Daisy." Connor said from the passenger seat of the tank. "As long as it doesn't make it on air, I'm fine."

L.A. would never make any sense to me. I'd been driving up some street in hills north of Beverly Hills filled with regular two and three bedroom houses in between a lot of construction, knock downs and the like. Then I followed Connor's directions, and there I was in front of some mansion with grounds the size of a nine hole golf course.

"This is it?" I asked.

"Yep. This is where you'll be for a lot of the next eight weeks, so you may as well memorize those turns off of Benedict Canyon," he said.

This was like a million bedroom, million bathroom Southern California mansion. I'm sure some real estate agent would have called it Mediterranean or something like that, but it was the same as most of the new houses you saw going up on any residential street, all elaborate arches and pretentious columns, only about ten times bigger than those.

Scores of people milled about, every last one decked out with name badge lanyards and bottled water. I eased into a parking space between catering trucks, dragged out my own CBT badge, and got out of the car. What in the hell was I supposed to be doing? This was the most fraudulent I'd ever felt. Thank God for Connor. He strode up to a young looking girl with a clipboard, full of authority.

"Connor Quinlan, Program Practices, CBT. Where's the EP?"

She gestured toward a guest house bigger than my parent's regular house. "Production's in there."

I followed Connor across the vast lawn. Ten fully made up people were perched casually against a huge fountain, a photographer snapping pictures. "I think we've got it," she yelled, hoisting her camera aloft, and the group broke up.

"Those are the contestants," I pointed out to Connor. I'd seen their headshots enough times that I knew them all by name and face. I also probably knew more about them than their parents. It was amazing what people were willing to reveal for a chance to be on television.

I couldn't help but look for Raphael. And there he was, skin tan, hair flawless, lean body wrapped in a tight t-shirt and skinny jeans. What I was beginning to think of as his trademark checked Vans were on his feet. We locked eyes. My heart sped up and sweat started to trickle on my lip, under my arms, between my breasts. I fanned myself with the directions I'd printed out. I'd kept the papers in my hand so I looked like I had something official to do on set.

I looked away, closing my eyes to obliterate him from my mind. I stumbled on the meticulously groomed lawn. More heat crept up my face. I could only hope that my embarrassment at making a fool myself in front of this guy was hidden by my clumsiness.

"You okay?" Connor asked casually.

"Fine," I said through gritted teeth. Sweat streaked from my hairline.

My laser focus was on reaching the executive office without humiliating myself any more than I already had, when a hand grabbed my upper arm.

I started to tell Connor that I was really okay to navigate grass in flats, when I felt lips descend on my cheek.

"Good to see you, Bronwen," Raphael said. His deep voice lifted the fine hairs along my ear, jawline. I held my body stiff, willing it not to shiver.

Connor's eyes grew as big as saucers. Looking around with alarm, he herded us into the space between a line of cypress trees and the garage of the guesthouse.

"Daisy," his usually cheerful voice was suddenly all business. "You know a contestant on the show?"

My heartbeat went from fast to erratic. I'd debated telling Connor and Isabella that I knew Raphael. But they'd have tossed him from the show, no questions asked. And he probably needed the money to pay for that lawyer who got him off. I knew what it was like to be cash poor.

I was getting ready to formulate a lie when a guy in pressed jeans and a blue button down oxford came outside.

"Connor? What's going on here?" He didn't sound casual by any means. A few people stopped what they were doing to look in our direction. Blue Oxford herded us into the house and closed the door.

Cool air enveloped us. All sound from outside disappeared. We followed him meekly to the kitchen. I was crap at lying and was trying as hard as I could to figure out what in the hell I was going to say. I had to speak first. If things kept going well with sultrynewcummers.com, I wouldn't need this job. But I wanted to quit on my terms, not be fired a month into the thing. I was starting to like the steady income, the health insurance, looking at people who were fully dressed.

"Care to explain what I witnessed out there?"

I thrust out my hand. The charm bracelet that had seemed like the perfect accompaniment to the blue and green print dress this morning made me feel childish in front of these executives. "Daisy Fletcher." He shook my hand limply and continued to look at me expectantly. I didn't even know his name. Introductions weren't forthcoming.

"I met Raphael at a bar a few weeks ago," I said. Truth, so far. "He was at a bachelor party with some friends. We shared a booth." I fell silent. I wasn't going to tell Blue Oxford about the bad drunken sex. No job was worth that.

Blue Oxford looked at Raphael. "What bar?"

"MJ's on Hyperion," Raphael said. His deep voice cut right through me.

The producer looked from Raphael to me and back again. He went into a room and came back with a stack of papers. It looked like a copy of Raphael's application. He slapped it on the granite counter and paged through it.

"You gay?"

Raphael hesitated. I willed myself to have no reaction, but my face got hot again. Blue Oxford watched me squirm then addressed Raphael. "I didn't just read this application. I saw your tapes. The Vogue Rafe dance you've done as a closer is all over YouTube. Is it an act?"

Raphael swallowed visibly. "Rafe's an act. I retired him. I was hoping to press the reset button on my career while on this show."

"Obviously," he said, waving his hand in a broad sweeping motion. "Everyone's here to try to change the direction of their career." He pointed out the window toward the fountain. "That guy's spiraling downwards. Off drugs, but not funny anymore. That girl's funny as shit, but hasn't caught a break. Every last one has a redemption story. So what's yours going to be?" He leaned against the countertop and leafed through the papers again. He pulled a pen from behind his ear and turned the pages over.

"Why'd you kiss her—Daisy?"

"I want to see her," Raphael said. "I didn't want her to forget that while the show taped."

Connor, who'd been watching the three-way ping-pong match, spoke up. "But you know you can't date her during the show, right?"

"Of course not," we chorused.

Blue Oxford pulled Connor into a dining room where a bunch of guys in t-shirts and jeans sat around a table, eating and drinking.

I wheeled on Raphael. "Why did you do that? Can you not keep it in your pants even one second?"

The squint of his eyes told me I'd hurt him. I felt both vindicated and crappy. I had no reason to be mean to him. We weren't compatible. I should just leave it there. I'd just wanted so much for us to be compatible. Looking at him made my belly twinge down low. If only he'd been....

Connor and Blue Oxford came back with three other men in tow. "We're going to reenact what happened there. Daisy, you go back to the head of the driveway. Connor will stay here. Raphael, you'll lean against the fountain." He lifted a walkie-talkie to his mouth. In between static, I heard the words 'makeup' and 'establishment shot.'

I looked at Connor. His nod was nearly imperceptible, but his eyes held a glint of steel. Arms like iron banded across his chest. No one had sought my opinion. If I wanted to keep my job, I would have to become part of the story. I pulled my shoulder bag tighter and walked out, preparing myself for my first close-up. Raphael trailed in my wake.

When I got to the gate a woman with a small black bag stopped me. "Makeup," was all she said before she pulled off my sunglasses, powdered my face and slicked gloss over my lips. Scissors flew across uneven ends and another woman brushed and sprayed my hair. They swept me clean with a wide paint-brush and pushed me forward.

"Quiet on set," boomed from somewhere. "Action."

As I walked from the parking area across the lawn, memories of green slime from that Nickelodeon show filled my head. I put one foot in front of the other expecting a pie in the face at any moment. Instead, Raphael appeared by my side, grabbed my arm again and kissed me. This time full on the lips. My palpable shock was real. Two producer types zoomed out, each grabbing one of us. "Cut!"

The producer let me go. Connor came to me. "You have to tell me whenever you know anyone on a reality or game show, understand?" I nodded, still wondering if I was going to be fired. "We pulled this one out of the flames, but you could have been fired or that guy you like could have been bumped from the show. Got it?"

"Yes. Connor." I should have stopped there, but I couldn't help myself. "I met him in a bar. He did that striptease the guy was talking about and I caught his shirt. I met him a few weeks later to give him back the shirt."

"That's it?" Connor asked.

"That's it. He's cute, but I actually thought he was gay, so...."

"Okay, cool. That's fine. It would have been fine if you'd told me. If the producers had really wanted him, Legal, Isabella, and I would have figured out a way to keep him. You would have probably been reassigned. Water under the bridge." He pointed at my chest. I tried not to curl up like a naughty child. "But there are no secrets here. There can't be. If he wins the show, we wouldn't want the liability of some other contestant coming back and saying he got favoritism from the network."

"There's no worry that'll happen now?" I didn't relish the idea of being cross examined on the stand by some disgruntled contestant's lawyer.

"No. It's nipped. That little scene you just taped there will show that Raphael is some big swinging dick. Viewers won't expect it because he's Asian. They'll also play up the angle that he may be gay and covering it up. Either way, you'll just be the start of his story arc on this show."

I hoped that girl he'd had sex with was the only young one because by my estimation they were about to come out of the woodwork.

"You'll have to sign a release," Connor was saying as we walked back to the guesthouse. I was going to formally meet the producers for real this time and get a handle on how I was going to do this job.

EIGHTEEN

RAPHAEL

I CLOSED the door to my bedroom at the House, thanking the deities that I didn't have to share a room or bunk beds like other stupid reality shows. It was enough that every action outside the bathroom was being filmed. I wanted to sleep in comfort, keep my game sharp. I went into the dressing room next to the bathroom and changed into long johns. I'd paid a pretty penny at Neiman Marcus, but they made me look as good as those Korean soap actors that sell everything from ramen to phones.

I laid down and let my mind drift. Dinner was in half an hour, so I didn't want to nap. But I could stand a minute of rest. They had run us ragged this first day in the House with endless forms to fill out for taxes, and releases, and insurance and more insurance. Then we took pictures, thousands of them. All of the contestants on stage, all of us by the fountain, the bunch of us together making goofy faces. I knew the results would be worse than the most cliché comedian headshots. Anything for the money. Being off the road was a godsend. And given my trouble in Topanga and Cleveland, this being in one place was exactly what I needed right now.

Bronwen. I shifted uncomfortably in the tight underwear. I

wanted Daisy, though I didn't know why. She wasn't easy, wasn't an airhead, wasn't overly impressed by comedy, my career, or my looks. But she was interesting. Her favorite drink was a Brooklyn; not a Sex in the City copycat cosmopolitan or the Westside special, a fourteen dollar chocolate martini.

And I'd been horrible to her. I must have been drunk and stupid that time we'd had sex. I'd wanted her so bad and got the living, breathing woman under me all mixed up with the porn movies I'd seen. Ever since I'd been young, I'd thought women were there to make me feel better about myself. Until Daisy, I'd never wanted to make someone else feel good beyond the next orgasm, and I'd blown it.

I had no idea how I was going to get her. I cataloged our encounters, trying to imagine what her impression of me might be. First I did the gay dancing shtick, then I got arrested, and then I got drunk and disrespecting her in bed. I cringed at each and every memory. I'd never gone after a girl I'd really liked. It took a lot less to conquer the easy targets. They were easy to spot, too much—

The loud knock at the door got me out of my own head for a moment. It was probably a producer herding us for dinner early. I reached down to grab my jeans. Before I could pull them on or get up to open the door, the heavy iron knob hit the wall. Two cameramen and a sound guy, furry boom mike in hand, strode in. Three girls, who looked like strippers from 4Play, followed.

"Rafe?" a blonde with barely covered tits asked.

I closed my eyes for a second. When I opened them, she was still there. And I was now Rafe, lady-killer mask firmly in place. "Ladies, ladies, what brings you here?" I put my hands on my hips, thighs spread wide—macho guy stance.

A couple of the other comics filed in behind the two remaining girls, a redhead and a brown-skinned girl of ambiguous ethnicity.

"There was petty cash in the kitchen cookie jar," one comedian, Dillon Keen, started.

"And we debated between pizza and strippers," another contestant, Zach Rubin said.

"So there's no pizza?" My stomach was suddenly rumbling. A girl crush always stole my appetite, and I'd skipped the lunch buffet. I didn't have a lot of fat to spare.

The girls started twirling out of the room as if on some imaginary poles. "Nope, we got both," Zach said, hooting. "Pizza party!"

I followed them all out of the room.

The living room had morphed into a carbon copy of Déjà Vu, a strip club I used to frequent in the Valley. The lighting cast a deep red glow across the vast living area. Someone had brought in strobe lights. Reality TV, my ass. I didn't know a single person with strobes, and I lived in West Hollywood.

A producer stepped into the middle of the room, while caterers set up the tomato pies making sure the pizza company's logo was prominently displayed. He introduced the strippers and told us they'd be serving us dinner. I wasn't the only one in pajamas. A couple of the other guys were in boxers. The fat guys were in flannel shirts and tank tops, and the guys who looked like they worked out were hardly dressed. It was no accident they'd told me to relax. The producer admonished us to, 'keep it funny and lively,' and stepped back into another room.

I ate my pizza quietly and watched the show. Even though I knew I should be hamming it up for the producers, judges, the home audience, whomever, I didn't have the heart to do this right now. Like a teenager, I wanted to go back to my room and moon over a girl. Write a crappy love song or two. I'd dutifully completed years of piano lessons at my mother's admonition. Maybe I could finally put that knowledge to good use. I'd put my second crust down, when Zach poked me in the ribs.

"You gay, man?" My shoulders tensed, arms ready to throw a punch. I'd defended Gabe so many times as a kid, I was easily provoked. "How is it you're not taking what's being offered here?" Indeed, one of the girls was sitting on Dillon's lap. Even the one girl comic, Glenna, had her face ear deep in cleavage.

I didn't say anything. Last week, this would have been right up my alley. I didn't hear the chant at first. I thought the guys were egging someone else on. Then it got louder than the music, "Gaysian, gaysian, gaysian!"

Everyone was looking at me expectantly. I had to do something. Spectating was not an option. I dredged Rafe from the grave. I grabbed the redhead from behind and did my best bump and grind. She caught my rhythm and pushed her bottom right into my crotch. It felt good. I won't lie. But I wasn't ready to stand up and salute. Thinking of another woman, no matter how available, suddenly smacked of cheating.

Taking a deep breath, I overcame my scruples and turned the redhead around. I looked into her hazel eyes, trying to gauge her willingness. Her wink was for me, not the cameras. I took the invitation and pulled her up, straddling her legs around my hips in a mock lap dance. This girl was a pro, doing it up for the camera with all the gyrating, hair tossing, and smiles. When the song ended, she planted a big ol' kiss on me. I was sure after tonight they'd no longer call me the Gaysian.

NINETEEN
DAISY

RAPHAEL and I never spoke again. Despite my fervent prayers, he was hanging on to the very end. I refused to give in to the idea that he was doing this to torture me. Every week I dutifully turned up to the set, watched the live performances, scoured the taped segments for red flags, and waited for him to be kicked off the show. But he met every challenge head on and won immunity from elimination or the audience popular vote.

I was sitting with a bunch of CBT network brass, set apart from the general crowd in the Wiltern Theater. Tonight was the final showdown. Each comedian had to perform twenty minutes of new material, and the audience and some celebrity judges would vote on the show's winner. It was between Raphael and Dillon Keen.

Dillon was one those silly comedians whose act bounced between jokes about bodily functions and his supposedly hot wife. He'd been edited heavily to make him safe to go on air. I knew I'd have to keep my trigger finger on the Futter button in case he got out of hand during the live performance. Raphael had been pretty clean the whole time, and very charismatic, if not always super funny.

I pinched my stocking clad leg. All these weeks later, he still pulled me in with his electric smile. I still wanted to smooth down the thick black hair that tended to stand up despite his best efforts. I itched to smooth the collar of his shirts, when they weren't quite straight. But I was really starting to like this job and wanted to keep it. Everyone on the show had overlooked that first fuck up, and I had Connor to thank for not bringing Isabella into that loop of stupidity.

There was a reason, 'hurry up and wait,' was the motto of movie and television making. I looked at my watch. The show would air live. It had to start promptly at six o'clock. I pulled a couple of scripts out of my bag. I could do double duty for the half hour I had left.

Feedback filled the auditorium with screeches and scratches. Rafe and Dillon marched up on stage while technicians checked lights and sound. I looked down, pretending to be immersed in the script blurring in front of my eyes.

I heard: "I like this girl."

My head snapped up. Dillon had been making farting noises into the microphone. I hadn't been aware of the switch from one performer to another. Through someone's walkie-talkie I heard the sound technician say something to the director. The stage manager directed Raphael to try again. He cleared his throat and started again. "This girl is so out of my league. She's the Yankees, and I'm the Bad News Bears."

Who did he like? Was it me? I wanted it to be me. I pinched my thigh again, trying to clear my head. Cute Korean kryptonite had no power over me. None. If I said it one hundred times, maybe it would carry some weight. I was losing my single-girl cred. How could I even think about being with a guy who didn't respect me, my job, my boundaries. My face heated when the drunken sex episode came to me. Porn was like a cancer. It affected everyone who'd ever seen it—and not in a good way.

I turned back to the thin action show script that I'd taken over for someone on vacation. Explosions and car chase shows were much easier than the angsty walking talking dramas. In the last two months, I'd discovered something. TV was boring. Glossy hosts, endless reality contests. Fat guy in plaid flannel, hot wife sit-coms. Medical dramas. Legal dramas. Forensic dramas, which combined the two. So I zoned out during the first twenty or thirty minutes of the show.

The host was an old pro, newly sober and interested in keeping his job. He was not going to do anything profane. Dillon was another story. Even with an eight second delay to clean up his act, I sat shoulders hunched, keeping my finger ready. He only made one slip, using the word penis one too many times. I bleeped him in time, keeping the ears of America safe.

A long commercial break, a pre-approved video segment gave me a moment to relax. Then it was Raphael's turn. He'd never gone off the reservation, so I eased away from the button and watched the performance. The show's rules had him doing a twenty-minute set tonight. Ace this and he had a fifty-fifty shot of winning it all.

The heat of the lights, the noise of the crowd, the chatter from the director's booth all faded away when the blue and red spotlights came up on Raphael.

The trademark designer casual clothes were gone. He was all dressed up. Black, double-breasted suit, in what looked like linen. I sat forward in my chair to get a closer look at the loose weave. Yup, linen. Square-toed leather shoes replaced the slip on sneakers. He looked like every well-dressed Korean drama star I'd ever seen. His dark hair was mussed just so. The audience's applause break went on for longer than Dillon's. Keen was the crowd favorite tonight. Though I knew it was probably futile, I crossed my fingers for Raphael.

"I met this girl that I really like," Raphael started.

The audience gave him one big "Awww."

"Don't worry. It gets worse." He paused a beat, drawing the crowd in. "So I'm cozying up to this girl in my apartment after a date. I'm all leaning in to kiss her, and she's leaning back. I ask her, 'What's wrong baby?' She blinks. Blinking is not good unless you're wearing contacts or at the beach. Blinking means back off. Anyway, she says, 'You play for the other team.' And with that, she leaves." Raphael waited a second. "That's the last time I meet a girl at a gay bar.

"Same girl, different night. I've set the scene this time. Good friends, great cocktails. I'm cozying up to this girl in my apartment, ready to try the kissing thing again. Then someone starts banging on the door. The police barge in. And they arrest me. Handcuffs, reading me my rights, the whole bit. I have to tell you if it hadn't been me, this would have been a very cool episode of Law and Order." Everyone in the theater cheered. "Surprisingly, she didn't want to sit shotgun on the way to jail. That's the last time I invite a girl to my house when I have an arrest warrant. Cops kill the mood."

I looked away from Raphael. I swear he was looking directly at me, although there's no way he could see me through the booth's reflective glass.

"After all this, she invites me over." Everyone gasps. "What can I say, I'm that good. Anyway, this is my chance. Probably my last chance to show her what I can do. Two or three vodkas in, I'm good to go. I get her to the bedroom. I'm ready to make my move, and nothing goes right. I was as useless as a three-legged horse. A little alcohol can be good, a lot of alcohol will kill your dick."

"I know I should give up, man. Finally, I get my chance. I'm looking good. Nearly this good." He gestured to his well-put-together self. The audience clapped approvingly. "She happens to be walking across the grass toward me. It's like I'm in a tampon commercial, but I don't care. There's only one other guy around. He's old, not my competition." He opened his hand to tick off on his fingers "I'm not gay, I'm not drunk, not under arrest. So I make my move and kiss her. She almost gets fired. Note to self: don't kiss a girl in front of her boss. Especially when you want him to be your boss. Never make a move during a job interview."

There were other jokes, I was sure of it. I hoped he didn't swear, because I didn't hear a word from the rest of the set. Raphael had talked about me. I was that girl. The girl he wanted to be with, but always screwed up around. I didn't even know if I wanted to be that girl. And like that, it was over. Through the roaring in my ears, I heard the host throwing it to commercial. I stood, glad my legs could hold me.

I joined the network execs and producers in a small room backstage. I put my trembling hands between my stocking clad legs. Now was not the time to betray my feelings. I was there to protect the network from embarrassment, from fines, from the Christian right's postcard campaigns. I needed to be cool, rational, in charge.

"Hey, there," Connor said, dropping into the seat next to me. This was my first contest finale and Isabella wanted a member of the senior staff to walk me through it. I was grateful for his presence. Muddle-headed, I didn't want to be solely responsible for my decisions. "You got a copy of the rules?"

"Yep, here," I said, dropping the packet before I could put it in his hands. Isabella and Connor must think I have the coordination of an orangutan.

"Are you nervous about tonight?" I was, but not about Heir. Connor didn't have the time to probe, because Blue Oxford, who was wearing green today, and whose name I'd learned was Seth, called the meeting to order. We only had nine minutes, while the producers aired another pre-approved segment—a highlight reel of the season.

An auditor read the audience tally. Kevin Dillon had prevailed by a few percentage points.

"We are going to override this one," Seth said.

"Override," I blurted out before I could help myself.

Seth looked at Connor then at me. He did not look pleased. I wanted to tell him I wasn't questioning his authority, I couldn't process what was going on, was all. But I knew the rules, I'd merely forgotten them in all the excitement of the show. The judges and network executives had final say. The audience opinion was a courtesy more than anything. The producers took a vote amongst themselves and as quick as that, Raphael was the winner.

"Raphael is going to be crowned the winner tonight. Audience preference aside, his pitch idea works better in the lineup than Dillon's." Seth went on to list the bevy of fat flannel guy, hot wife comedies that were airing or had just been cancelled. "Augustine's pitch, of a send-off of his single straight life compared to his brother's gay life, is a good one. Kind of like 'gay' *Friends*—only they're brothers. American demographics are changing. Asian is the new white. More disposable income, growing population. There's hasn't been a Korean on TV since Margaret Cho."

That wasn't exactly right, Rex Lee, John Cho, Daniel Dae Kim had done a lot of fine work. But I doubted anyone wanted my recitation.

After a quick consultation with Legal and some muckety-muck VP in Programming, I nodded when they asked if Program Practices would sign off on it. A production assistant picked up one of two envelopes on the table and rushed to deliver it to the host.

Back in the booth, I watched as both men were corralled on

stage. The stage lights came up then the red lights on the camera letting everyone know we were live. When the hoots and hollers from the audience subsided, the host announced the prizes again and took the envelope from his breast pocket. Over the drum roll effect he said, "And the King of Comedy is...Raphael Augustine!"

Before the PAs rushed out with an actual crown, scepter, and robe, the cameras switched to Dillon who did an elaborate bow. His Miss America runner up kiss and wave had the audience laughing at his exit. Raphael, fully outfitted, posed with a larger than life check. Then it was over. The audience spilled out, the house lights went up, and it was time for me to go home. I let Connor introduce me to producers and various industry people I hadn't met. With my thoughts full of Raphael, I was sure I wouldn't remember a single name.

"Let me walk you out," Connor said. Not that Connor wasn't chivalrous, but it was broad, sunny daylight. I wasn't looking forward to the reprimand that was surely coming even if I didn't know what for. I'd stayed away from Raphael. I'd done my job scrupulously.

Down the winding backstage corridor, I chewed the inside of my lip. Maybe he'd Googled Images of Harmony. I pulled my sunglasses from my tote and put them on before we hit the sunlight. I frantically plumbed my brain for an explanation of why I was tied to hundreds of porn sites. These dark lenses would hide my eyes if a lie betrayed me. He patted the hood of my car, and I leaned my butt against the warm metal.

"So..." I prompted.

"The coast is clear," Connor said.

Had I fallen into a spy novel? "I don't understand."

Connor pointed to a lone figure weaving through the lot to his car, a few spaces down from mine. Raphael. "You can go out with him if you want. There's no conflict of interest anymore."

"But I don't..." I didn't. At least I shouldn't want to....

Connor smiled at me like I was his doddering senile aunt. "Have a good weekend." He waved over his shoulder, his back already to me.

I turned back and Raphael was still walking in my direction toward his car. Nothing could have moved me from that spot on my hood. I was hooked to this like I would be to a good television drama. I had to know what was going to happen next.

"Bronwen?" My name was a question on his lips as he approached and leaned his hands against my hood, only a few inches separating us. I turned slightly to look at him, and I knew. I was a very good girl falling for a bad, bad boy.

TWENTY

RAPHAEL

NO COPS, no vodka, no gay men, no Connor. It was me and Daisy.

"Where's your brother or...Joel?"

My brother and my manager had dutifully come out for the show tonight. When *Heir to the Throne* needed reaction shots of friends and family, they were there. "They scattered to the four winds. Ted's got a work thing. Joel had a kid thing."

"Oh," she said. I didn't know what to read into that purse of her lips. She didn't make a move to get into her car. I was still in the game. Didn't have a clue about my next play, though.

I had talked more girls out of their panties than Hugh Hefner. Okay, maybe not more than the Playboy magnate, but I'd made my share of conquests. Daisy was a mystery. Maybe not a mystery, exactly. All of my blunders had led me down this path of uncertainty. I knew what not to do. I couldn't and shouldn't kiss her again. I promised myself, silently, that I wouldn't touch her unless she gave me an explicit invitation. Suddenly, the lips I'd been unwittingly focusing on were talking.

"Why do you drive a Japanese car?" she asked, pointing to

my midnight blue Infiniti parked a few rows from hers. The air shimmered with exhaust heat as one car after another left the rapidly emptying lot. I craned my neck to look at my potentially offensive car then swung my head back to Daisy.

I pushed myself from her hood and turned around, leaning my butt against it in an imitation of her pose. What answer was she looking for? The price I'd paid, whether I'd ever done it in the car, if she could drive it? Was she still fighting World War II? Did she have one of those families? Nope, that couldn't be it. I was leaning against her very German made, Axis Powers car.

"I liked how it drove," I said, fighting the urge to seek out validation for my choices. "It handled smoothly."

"You're the first Korean I've met who drives one," she said.

"I never thought about the car being Japanese. Korea and Japan are allies now," I said, walking a fine line between what I knew and what I didn't know. "Hasn't Japan apologized for its part in colonial rule?" I added. I was sure I'd seen that Japanese president with the long hair prostrating on an airport television while I was delayed somewhere in the Midwest.

Daisy banged her fist on the car's roof, not making a dent in the metal. "Naoto Kan's apology wasn't the least bit sincere. Every few years some official flies over the Sea of Japan, lands in Seoul then makes some superficial apology. What about the exploitation of the thousands of comfort women abused during that time?"

"You're coming to the defense of Korean comfort women at the same time you sell women having sex." Daisy nodded as if this weren't the oddest dichotomy ever. "But you think I shouldn't drive a Japanese car?" She nodded again. "Honey, one day I'll talk to you about politics. I'll talk to you about whatever you want over breakfast. But for us to talk, there has to be an us."

"What do you mean, Raphael?" Her eyes, which up until

now has been focused on me like lasers, couldn't meet mine. Everything—the asphalt, the sky, the art deco theater— was more interesting than what was going on between us. I wasn't exactly sure what that was, but it was something. That, I knew as well as I knew my name.

"I think I've been as plain spoken as I can. I want to see you, date you, kiss you, wake up with you, Bronwen," I said, risking the worst rejection I'd ever feared. Every day since I'd hit puberty, I'd stared rejection in the face, laughed at it. Defied it. I'd had nearly every women I'd set my mind to having.

"What do you want me to say?" Her voice was quiet as mouse.

"Yes."

But she didn't say yes, because this was my lot with this girl.

"Have you ever had a girlfriend?"

Why did women always ask that question? We were only relationship material if we'd been in a relationship? "Past performance is no indication of future results."

"Don't quote brokerage disclaimers at me."

"How many boyfriends have you had, Daisy?" I regretted the question as soon as it left my lips. I didn't want to know that she'd loved anyone. That she'd let men into her heart and her bed, when I couldn't do either halfway right.

"This is crazy," she whispered. Her eyes once again met mine. "I am who I am. You are who you are. We exist in different worlds."

"Our worlds collided."

The sun sunk low, disappearing behind the dense concrete maze along Wilshire. The sky was pink and I broke my minutes-old vow. I put a hand on either side of her jaw and pulled her toward me. One kiss, I promised myself. I touched her lips with mine, tentative at first. When she didn't slap me or push me away, I let out a deep breath and opened her lips with mine. I'd never seen her eat candy, but she tasted like butterscotch.

I wanted to pull her body to mine, have her feel what she was doing to me. But I'd already showed her crude. I only wanted to show her kindness. The kindest thing I could do was to pull back. I brushed one last kiss across her lips, taking all the gloss away. I gently pushed her back to take away temptation. This time, I would hold to my promise. No more touching, no more anything without invitation.

"What happens now, Raphael?" Daisy whispered.

"That, my dear Bronwen, is entirely up to you." I kissed her cheek, willing myself to walk away from the smooth skin and wonderful smell of perfume that brought pink, green, badminton and croquet to mind. I made it to my car. Never once did I look back. The ball was in her court.

TWENTY-ONE
DAISY

I STUCK a DVD into the computer. There had to be something there I could use. I had that unsatisfied feeling in my body. Despite my efforts to ignore it, I got turned on when I worked. The easiest way to get stuff done, was to get it over with. If I waited all day, the need for relief only got worse.

I double-clicked the icon, glad that no one could see my heated cheeks. Like a drug dealer who craved their own product, I was slipping. More and more often, I was using the pictures I used to hook my customers, to satisfy myself. I'd sworn never to do that, but I was like a crack addict on a pipe.

You don't spend nearly ten years in the sex business without figuring out what turns you on. I found my cache of 'real girl-friend' videos and clicked one open. I hated all the degrading sex, bukkake, gag job blow jobs, and endless ways men found to humiliate women. It was exhausting. I like my sex real, or as real as you could get from people willing to expose themselves in front of cameras.

I watched as the young lovers kissed a lot. I missed kisses like that. The last person who kissed me like that had been sixteen when I had. After that, one kiss and they wanted a blow job and straight sex, if a girl was lucky. I'd had more than one person tell me that foreplay had gone out of style after the year 2000. The breathing was getting heavy, and the young guy was slipping a hand under the girl's shirt, when the phone rang. I paused the video, hitting mute for good measure and answered Nari's call.

"Can you come over?"

Because I was still in the doghouse, I readily agreed without asking what was so urgent. I finished what I'd started in the shower, dressed, and drove like a mad woman to get to Nari's apartment. I hadn't been there since that last day. I was so nervous that I was going to be confronted with a used dildo, that I missed her floor. I got off on the top floor and had to walk down a flight of stairs. Approaching her door, I was half convinced a wayward bottle of lubricant had ruined her bedroom rug. I was calculating the cost of new carpet in my head, when I walked up to Nari from behind. She had been waiting for me to exit the elevator. She pulled me in and slammed the door.

"Are you okay?" I asked.

"No." She shook her head. "Not one little bit." I looked around. Piles of stuff covered the living room. 'Large Brown Bags' from Bloomingdales, shiny silver Nordstrom & Neiman Marcus bags, and even a red and white bag from Harrods lined the floor. She hadn't been to London in ten years.

"What are you doing?" Maybe there was some charity that took designer stuff. That would be so L.A.

"You know my cousin Eunji?" I nodded. Of course, I'd known Eunji for years, but would probably never see her again.

"What about her?"

"She's coming here today with my parents."

"What? Why? Isn't she back in Seoul?"

"She got accepted to USC off the wait list."

I gestured out the window with my thumb. "I thought she was going back east to Cornell."

Nari sat, a stray hank of hair falling in her face. The girl had more bobby pins than an Olympic gymnast. Her hair never fell out. She tucked the wayward stands behind her ear. I looked a little closer. Her bun was coming undone. How had a visit from a cousin shaken her up so much?

"On second thought, she decided small town Ithaca wouldn't be much fun. Why not live in the big city where Auntie Nari lives? But my precious cousin can't possibly live in South L.A. Oh no. So my parents volunteered my place."

"So say no."

Nari's sigh was long and sad. "And how would I do that? It's bad enough this Korean daughter isn't married, lives alone, doesn't have a kimchi fridge...isn't Korean enough."

"But it's your place. They can't make you take her. This is what dorms are for," I said, indignant on her behalf.

"It's not exactly mine. You know that better than anyone."

Nari's parents had put a down payment on the condo and made the payments while Nari was in medical school. But that was, I counted in my head, nine years ago. "Who's on the title?"

"All three of us. I insisted they add me when I started making the mortgage payments."

"So is it not legally yours?"

"Apparently. They have a key. They have the lion's share of the title. And they have control. But I don't want to talk about this. I can't change it. I need you to get this stuff out of here." She made a sweeping gesture encompassing all the bags, like Vanna White displaying prizes.

"What is all this?"

"The shit I don't want them to know I have."

Nari liked to shop, all the time. It was what she did with her weekends. She liked expensive clothes, shoes, and purses. She had a great body and looked like a mannequin in everything she tried on. Even though I knew she'd turned my old room into a big closet, I'd never much thought about how much stuff she had. I guess it was weird that she had more clothes than Princess Diana, but never went anywhere. Who was I to judge, though?

Nari always seemed content. She didn't have many friends. She didn't date. I rarely thought about it, but she must have some hole that needed filling. And she did it with designer goods. Even though I had no storage space to speak of, I dutifully took load after load down to my car. The Tank had one of those bottomless trunks, but we nearly filled it.

Tired, we split some leftover *seollongtang* Nari pulled from the fridge. I helped myself to the rice she always kept warm in the same red Japanese cooker her mom had. Quiet as we added salt, scallions, and chili paste, we pulled up stools to her tall two person table and slurped our soup.

"I can't wait to live with a teenager," Nari said, full of sarcasm.

"Do you want me to talk to them? They might listen to me." I'd had good luck talking her family out of some of their overprotective behavior. Sometimes I think if it weren't for me, she'd be practicing medicine in Riverside and on display every Sunday at the Korean church.

Nari's glare stopped the spoon midway to my mouth. "No, Daisy. I don't think they're going to take advice from you."

Like that, I'd forgotten about my little film session gone wrong. "Sorry Nari," I said. I needed to find a new way to apologize to her. She wasn't smiling at my rhymes, though.

"Believe you me, I thought about you talking to them. I'd worked it all out in my head this morning, then I remembered that they wouldn't listen to anything you said."

I put my spoon down. The churning guilt in my stomach had ruined my appetite. I'd gone off the ox bone soup.

"Have you quit?" Nari asked. I wanted to play dumb. Pretend I hadn't heard what she'd said. I stirred my soup, watching the bright green onions swirl among the chili flecked broth.

"Almost."

"It's all or nothing, Daisy."

"I'm trying, Nari. I want to bulk up my bank account a little. Make sure I have money for the assessment. A little something in case my car needs repairs. Maybe take a vacation to Hawaii or something like that." The last was a stab at the trip she'd failed to invite me on this spring.

"Why do you do it, Daisy?" Her deep brown eyes pinned me to the back of the stool. I squirmed under her scrutiny. "There's something else going on," she concluded.

"Is it a crime to like your work?"

"Do you like the job at CBT? You've been there a couple months now."

I did really like the network job. "Who wouldn't want to get paid to watch TV all day?"

"So why isn't it enough?"

I could have asked her the same thing. I mean, who in the hell had a thousand pounds of clothes they had to hide from their family? "It's fine, Nari. A lot of people have two jobs. I'm not actively adding sites. I have passive income, like a nice stock portfolio."

"Exploiting women."

The gloves were coming off. Nari and I had remained best friends for years by not talking about certain things, sex among them. We each came from a culture that didn't talk about sex, ever. The Puritans could have taught the Koreans a little something. I didn't know why Nari didn't date, beyond the superficial. I didn't share my solo sex life with her either. And our little détente had worked perfectly, for more than a decade.

"I don't exploit women, Nari. It's not like I'm some trafficker peddling ten-year-old Taiwanese girls to sex tourists." I'd gone over this in my head hundreds of times. "The women are over eighteen and working. They trade sex for money. End of story. And with video, they only do it once, no matter how many times men watch it. It's not like there's a brothel in my living room."

"Do you do it to get off? You haven't gotten laid since that smarmy so-called producer in two thousand six."

I did not want to think about that guy, so I said, "You forgot about Raphael." And regretted it immediately when she looked at me like I'd kicked her dog.

"Ah yes, you haven't gotten laid since the local pedophile did you."

I could feel anger and humiliation heat my cheeks. "The charges were dropped," I said, my voice rough. I would not cry. She was being mean because she was feeling powerless. Any Psychology 101 student could see that. If I were another person, I would point out that she hadn't had sex since forever, either. That if she got laid, maybe she'd stay the hell out of Fred Segal. That she was abnormally tied to her family. That she let her parents run her life. But I wanted to keep the one friend I had. I pushed back from the tall table, stepping down from the stool. "I'm going home before we say something we can't take back."

TWENTY-TWO

RAPHAEL

"I MISS THE ROAD," I said to my manager. We were sitting at the crepe stand in the Farmer's Market, just south of the network.

"What's up?" Joel inquired dutifully. If he were any more laid back, he'd have fallen off the stool.

"Why did they pick me? I'm just a cog in the network wheel. They've picked the writers, dumped the actors on me who already have holding deals, and have given me notes on everything I've turned in." I lowered my voice when the guy swirling batter on the griddle turned to look at me.

"This is how it works," Joel said. Was he high already? I was looking for a little more outrage and sympathy on my behalf.

"Fuck this. I'm going to walk off this show. I mean, they're breaking story and the freaking characters are already going camping and ending up in jail."

Joel's eyes met mine. "Well, that last one's real."

"Don't be an ass. You know what I mean. Name a sitcom where the damned characters didn't end up in jail. And those fake set camping episodes. Seriously. It's not nineteen eighty five. I don't want to do an Asian Friends or an Asian King of Queens. I want to do the idea that the network bought."

"They didn't buy an idea, Raphael. They bought you."

I threw down my napkin in disgust. Then they'd paid too damn little. Joel could pay for the breakfast from his ten percent. I was through.

I stalked around the block, past the network and the health food store with ten aisles of nothing worth eating. Past the post office and a million new stucco block apartments. By Kmart and another market whose crap would eat your whole paycheck. By the time I got back to the network, I'd cooled down.

I needed this money. Network executives weren't idiots. They paid out money in dribs and drabs. Enough to make you feel almost rich, but not enough that you couldn't live without the next payment.

The head writer pulled me aside before I could go into the room.

"Man, I'm glad you're back, bro. The network execs are trolling around, asking to see more scripts. I told them you went for coffee, but that excuse was wearing a little thin."

The guy was a hack. But I was still grateful that he'd had my back. I put on my confident face and strode into the room. When I looked at the line of executives, I almost lost my carefully cultivated cool. Daisy.

An acting coach and some other people were introduced. "And this is the Program Practices exec assigned to your show," someone said. I didn't look to see who was speaking because I couldn't stop looking at her.

I stuck my hand out, looking for a handshake. No one else had extended their hand, but I would take any excuse to touch her. Her warm, soft hand grasped mine. I knew her manners would win out over any aversion she would have to touching me.

Every night I'd had to resist calling her, texting her. I'd left the ball firmly in her court, stuck to my guns. It hadn't been easy. In my horniest moments, I'd even thought of calling some of the other girls in my little black phone. But I couldn't bring myself to do it. Because of Rose, because of Jude...because of Daisy.

The writers were their most charming selves, shooting the shit with their bosses for an hour or so. Every time an executive looked over my way, I shot him the evil eye. Joel who couldn't have been hungry after eating that plate-seized crepe, seemed to sense he needed to smooth things over. My manager made a big deal of us all lunching together. Joel's wife got us a private room at Tart, the restaurant at the Farmer's Daughter's hotel across the street.

I angled my way to a seat next to Daisy. It wasn't hard. The writers were too busy sucking up to network producers. Joel spent more of my money on the house special, bottomless mimosas. The more alcohol, the greater the volume. No one could hear me when I leaned over to whisper in her ear.

"Were you ever going to call me?"

Daisy put down her fork. She'd eaten nothing of the slow roasted pork she'd ordered. I pierced a piece of her fried okra. It was as good as it could be. L.A. didn't do 'down home' cooking well. I'd had better on the road.

"You haven't had much of your drink," she said, pointing to my mimosa.

"I was drinking when we were together that night. I don't intend to repeat that performance," I said. Her head rose sharply. She surveyed the table to see who was listening to us. No one. Her nose flared in indignation or shock that I'd cop to being a shit that night. "It will never be like that between us again," I said, glad that my bravado hadn't slipped. Years of practice served me well.

Daisy looked around the table again. "There is no us, Raphael.

She gave her nearly full plate to the waitress, declining a doggy bag. She was so cool. While I was so hot and bothered. The next words slipped out before I could check my brain.

"Did you quit yet?" I said loudly enough for the entire table to hear.

"Quit what?" someone asked, laying a protective hand over their drink. Shit. I didn't want her coworkers thinking she was an alcoholic or worse, some kind of drug addict.

"Carbs. We were comparing Atkins, Paleo, and South Beach," I said.

The nameless legal exec pulled her hand back from her drink. Conversation resumed, mostly about the evils of carbs while they poured over the dessert menu. That could go on forever.

"No," she said, shaking her head. "I haven't exactly quit."

"Why?"

"I'll tell you later," she whispered, turning toward the guy on her left. Later. That had promise.

Later was now. I'd waited long enough. I loitered near the security doors after the suits left. Not one rent-a-cop asked what I was doing there. Asian invisibility, blessing or curse; I could never decide. Maybe I could make a bit out of that. I stashed the thought. There was Daisy, fishing through that huge brown tote she always carried. Her car predated automatic fobs and keyless entry.

I cleared my throat. She looked up. "Geez Raphael, I thought you'd left."

"It's later now," I said. Yep, an 'F' for original.

"What does that mean?"

"We should talk. Have a drink."

She looked at the white Timex she always wore. Did she

have a date? Had I waited too long? I was ready for a round of self-flagellation. Then she rescued me.

"Where?" she asked, her face inscrutable.

I never thought she'd agree on the first try. For a moment, my mind went blank. All I knew about Daisy was that she liked Koreatown. I didn't.

"AOC," I said. It was a crowded after work wine bar that served single glasses and fussy appetizers to an upscale crowd. I looked at her severe grey dress. Miss Connecticut was made for that place. She'd fit right in. We agreed to meet there. I got in my car, hoping she didn't change her mind along the way.

I stood outside at the valet stand for nearly ten minutes. Checked my phone. Nothing. I should have known I'd lose her in the mile and a half between there and the wine bar. Her agreement had been too ready.

The men in the red vests started to look at me oddly. Took the hint and went inside. I asked for a quiet table in the back, hoping it would make her escape—should she show—that much more difficult.

A couple of women waved at me from the bar. Since I'd done the *Heir to the Throne*, I didn't have to work so hard to get a woman's attention. How was I so lucky now, when I didn't want to pull birds? God was a comic. He was laughing somewhere. Then there she was, striding toward the table in sensible shoes. Daisy had missed the memo on the spikes that made even ugly legs incredible. Not that she needed anything to make her legs look better. I remembered those legs spread wide and immediately shut down those thoughts.

Dropping her bag on the floor under her stool, she perched warily on the square leather seat.

"So, what's good here?"

I pushed the menu across the table. I had no idea what was good there. I'd only wanted to spend time with her and this place seemed acceptable. I glanced at the long menu descriptions, the descriptions overwrought even upside down. This had been a bad idea. How had I not seen this? Bacon wrapped dates? Ten types of focaccia? Aïoli? What had happened to Best Foods mayonnaise? "Let's go. I'll make you something."

One questioning look and she followed me outside the restaurant. Twenty dollars slipped from my hand to the valet's while Daisy's head and shoulder disappeared into the depths of that purse. Her Mercedes was at the curb before she could lay hands on the claim ticket. Hearing the diesel sputter, she looked up. "How?"

My car was right behind. "I'll follow you back to CBT. We'll take one car."

Daisy's car safely tucked in a corner of iron gated Broadcast City lot, she slipped into my leather bucket seat. I'd put on the local jazz station, and she didn't protest.

My mind made up, we drove in silence past dozens more upscale eateries, past the tony houses of Hancock Park, and into Koreatown. The lot at Han Kook was crazy busy as always. Unlike the sterile exterior of Ralph's, the sidewalk outside this store was chock full of vendors selling odd combinations of prepared food and ladies' underwear. For a moment, I flashed back to my childhood trips to Busan. We pushed through the crush of middle-aged women perusing a Lock&Lock sale like their life depended on storage containers. I picked up a basket.

"What are you getting?"

"Shh. It's a surprise," I said. It would be a surprise to me as well. I was rifling through my brain thinking what I could make. I couldn't remember the last time I'd made any kind of Korean food. We walked down the produce aisle and I threw a bag of peeled garlic into the basket. Whatever I picked, I knew from watching my mother all those years, I'd need garlic. A display of jujubes caught my eye, and I picked up a handful. "Can you get a bag of sweet rice? I'm going to get something else."

I scoured the produce section for ginseng, kicking myself for quitting Korean school as the familiar characters failed to come together into words I could understand. I finally located the roots when Daisy joined me, white bag in hand.

I could barely follow the small talk in my car on the way back to West Hollywood. I tried to control my nervous hand by gripping the gear stick tight. Unfortunately, the car was an automatic and I knew I looked stupid doing it. But I didn't want Daisy to know how fast my heart was beating or how hard it was to keep my left knee from bobbing wildly. No girl had made me this nervous since my first date in seventh grade.

While I hauled the bags to the kitchen, Daisy loitered by the front door. She came to the kitchen, bare toes painted pink. I looked up at her legs, also bare, and tried not to think about what else disappeared under that prim dress of hers.

"What are we making?" she asked.

Thank goodness she'd spoken, asked something normal. I looked away, taking a deep breath. "My mom's *samgyetang*," I said in perfect Korean.

"Ginseng. Wow, that's cool. How do we get the rice in the chicken?"

Why was I not surprised that her Korean was better than mine? "Can you wash the ginseng?" I asked her while I banged around the cabinets trying and failing to locate some kind of soup pot.

"What are you looking for?" I looked back seeing that she'd laid out the roots on some paper towels.

"One of those stone pots. The kind with the metal band?" I opened more cabinets. "Gabriel would have one," I muttered under my breath.

"He lives upstairs, right? Do you want me to go ask?" No, I

didn't want a third wheel down in my apartment, a cock blocking brother no less.

"No, I'm sure I have one," I said, moving on to the utility room.

"Does Gabriel cook?"

Of course Gabriel cooked. My brother was an excellent cook of Korean cuisine. Not because he was gay, but because he'd been the favorite child. He'd spent hours at my mother's side, chopping onions, smashing garlic, pounding kimchi. The two of them speaking Korean like a secret language. When he wasn't there, he was running errands with my father, working on cars, fixing stuff around the house. I shook my head clear and bent down to the bottom shelf. There, across from the washer and dryer was a little stone pot.

"What else can I do?" Daisy asked. Little Miss Enthusiasm.

"Can you put a handful of rice in some water?" I heard the sink go on again, cabinet doors opening and closing.

The look in her eyes stopped me when I came back to the kitchen. Was I imagining things, or did she look like she wanted to kiss me? I was probably projecting. "I have to wash this out. Can't remember the last time I used it." I jumped, nearly burning myself under the scalding water.

Daisy was immediately at my side, towel in hand. She pulled my reddening arm toward her and dried it with the towel. My dick stirred. How had I thought this a good idea? Why had I put her in the driver's seat? "Thanks. I'll do it," I said, snatching the towel from her hands.

Wincing at the wounded look in her eye, I turned away to dry the pot. "My mom always told us if we ate ginseng, we'd live another year for each root we ate."

Recovered, Daisy leaned against the counter. "Where's your mom?"

"La Crescenta."

I stuffed rice, the smaller ginseng, garlic, and jujubes into the chicken, jamming the fowl into the pot. I suspected I'd bought a chicken on steroids, instead of the anorexic chickens my mom had favored. It would have to work. I forced it in farther.

"Isn't that somewhere around here?"

"Up near Glendale," I said. I knew what was coming next. Guilt and anger flooded my gut.

"How long do we cook it?"

My eyes slid from hers. "About an hour or so. Until the chicken is done. Everything else will cook in the broth, I think."

"Should you call your mom? Nari's mom knows everything. She's always sending us home with cartons of food. Her kimchi is amaz—"

"I don't speak to my parents."

"Oh." Daisy deflated. "That's too bad." The chicken boiled. I walked to the stove to turn down the fire. I waited one beat, two. "Why don't you talk to them?"

"I disowned them when they disowned Gabriel."

TWENTY-THREE

DAISY

I JUMPED up on the counter next to the coffee maker and watched the soup bubble, turning cloudy. Raphael leaned next to me, arms crossed.

"I'm sorry," I said after a long moment. I couldn't imagine life without Doris and Hugh to fall back on.

"Don't be. They made their choice."

"Is it because he's gay?"

Raphael nodded. "My dad didn't want a fag for a son, and my mother didn't want a life without my dad." I imagined his voice, spitting out the epithet, a bitter imitation of his father's.

So the brothers were on their own. Only having each other. I'd never wanted a sibling, but was infinitely glad Gabriel had his brother.

He turned to look at me. His hand reached out to tuck my hair behind my ears. The last time I'd been there, I'd wanted him to kiss me, but I thought he was gay. This time, I knew he was straight, and I knew he liked me. I knew I liked him. I had no idea how to get what I thought I wanted. Then he spoke.

"Can I kiss you?"

Those four words melted any resistance. "God, yes," was what I thought I heard come from my mouth. Then we were kissing, and there were no more words.

I wanted to pull him closer and shove him far away at the same time. My insides were melting and that was good. But the guilt of my lips and now my tongue melding with the wrong guy was bad, very bad.

Raphael's hands bracketed my hips and next thing I knew my back was against the wall. The sting of cold granite hit the back of my knees, my thighs spreading as wide as the stiff dress would allow. He pulled away, looking at me. His warm brown eyes thawed a little bit of the ice around my heart. I smoothed back his hair like I'd wanted to do so many times. He had so much of it, the thick strands brushing against my fingers.

His head dipped in question, mine answered and we were kissing again. My arms banded around his waist, pulling him between my legs. Arms that had pushed me back, pulled me close and my legs wrapped around his hips. We waltzed across the tiny room, and my back hit wood. There was no mistaking the hard ridge teasing me where I wanted to be touched. He was enjoying this kiss or whatever it was.

The lid clanged. We broke the kiss, both looking at the stove. I hurriedly dropped my legs, so he could put me down and turn down the flame. He pulled chopsticks from a drawer and poked around the bird.

"It's nearly done."

"Can I set the table?" It seemed the least I could do. Raphael looked at me and laughed, a genuine belly deep laugh. "What's so funny?"

He didn't answer, only shook his head. "Dear Miss Connecticut, the bowls and stuff are next to the sink." I opened and closed a few cabinets before I got it right, but I pulled out wide bowls, spoons, and napkins. I hauled my find to the dining room and set us across from each other. It was safest that way.

He brought in the bubbling soup and set the bowl and trivet on the table. I sat in my chair by the window. "Come closer, Daisy. It's difficult to share soup five feet away." I slid my stuff down the table and picked a chair next to him. My hands remained folded in my lap. "I don't bite, Bronwen. Unless you ask me."

Shivering, I brought my hands up, spooning broth and chunks of meat into my bowl. "Why do you call me Bronwen?"

Raphael glanced at me before turning back to his bowl. "It's your name."

"Everyone calls me Daisy."

"I'm not everyone."

"What do you want, Raphael?"

"I think we've already covered that in more ways than one."

If I hadn't kicked off my heels, I would have run out the door. Just because a man was your catnip, didn't mean you had to indulge. I pushed back the chair and walked to the living room. Shoes or no shoes, I needed to leave. But indecision kept me from crossing the threshold. I don't know how long I was standing there, but I was surprised to find Raphael behind me. His hand grasping mine, he pulled me toward the couch.

I sat ramrod straight, determined to have an adult conversation. Then I looked down. As serious as I could get barefoot. They never showed people's feet during the emotionally wrought scenes on Korean dramas. The tension would be broken by images of feet. I tucked mine under my butt, which threw me off kilter, and I bumped against Raphael.

Grabbing my upper arms, he set me straight. He broke his own rule and kissed me. Oh God, was all I could think. I needed to get out of there. Fingers unclasped my arm and brushed the side of my boob. I gasped, my nipple tightened and then our tongues were mating. Ten more minutes of this, and we'd be in bed again. That stopped me cold.

"I have to go."

Raphael blinked. He looked foggy. "Why?"

"I'm not thirteen. If we keep kissing, we're going to end up in bed."

A palm slipped from my side, past my hip, along my thigh. "That's a bad thing?" His voice was low and husky. My thighs squeezed together involuntarily.

"It was last time."

He stood then knelt before me. "I apologize. I'm not that guy. I was drunk and—"

"And what? That gave you license to treat me like a..." Whore was the word I wanted to say, but Nari had already pointed out that I was unfairly judgmental of the women in the sex industry.

"If I'd known you weren't down, I'd never have done that."

"So if we have sex again, will I have to worry that I'm not enough? That plain vanilla missionary will get boring—"

"Bronwen—"

"That you'll be unsatisfied. Run to the next eighteen-year-old groupie willing to do anything to get your attention."

"Daisy! This is about you and me. No one else."

The good feeling that I'd had kissing, and cooking, and kissing some more disappeared. I was filled with jealousy and envy for the girls that came before me. This made no sense. "I'll see you later, Raphael."

And like every damn Korean drama I'd watched, I had to fit my tight heels on my swollen feet and stalk out the door. I was practically running toward Sunset Boulevard, wondering how in the hell I was going to get home when I heard him behind me, reminding me that I didn't have a car.

"I'll drive you home."

By the time we got to Beverly and Fairfax, I was wiping tears from my eyes. Why did this guy rile me up so much? I needed to leave the entire situation alone. Everything in my life was a mess. Nothing was working out. I couldn't figure out what I was doing wrong.

One hand on the handle, the other on the lock, I was ready to make my getaway, when a hand touched my arm.

Knowing I didn't have sunglasses to hide the tears in my eyes, I nonetheless looked at the man next to me.

He put the car in park. "Why are you crying? We were... Things were okay back at my place."

"It's me," I said. I wanted a normal life, with a nice boyfriend. And what I'd gotten was porn, a would-be criminal, and alienation from my surrogate family.

"Let's try again, Daisy."

"What? Why?" I pinched my nostrils.

"A real date. Dinner, entertainment. A plain vanilla date."

"I don't know."

"Yes, you do. Next Saturday. I'll pick you up at five."

"Where—"

"Let me worry about all that."

He practically pushed me out the door and drove away. I buzzed the gate and the guard let me retrieve my car.

AFTER I GOT HOME, I put on my pajamas. I fidgeted for a bit before I woke my computer. The anger was gone and in its place was an ache I wanted to ease. *Sexychatpad.com* was full as always. I didn't announce myself as I usually did. Instead, I watched the chat scroll by. A guy looking for short black girls lit up the screen every few seconds, a woman claiming to be a real lesbian was looking for the same.

Watching all this usually titillated me. I liked the men seeking out my attention, the constant private messages flying my way. Today, it left me cold. I could have said yes. I'd said no to Raphael and I was alone.

TWENTY-FOUR

RAPHAEL

BEING out on Saturday night among civilians was strange. I couldn't remember the last time I had been in a bar or club on a weekend that wasn't focused on comedy. I buzzed Daisy's place. Fifty-fifty chance I'd strike out. Looked at my phone. Gabriel was dying to go see *The Book of Mormon*. I knew he and Ted were sitting by the phone, waiting for my call. They'd promised to meet me at will call if my date was a no show.

Geez, who used the word date? I rubbed my damp palms against my pants, banishing my inner fourteen year old to oblivion. Before I could press my lips to the call box, the door unlocked. I walked the empty corridor to the elevator and shot up to her floor.

I was reciting my agenda under my breath when Daisy opened the door. I wanted to send Gabriel the tickets by carrier pigeon and take this woman back into her bedroom, never to leave. Jesus. She was going to kill me.

She was in an all black sheer something and high heels. Apparently she did know what shoes did for a woman's legs.

"Hi," she said, more confident than I'd ever seen her. She

kissed me on the cheek and ushered me out the door. "Where are we going?"

She slung a small bag over her shoulder. What happened to that thing she'd bashed people with in MJ's? I went through my mental list again. "Dinner, Pantages," I said.

"You look...great," she said. I always looked great. What she meant was that I looked appropriate. Tonight I'd tried to dress like I was meeting a girl from Connecticut. The conservative clothes probably shocked her.

I pulled out my phone after we got into the car. "Who are you texting?" she asked, eyeing me with suspicion.

"Gabriel," I answered honestly. "If you didn't answer your door, he got the tickets." I snuck a glance at her. A small smile tilted her lips up. She wasn't planning to stand me up. Things just took a turn for the better.

I pulled up to Delphine, and escorted my date into the restaurant. We perused menus, marveled at the color and bouquet of wine, and unfolded crisp napkins in our lap.

"How's work?" I asked.

"It's time to quit," she said.

"You're quitting CBT?"

"No, the other," Daisy said, leaning back and taking a long drink of wine.

"Why now?"

"It's killing my sex life," she said matter-of-factly. The waitress served Daisy her scallops and me my short ribs. I tamped down my hopes. She wanted a sex life. The issue wasn't dead in the water. God knew, I was willing and able. But she may not be ready to resume her sex life tonight.

"How so?"

"After watching sex all day, it's the last thing you want to have."

That probably wasn't true for men, but I held my tongue.

"How's CBT?"

"Fine. I watch TV. It's not too hard. Not a lot of nipples or swear words to weed out." She paused, looking around the restaurant. "Nice here. How's your show?"

I debated between a lie and the truth. "I regret doing the show."

Daisy nearly dropped her fork. "Why? Thousands of other comics would kill for a development deal. From talking to Connor, they used to hand them out like cookies at a church social. Now, it's like finding gold in a river."

"That's true. They're trying to put me in a box, though."

"What box?"

"The neutered Asian box," I said. Then regretted it. I wanted to bolt. All I could see was dangerous territory ahead.

Daisy waved away a doggy bag when the waitress gathered the remains of her meal. "What was your original pitch?"

"A send-up to my life. Like C.K., or Maron."

"Ensemble, right? You, your brother, both looking for love. And you're some cocksman who breaks girls' hearts, while Gabriel gets his heart broken time and again looking to settle down?"

"That's about the size of it," I said.

"Kind of like your real life, I guess." I nodded and she paused, looking thoughtful. "Have you ever had a girlfriend?" I explored the table, looking for something to hold on to. The conversation had taken a hard left.

I'd avoided it before. I answered it now. "No."

Daisy's eyes grew wide in surprise. "You're what, thirty-three and you've never been serious? Jesus." She shook her head. "How many—"

I held up my hand. I would never answer that question because I didn't know and didn't care to tally it up. It was too many, I knew that... now. "How about you?" I asked.

Daisy sat back again. She fiddled with the empty wine glass then her skirt. "I dated a guy in high school that carried over into college. And I dated one other guy out here. That's it."

How did women do it? "You're smart and gorgeous," I started to say then stopped myself. Geez, dorking out much? Well, I couldn't back down now. "So why don't you have a boyfriend?"

"I see the worst in men every day. That doesn't make me want to get dressed up and troll a bar," she said. "I don't want to be some guys' one night stand."

I looked at my watch, grateful that the play was going to start soon. I did not need to go down the one night stand road. We walked the two blocks to the theater. I drew her close when she shivered outside the Will Call booth. Rubbed my hands down her bare arm. It was probably the only part of her I'd see naked today.

I had no desire to run to the bar or scope out women, my usual pastime during intermission. Instead we talked about the musical's irreverent take on an unpopular religion. When the house lights flickered, she sat back in her seat, leaning toward me. The minute darkness overtook the theater, and spotlights went up on the stage, she sought my hand, intertwining our fingers. Goofy butterflies went off. I squeezed her hand like the teenager I was channeling.

Daisy was fine with waiting until the aisles cleared out a bit before leaving the Pantages. She was looking down and fiddling with her program a lot. I lifted her chin, so I could see her eyes. Tears streamed down her cheeks.

"What's up? It was supposed to be a comedy."

"It's not that. The actors look like they're enjoying themselves so much. They're so passionate about what they're doing. I wish I could feel that passion in my life. What I'm doing is not exactly a calling."

. . .

"WHERE TO?" I asked jokingly when we got into the car. I needed to take her home, kiss her on the doorstep, and get the hell away before I fucked this up.

"Home," she said. It was the right thing. I ignored the punch in the gut that came with the worry that she'd never want to spend time with me again.

I did what I promised myself. Parked, opened her door, escorted her upstairs, and kissed her cheek on the doorstep. If she hadn't been there to witness it, I would have patted myself on the back for being so noble. Good thing I hadn't lifted my hand, because I was done with her next words.

"Please come in."

I could feel my head shaking. This was a bad idea. I needed to turn right around and walk out that door. "We won't do anything that you don't want," I heard myself saying instead. At the same time, I knew I was getting hard. Blood was leaving my brain.

"Okay," she threw over her shoulder, cryptic. She pushed the door open and draped her shawl over the chair. A few lights came on as she walked through the living room toward the bedroom. I didn't know what to do, so I sat on the couch with my hands folded.

"Do you mind if I get some water?" I called to her.

I heard the sink go on then off. "Help yourself to whatever you'd like." I didn't take that advice. Poured myself some pomegranate juice, instead.

She came back in wearing something that looked blue and soft. Glad I had the glass in my lap, I gripped the juice harder. Daisy looked at me for a long time before saying anything. "Can I ask you something?" I could only nod, willing at this point to do anything she wanted. "Can you kiss me?"

TWENTY-FIVE

DAISY

I COULDN'T BELIEVE I'd done it. It had taken me long minutes of heavy breathing in the bathroom to get up my courage. I wanted to be able to do in real life, what I could only do online as Lexi.

Raphael only hesitated long enough to put down his glass.

"Yes." He turned toward me, a half-smile playing around the lips I wanted on mine. The first touch was light, almost nonexistent.

"Please," I begged. Raphael pulled away. His eyes shifted away from mine, unsure. "I want to kiss you, Raphael. That's all for now, just kiss."

His eyes met mine again. I tried not to get lost in their depths. I watched full lips purse slightly, his nose flare as he breathed out. I think he looked almost relieved. Then he kissed me for real.

All the awkwardness I'd felt asking for what I wanted, slipped away on a single breath. He tilted his head just so, and we fit together. But he was still too far away. Cool air slipped between our bodies, pulling hard at my nipples. I wanted the heat of him near me. I eased my hands under his jacket, the hot flesh of his back searing my hands. Instead of pulling him closer, I put one leg on either side of his waist and slid nearer to him. I let the scent of his cologne intoxicate me.

Raphael's lips on mine, our mingled breath, the slide of his tongue weren't enough. I don't know why I thought they would be. Reluctantly, I pulled away. "I ..." I closed my eyes, blocking him from my view, hoping to lessen my embarrassment. I took another deep breath and pretended I was Lexi. She always knew how to get what she wanted. "Can you touch me?"

I closed my eyes again as he leaned toward me. First, he released a single button then a second. A warm palm slid along my collarbone then across my nipple. My jump was involuntary. Raphael pulled his hand back. "I'm sorry," he said.

"Don't be. It felt better than I thought it would." I slipped the few remaining buttons from their holes, pulling open my shirt. I'd taken off my bra when we'd come back from the theater. I put each of his hands bare breast. "Don't stop."

Raphael pulled his hands away, shucked his jacket, and those long, elegant fingers were back before I could miss them. He slid each hand back and forth against a nipple. The heat and a telltale blush rose up my chest. Each of his thumbs zeroed in on its own nipple. I wanted his mouth on me. I ached for the sweet, hot, wet feeling of warm heat on me.

"Come to bed." I stood and pulled him toward my bedroom. I lay on my side, elbow propping me up, but he didn't come past the door.

"Daisy, what are you doing?" My name was a little jarring. Daisy was not this wanton girl who'd tell a guy how to pleasure her. That was Lexi. Lexi was in charge in the bedroom. Lexi wanted to feel good tonight. "Asking for what I want, Raphael." I tried to make my smile as come hither as I could, how Lexi would. "Come here. I want your mouth on me."

Raphael came to me, sitting on the side of the bed. He oh-so-slowly took off his shoes, socks, and those dress pants he was rocking. He hooked a finger in my hair, looping a hank of hair behind it. The look he gave me was odd. "Are you sure about this? Bronwen?"

I lay back against the pillows, arranging my legs, so nothing was left to the imagination. "I'm sure."

His tongue explored the whorls of my ear first then the corner of my lips. I tried to catch him, pull him down to me, but Raphael was elusive. He held my two hands with one of his. Finally, finally he pulled a peak into his mouth. God, that was what I needed. Raphael released the peak with a delicate scrape of his teeth. My hips bucked off the bed. His other hand pushed them down, easing my plaid lounging pants off my hips.

I wanted release so badly I could almost feel its elusive pull.

"Please, Raphael. Please put your mouth on me," I begged.

He released my hands, sliding down the bed. He spread my legs, and his breath tickled the hairs on my thighs. My heart sped up, and my head swam. I was going to die from anticipation.

Then his mouth was there where I needed him. He made slow work of pleasuring me. First his lips gently abraded my flesh. Then his tongue zeroed in on my core. I needed to say no more to guide him. He was exactly where I wanted him. I took hold of the hairs on the back of his head and held on for dear life.

He went slow then fast, keeping me on the edge of insanity. My hands slipped from his hair and down his arms until I was gripping his hands. He interlaced his fingers with mine, and I melted a little. I was getting so close.

"Oh, God. I want to come," I said, seeking release.

His mouth had no mercy, and before I could take a breath, I was spinning uncontrollably. My bedroom went all hazy before

I squeezed my eyelids shut. Raphael didn't pull away immediately. He gentled his tongue, prolonging the pleasure.

The bed dipped and squeaked, and Raphael was next to me, cradling my body next to his. The fronds of the palms whispered against my windows. The clock next to the bed ticked loudly. His warm breath stirred my hair. I peeked through my lids. It was still me and Raphael in my bedroom, naked. Lexi and her bravado had fled.

"Daisy?" Raphael whispered against my neck. I could feel the ridge of his erection pressing my back.

"Can you please leave?"

Raphael scooted back. "I'm not asking for anything here. Don't push me away again."

"Please," I pleaded. Lexi was long gone, and Daisy needed to process what had happened—alone. The bed dipped again. Cold air raised the flesh on my back. I pulled the duvet over my body.

He put on his clothes, eerily silent. I watched his broad back as he left my room, hearing the front door close with a quiet snick. I flopped back against the headboard. I'd never been so thoroughly satisfied, yet felt so empty.

TWENTY-SIX

RAPHAEL

WHAT THE HELL HAPPENED TONIGHT? I should never have gone up there. Never. I should have stuck to the plan: dinner, show, one kiss—done. The steering wheel took a beating on the way home.

I bypassed my door and walked around the building to Gabriel's. I twisted the knob. Locked. I used the meaty side of my fist to pound on the door. Gabriel answered in sweats. Ted brought up the rear in a bathrobe. I pulled my phone from my pocket. When was midnight late? They must be creeping up on geriatric getting ready for bed this early.

"Please tell me you're not in trouble," Gabriel said.

"No, I'm not in trouble, big brother. I'm not some teen starlet who gets arrested every other day."

"But when you did, it was a doozy."

This was the problem with family. They never let you forget shit. "I'm fine."

Ted and Gabriel exchanged some kind of look. Gabriel shrugged. "You want some *sikhye?*"

The thought of the cool rice and barley malt drink calmed me. I nodded, and Gabriel went to the kitchen. "We were kind of in the middle of something," Ted said as my brother came back toward the couch. For the first time, I noticed the candles and slow jazz. I looked back at them. Fuck. Bad timing.

I put my drink on the coffee table. "Sorry, I'll talk to you later," I said, starting to rise. Gabriel's hand was heavy on my shoulder.

"Sit. You never come up here. What's wrong?"

My shoulders started creeping toward my ears. "Nothing."

Another look passed between Gabriel and his husband. Ted disappeared from the room. "What's with the clothes?" he asked, fingering the lapels of my jacket.

"Book of Mormon, your tickets."

"I know that part. Why are you dressed like this? Is there a country club next to the Pantages?"

"Don't quit your day job. You'd never get a spot at the Comedy Store." He didn't laugh even though my joke was funnier than his. "I had a date."

My brother's hand immediately went up to his mouth. "Jesus. Seriously?"

I nodded.

"Daisy?"

I bowed my head again.

"Figured," Ted said from their bedroom doorway.

What the hell? "Why would you figure?"

"She was at your house, and she wasn't horizontal," Ted said.

"Gee thanks. You make me sound like a fuck 'em and forget 'em kinda guy."

"C'mon, Raphael. You're more promiscuous than a gay man."

"That's not fair." I turned toward him. My hands were trembling. If he wasn't fucking my brother, I'd have punched that smug little face of his.

Gabriel put another steadying hand on my arm. He'd been doing that since I could remember. My old man would make fun of me for listening to comedy records in my room or wearing mousse in my hair and my brother would be there making sure I didn't deck my father. "What Ted means is that you've never been in a relationship."

"Did you all have a secret meeting?" They looked at me, perplexed. "Daisy keeps asking me about girlfriends."

"You never had one," Gabriel said.

"So?"

"So? Who wants to take a chance on a guy whose idea of a relationship is staying the night?"

That was harsh. I hadn't had a girlfriend, because I hadn't wanted one. You don't meet girlfriends on Twitter or in a bar. And definitely not those comedy groupies. I'd seen guys date those girls. Those chicks were always crazy, never ever worth the pussy.

"But she's different."

Ted came into the room and sat down next to me.

"I'm sorry. It's just that you've never been remotely serious before."

"I am now." You'd have thought I farted, with all the stoicism hiding smirks from the boys.

"Geez," Gabriel said. "How did your date go?" I didn't know how to answer that. Shook my head. "Are you going to see her again?"

"I wish I knew."

"All kidding aside. What's up?" Ted asked.

"She's..." What did I say? We had crappy sex one day when I was trying to fulfill my drunken fantasies. I tried doing it her way tonight, now I was on the receiving end of being used. "I made her *samgyetang*."

Gabriel got a faraway look in his eye. "Mom loved to serve

us that. It was the next best thing to sending us to get our flu shot."

"Ginseng will make you live one more year," I said in a perfect imitation of Mom.

"You should call her," Gabriel said. "She always had good dating advice."

"She thought you were dating girls when she dispensed all that wisdom."

"It worked, though."

"I promised you I wouldn't talk to them until they accepted you, bro."

"I never asked you to do that, Raphael. They're your parents, too."

"I don't see Dad knocking down my door."

"Dad and Mom are not the same, you know. Mom was always a big supporter of you and your comedy."

"Is that why they stopped paying for college? Was that how they supported me?"

"It was stupid what Dad did."

"You were Mom's favorite. And Dad's too. They're not the least bit interested in me. Anyway, my first conversation with Mom in twelve years can't be about a girl."

Gabriel dipped his head. "You're probably right about that," he acknowledged.

"So what do I do?"

"Why this girl?" Ted asked.

Visions of the pointy ends of Daisy's hair brushing against her cheeks, her spiky lashes wet with tears sweeping down over her blue eyes, her nipple hard and dark pink with desire, floated before my eyes. "Do I need a reason?"

"God damn it, Gabriel, I think your brother's in love."

I shot up from the couch and stalked to their kitchen. I poured myself a water with a lot of ice.

"I'm not in love," I said. "I hardly know her."

"Have you slept with her?"

Heat suffused my face, I could feel it. I couldn't believe I was blushing. I've had sex a million ways with a million people, and I was blushing. Fuck it. "Yeah," I mumbled.

"Then I think 'hardly know her' is not an accurate description."

"Was the sex good?" Ted asked. I was not a fan of Ted. I tolerated him. I didn't want to tolerate him much more tonight.

"No, it wasn't good, and I can't figure out how to fix it," I admitted.

Ignoring Ted, I poured out the whole story to my brother. His wincing and face contortions nearly did me in. "Sounds like you both need therapy."

"Gee. Thanks."

"Seriously. This is the most emotionally retarded crap I've ever heard."

"I could have felt like shit alone in my apartment, you know."

"I'm telling it like it is. You like her. She likes you, but the two of you can't meet in the middle."

"I think it's the porn."

"What?!"

Maybe I'd left something out. "She does porn websites for a living."

"I thought she worked at CBT."

"That job is a concession to her best friend."

"What's the problem with the porn? Everyone enjoys a little porn now and then."

"Not Christian fundamentalists or Mormons."

"I think I read somewhere that Mississippi and Utah were net importers of racy DVDs," Ted threw in.

I resisted the urge to pull out my phone and disprove him.

The one-upmanship had to take a backseat. I really needed my brother's advice. "It's like the porn is ruining everything," I continued.

"How? Everything I've read says porn could spice up a relationship. You have a little wine, press play, get the juices flowing, so to speak...."

"It's the opposite, though. She's nervous around me like I'm gonna pounce at any minute. Like I can't control myself." I deliberately left out the part about my lack of control that night.

"A rape charge will do that," Ted said.

My hand went to the opposite ear as I pulled my head one way then the other releasing tension. That had been uncalled for. "Gabe."

My brother gave his husband a look. Ted disappeared into the kitchen.

"I'm serious. I've seen this in other comics. They watch a lot of porn and think everything is on the menu, that every girl is going to fall at their feet. They start dating strippers, 'cause they have no boundaries, they need women who have little that's off limits. You get the drift."

"Sounds like you've already thought this out," Gabriel said. He was right. Saying it made it easier, though.

"What should I do?"

"Because despite all this fucked up shit, you like her."

I nodded like an ignorant fool. I'd tried forgetting about her, but I couldn't. Plus, I'd seen glimpses of the woman she wanted to be. I wanted to be there when she let her inner Bronwen free.

TWENTY-SEVEN

DAISY

CONTENT WAS KING. I was falling off the throne. In my first four plus months, I'd signed up a little over four hundred subscribers. The allure of new girls they'd never seen before and my nineteen ninety-nine monthly price was unbeatable. I'd only directed a small fraction of my sites there, and my bank account was already thirty thousand dollars healthier.

Then the e-mails had started as a trickle. New girls, black girls, Asian girls, they wanted it all. And that damned Goth girl, they'd loved her. If I were smart, I would set up a webcam site that was just her as a premium upgrade. Then the trickle had turned into a stream. I'd doled out the movies I'd made as slowly as I could get away with, but the well was nearly dry. Unless I bought some videos or shot new ones, the subscriber complaints would flood my box, and those twenty dollar recurring payments would disappear faster than water in the Mohave Desert.

I'd only been at the computer ten minutes before my mind drifted back to the previous night's humiliation. I wasn't fit for the world anymore. High school had nothing on adulthood. That was why people did drugs. I craved the sweet oblivion of heroin. I scanned my living room. Maybe a junkie, needle in hand would pop out of a hidden corner. Waited a beat. No luck there.

Up until this February I'd been okay being alone. I had my work, friends, lots of spare time to do whatever I liked. Now I wanted Raphael to fill the gap I hadn't known was there. How in the hell had this happened? I shook my head. It didn't matter how it happened. He was never coming back. We weren't right for each other. He wanted porn girl sex. I'd tried living out my Lexi fantasies and both had been a bust. So desperate I was for a distraction, that I made the mistake of picking up the phone without looking at the caller ID.

"Good morning Bronwen," my mother said. I felt like a Pavlovian three-year-old, thrilled to hear a voice as familiar to me as my own. Then thirty years of reality set in. "Is it too early?" my mother asked. "What time is it out there?"

I'd lived out in California for more than a decade, and Doris still hadn't learned to subtract three. "It's eleven."

"Are you busy?"

I was never busy. "Just working."

"On a Sunday? Even the gardeners around here take a day of rest. We're going to the club for dinner tonight."

I didn't mention that the employees at 'the club' weren't taking a 'day of rest.' Hugh and Doris went to the club every Sunday night, so this wasn't news. I asked the expected question. "Who are you having dinner with?"

"With whom, Bronwen," she corrected me. "Daddy and I are eating with the Loewes. Bianca is finally getting married. You remember Bianca, right?"

"Sure, Mom." Bianca was the ugly younger sister of Danica Loewe. Danica and I had graduated from the Hopkins School at the same time.

My mom took a sip. Martini hour had started early in Madison. I steeled myself for what came after every wedding announcement. "You seeing anyone? Have you been to an Ivy Plus social yet? You and your Asian friend Nari should go."

I'd looked up the Ivy thing. Drinks at the hot spot of the minute with over confident guys who wished they'd founded Facebook, did not appeal. "I'm seeing someone," I said before my brain censored my mouth.

Doris' bracelets jingled as she shook another cocktail. "Is it serious?"

"We're sleeping together. So I hope so." Bait. I'd just dangled it. My mother was a shark.

"Ooh, sounds juicy." I shifted uncomfortably. Doris loved to talk about my sex life. That I didn't have one was a constant disappointment. "What's his name?"

"Raphael Augustine," I answered.

"What do his parents do?"

"I don't know, Mom. He's not really in touch with them. They disowned his gay brother, so...."

Doris' sigh was dramatic. "Some people can be so provincial. Sorry to hear that. Where did you meet him? Where did he go to school?"

"I met him at a gay bar. He was there with his brother."

"Why were you there? Is there something you need to tell me? I'd be happy if you brought home a husband or a wife, dear."

"I'm not gay, Mom," I said truthfully. Then, I lied. "Nari wanted to go out and not get hit on."

"She is a lovely little slip of a thing. I'm sure men go gaga over her," Doris said to me, her not so little slip of a girl. "So back to your Raphael," she prompted.

"He went to Pomona."

"Oh, that's a good school," she said, her tone letting me know it was anything but, in her eyes. She was a dyed in the wool Cliffie from the days it was a separate school. Daddy had gone to Owen, of course. "What does he do?"

"He's got his own show on CBT," I said.

"Have we seen it?"

Even if it was airing, they wouldn't have seen it. Daddy's idea of fun was watching old black and white mysteries and Lawrence Welk on DVD. Doris sat with him, scrutinizing architectural and design magazines for kicks.

"It's not on yet. Maybe fall, or as a mid-season replacement."

"What does he look like?"

"He's cute. Brown hair and brown eyes," I answered then hesitated.

"What aren't you telling me?"

"He's Korean, Mom."

"Oh," she said. In the long pause, I could practically hear her struggle for diplomacy and tolerance. "That's nice, dear. Is he a friend of Nari's? She and her family are lovely."

"I've gotta go, Mom," I said. "Say 'hi' to Dad and the Loewes for me."

"Okay, dear," she said, disconnecting the call.

My mother was going to drip liberated Cliffie radical all over the dinner table. The fact that I was seeing someone Korean would spread throughout the club's gossip mill like wildfire. Moving to California, southern at that, had been exotic enough. Now, I'd stuck a toe in untested waters.

I pushed away from the desk, listening the casters spin on the hardwood floor. I didn't know which was worse, baiting my mother with Raphael's heritage or lying about dating. Begging for a little cunnilingus before pushing a guy out the door did not a relationship make.

The phone rang again. I was sure it was Hugh calling to warn me about the true nature of men. That had been one of his favorite speeches, and he would not miss an opportunity to make it again. I'm sure his lecture would have seen more action if I'd dated more. Little did he know I'd gotten a college degree and graduate honors in men's tastes.

My finger was already pressing talk when I realized it was Raphael's name, not The Fletchers on the phone. Shit. Shit. My stomach plummeted to my toes. Damn it. Against my better judgment, I didn't hang up.

"Hi," I squeaked like a mouse who wanted to disappear into a hole.

"Let's go to the Museum of Natural History," he said without preamble. My mind scattered in a thousand directions. Raphael, L.A.'s idea of a museum, last night. I brought it back to the present. My face flamed with heat at the thought of looking him in the eye. The phone crackled while I searched for any excuse, coming up dry. "I'll pick you up in an hour. Lunch is on me."

I placed the phone in the charger base.

RAPHAEL HAD an honest to God picnic in his trunk. After we parked in the museum's lot, I stood mute when he spread out a blanket and laid a basket under the shade of a broadleaf tree.

I sat, making sure to tuck my skirt under me like my mother had taught me.

He pulled out two plastic containers. "Do you want the ham and cheese or roast beef?"

I couldn't help laughing. "Where did you get regular sandwiches in L.A?"

He pulled a menu from the basket. "Apricot glazed ham and brie with mustard caper sauce, or grass finished roast beef with horseradish crème fresh," he finished with a flourish of his hand.

"That's more like it. I'll have ham and cheese." We ate in silence for a few minutes. A lot of things came to my mind, but I didn't want to say anything that reminded him of last night and Lexi Quinn. "I told my parents about you." Shit. Where had that come from? It was too bad we were drinking sparkling grape juice instead of wine. I could have used a little fortitude.

"What did they say?" The mild curiosity in his voice was belied by a crease between his eyebrows.

"Nothing much. Doris," at his head shake, I clarified, "my mom wanted to know what your parents did. Where you'd gone to college. That sort of thing."

"Did you tell her what I look like?"

"I told her that you're really cute." My hand flew to my mouth. I couldn't believe I said that out loud. I ran my hand along the blanket, looking for my inhibitions. Turning toward the screams and shouts of children, I hoped to hide my embarrassment. Kids ran around with booty from a snack cart. Families with strollers were coming and going down the long ramp leading to the museum. When I looked back, he was sweeping away invisible grass or dirt from the blanket. "You know, that you have dark hair and eyes, that sort of thing."

"It's not a bad thing that you think I'm attractive," he said. My whole body fizzed with nerves. Maybe it was adrenaline. I could have run to the coliseum and back without getting winded. I was imagining how I would do that in gold strappy sandals when Raphael spoke again. "I think you're cute, too."

"So what's for dessert?" I asked, concealing the nearly uneaten sandwich in the folds of my dress.

I could feel his eyes on me. When I looked up, his face was serious. "Did you tell them I'm half-Korean?"

"Yes."

"What did your mom, Doris, say?"

"Nothing, really." He winced a little. What answer did he want? I'd never dated anyone who wasn't white before. I'd hardly dated anyone. Okay, maybe I'd thought Mom would express a little more shock. He leaned back, trying to look casual, but I knew I'd been quiet too long. Even I thought it seemed like I was hiding something. "She was fine, really. Doris will be sure to tell everyone at dinner to show how liberal she and Dad are."

"Are you liberal?" he asked with a flourish of his hand. I looked at the museum's rotunda and columns and the big modernist additions comparing it to the museum in London with its bold homage to evolution. I turned back to Raphael.

"I'm not here because I'm liberal," I said. Attraction was so complicated. I didn't want to delve into my pull toward men who looked like him. I'd seen enough fetish stuff online. I wasn't like those men who could only get off on a very specific kind of woman. I found a lot of Korean men attractive. After the Korean Wave, who didn't? Raphael made me sweat just thinking about him.

He pulled two containers out of the basket. At the end of each outstretched hand was a dessert. I picked chocolate cake, leaving him with some mini apple pie or tart. "What happened last night?"

If I'd had any shred of appetite left, it fled. I dropped the cake on the blanket. Naively, I'd thought when he hadn't brought it up after the first fifteen minutes, I'd dodged a bullet. But there was the slug, right between the eyes. I looked at the orange, blue and green yarn of the wool blanket. Every fringe twisted to the right. Did all yarn have to twist the same way to keep it from unraveling? "I don't know," I mumbled into my chest.

Raphael had shifted closer. "Look at me, Bronwen." I looked up from the wool of the blanket, from the weave of my picnic appropriate dress.

"I don't know what you want me to say."

"Who was that last night? Because it wasn't you."

"Of course it was me."

"Who?" he asked, his question brooking no argument.

"Lexi."

"Who?"

"Lexi Quinn. She's my alterego, online."

"Why were you her? I don't get it. I thought we'd.... This is so fucked up." He rose. My eyes traveled up past his black shoes, tight fitting jeans, designer shirt. "Let's just go in."

It was like a junior high field trip. He held my hand as we walked through the rooms full of reconstructed dinosaurs and taxidermy mammals. At any time, I expected a teacher to thrust a clipboard at me full of questions about animals of the earth.

We went downstairs to the gem room. It was dark as a cave. Small halogens beamed at the crystallized structures, refracting the light into beautiful colors. Three kids ran by followed by a security guard, pushing us into a dark corner.

"Daisy?"

My heart nearly leapt from my chest. "What, Raphael?"

His head bowed, dropping toward mine. "Bronwen is the one I like."

TWENTY-EIGHT

RAPHAEL

THE MINUTE I walked into my apartment, I pulled out my laptop and plugged it in. One day I'd remember to charge the damned battery. When it got enough juice to boot up, I was typing 'Lexi Quinn' into Google as fast as my fingers could move.

Lexiquinn.com popped up first in the results. For not the first time, I wondered if siphoning off Gabriel's free internet left a trail of my browsing history. Ah hell, if he hadn't busted me for looking at porn yet, this wasn't going to cause a stir. I clicked on the link and found a single landing page. A reasonably attractive brunette with come and hither in her gaze seemingly pointed to a list of categories I might like. Admittedly, I'd sampled the complete palette of women in my life and didn't have a favorite.

Picking something, I clicked and was lured into the usual world of teaser pictures and video that would normally get me going. It wasn't that I was immune this time. Stirring was definitely happening in my pants, but I pushed aside thoughts of sex. I looked at every footer and every site in this little universe had been curated by Lexi/Daisy. Wow. If she'd made even a fraction of the money I'd heard about, she was doing quite well. I could see why she wouldn't want to give this up. It was like a syndication deal. You do the work, and if you hit the jackpot right, you could live off passive income forever.

When numbers stopped spinning in my head, I looked at the pictures and videos more closely. I'd never thought much about it before, but pornography was not exactly a celebration of women. Nearly every picture showed a penis jammed into one orifice or another. Unless the women were giving blow jobs, they were headless torsos. The videos were by men for men. Men in their basest form.

Teenage-like guilt flooded my veins. If you'd asked me yesterday, or the day before, I'd have said I was a nice guy. But looking at pictures of objectified women made me feel anti-feminist. I slammed the laptop shut. If a forty-minute tour of Daisy's world made me want to turn in my man card, it was no wonder she had such a low opinion of me. And I'd done nothing but live down to her expectations.

For the next couple of weeks I stewed. The morning we were doing the first table read, I pushed aside all the crap I'd wallowed in and took extra care getting ready. I got to my assigned spot at the long conference table and waited for everyone else to fill in. I was only half surprised this time to see Daisy among the execs filling half the room. She stopped by my chair, put a hand on my shoulder and leaned in close to me.

"Hey there."

Bronwen's light perfume enveloped me. I took a deep breath of her. "Surprised to see you here today," I said, neither original nor funny.

"Connor thought I could use some of the summer slowdown to spend more time with your show, get a feel for the hot button issues," she said.

One of the network producers called to Daisy before I could

say anything more. With everyone assembled, scripts in hand, we began. The scene was in my apartment located across the hall from my brother's, Friends style.

It opened with Gabriel knocking on my door at the same time I was pushing a half clad girl out. My brother sits on the couch, upset that he'd been dumped by his latest boyfriend for being too serious. I, on the other hand, play up the fact his coming over was the perfect excuse to eject last night's date.

Halfway through, an executive interjected. "Raphael, there are no parents in this show, right?"

I shook my head. "Nope. It's only the two brothers in L.A. One looking for love in a world of one night stands and the other looking for one night stands in a world of forever women."

"Have you thought of adding your parents?"

"No," I said firmly.

"You should think about it," the executive said. "Doris and Peter were a hit on Ray Romano's show."

Before my eyes, and without my input, the discussion evolved into how adding parents would be comic genius and what actors were available to play those roles. The writers, who knew which side their bread was buttered on, had their pens out, scratching notes on my script.

"Plus," one writer said. "We could do a whole rift on the cultural difference."

"Which one of your parents is Korean?" another asked.

"My mother," I answered, resigned. No one commented on my lack of enthusiasm. They bubbled around me, ready to bring fake parents into my life. Someone proclaimed hunger and before I knew it we were taking a coffee break while a production assistant scrambled for doughnuts and espresso drinks.

I pushed my way outside seeking fresh air.

"You didn't look happy in there," Daisy said, leaning back against the building, joining my pity party.

"It's not my show anymore."

"Because of your parents?"

"Here are two people that haven't so much as sent a card or lifted a phone to talk to me or my brother in years. And now I'm paying homage to them."

"It could be funny," Daisy said.

"How?" I wasn't in the mood for funny.

"I don't know. Maybe they don't know Gabriel's gay, or they think you are and for some reason you don't want to disabuse them of this notion. And Ray's parents were really funny on that show. The dad on King of Queens was hilarious too."

Great. She was on board with the best TV parents of all time shtick. My arms crossed in front of my chest.

"Look," she said. "In the last few months, you know what I've learned? TV is not real life. Us, here, now. That's what's real. The rest is all entertainment."

"And you know what I've learned in the last few months? What happens on the screen can affect us in real life."

"How? Every four-year-old knows that TV isn't real."

"Then someone better tell Lexi Quinn," I said.

"Oh, my God." She rounded on me. "That's so not fair."

I didn't move one muscle. "Really. How so?" I watched her sputter while her mind was probably whirling with excuses. Not one of which she was able to vocalize. "I checked out the Lexi Quinn little family of sites." That admission stunned her into silence. "The way I see it, Bronwen, ten of ten sites you have are full of men objectifying women. And years of seeing that has convinced you that's the way the world operates."

"Jesus." Epithets, but no objections. She looked at her watch. "We better go back in before someone realizes we're gone."

I followed her in, though they probably could have done the show without me.

More relaxed after getting some air, I had to agree with Daisy. Some of the stuff with the parents was actually funny. Maybe it would be better with an ensemble cast. With my limited acting skills, I was suddenly relieved the burden wouldn't all be on my shoulders, though the show would still carry my name.

And just maybe having loving, accepting parents on television would force my real life parents to do the right thing once and for all.

TWENTY-NINE

DAISY

AFTER PUTTING up the last of the original content I'd made, I got up from the computer, rubbed my eyes. It was nearing eleven, and I needed to get to bed soon or I'd be wrecked in the morning. Game show light and noise were hell on the tired.

My underwear drawer was nearly empty. I looked toward the overflowing hamper in my closet. Laundry had been a breeze when I was home all day. All the good pajamas were dirty. The only thing left in my drawer was a pink and lace nighty my mother had bought for me when I was dating Brett.

I was not a naked sleeper, so I pulled on the inappropriate gift. I looked at myself in the mirror. Clearly, I was not the sexy model the designer envisioned when sketching out this thing. I pulled at the fussy frills on the hip length hem. I'd need a C cup and a bedonkadonk butt for this to work.

I pouted at my reflection. Blew a kiss. Maybe. I sashayed over to my computer and opened a new tab, typing in *sexychat-pad.com*. When the men converged on me, I told them Lexi was in the house. The truth flew from my fingertips. I was all alone and horny as hell. I described what I was wearing from the matching pink and lace panties to the sheer peek-a-boo fabric barely covering my nipples.

Before I could type more, I clicked and found myself in a room with a guy named Phil. But no matter how many times he promised to bite my nipples or suck my clit, it wasn't working. I kept seeing Raphael doing those things to me, and then his back as he walked out of my apartment.

I closed the damned browser window and shut off the computer with a bang and a kick. I hoped the hard, space age metal case really held up to abuse.

Nothing was working. Not anonymous online sex, not sex in real life, nothing.

I got into bed unhappy and unsatisfied. The ding on my phone meant I'd received a text message. I picked it up from the nightstand and tapped the screen. Raphael. "Call me."

My hands shook as I reluctantly tapped the screen.

"Hey there," he said.

"Hey, yourself," I responded. Great, we'd graduated to seventh grade communication skills.

He cleared his throat. He couldn't be nervous, could he? He'd already gotten into my pants. "Want to go to First Friday over on Abbott Kinney?"

"Sure," I said, though I didn't know exactly what I'd agreed to.

"I'll text you Friday morning, Bronwen," he said.

On Thursday night, I was flipping through my closet and actually contemplating calling Nari for fashion advice. I was just working up to a good reason I'd need to look good without disclosing the date with Raphael, when the phone rang.

My heart sunk to the pit of my stomach. I knew it was Raphael calling to cancel. He'd changed his mind. Why would he want to go out with me? One kiss in the gem room at the museum didn't cure a relationship full of false starts.

"Bronwen, it's your father." One day I was going to learn to check the caller ID before I picked up the phone.

"Hugh."

"I know you're busy with your life out there, but..."

"What can I do for you?"

"Can you catch the red eye Friday night?"

I should have expected a 'big ask' the minute I heard Hugh's voice. Doris was much easier to refuse. "Why?"

"Your mom got roped into hosting an engagement party for Bianca."

Roped in my ass. My mother probably volunteered ten times over. "What happened to the Loewes' house?" They had a huge one on the water. Made my parents' home look like a shack in comparison.

"Some kind of renovation. Since we have the acreage in the back..."

He needed to say no more. Mom was planning a party for the daughter she'd never had. I backed out of my closet. I'd rather go on a date with Raphael than spend seventy-two hours playing Connecticut Miss. "I..." Why couldn't I manufacture an excuse from thin air?

"I'll send tickets," Hugh said.

"I have money, Dad. I can buy my own tickets."

"I had the travel agent overnight confirmation to you." Doris and Hugh had to be the last two people on earth who hadn't heard of online booking and e-tickets.

"I guess I'll see you Saturday morning, Dad."

"Good night, Bronwen."

I threw myself backwards on the bed. I knew exactly what I would wear. Dressing for a weekend in Connecticut was something I could do with both eyes closed. I tapped at the phone in my hand, dialing Raphael.

"I was just going to call you," he said by way of greeting.

"I can't go with you on Friday. I have to go home."

"Fuckin' A. I have a show at some school called Quinnipiac. It's why I had to cancel. Another comic broke his leg in an accident. Stand up and prop your leg up don't work together. Anyway, this will repay all my debts to everyone."

Because lawyers and bail weren't free, I knew. My dampened enthusiasm came back to life. "Maybe—"

He cut me off, speaking again. "We'll be in the same state, right? Maybe you could come down for the show. It's in some town north of the airport, Ham—"

"Hamden."

"Is that near where you are?"

I did a quick calculation in my head of not only the distance, but what being together outside L.A. might mean. "Maybe thirty miles," I answered.

"Let's meet up. I'll get you a couple of tickets to the show. Let me know if you can't make it."

By Saturday morning, I was only thinking of sleep. Tony Adams was right where he'd always been when I flew into this airport. The dark skinned man had been on hand to drive our family to and from the airport and into the city for as long as I could remember.

"Mornin' Miss Fletcher," he said with a two fingered salute from the brim of his feather adorned fedora.

"Daisy," I said as always. "How are you?"

During the thirty minute drive I relaxed. Tony regaled me with stories of his family. A lot had changed in the years I'd been gone. His kids now had kids.

"Anyone special in your life, Miss Daisy?"

"Maybe," I said, trying to sound more coy than unsure.

He pulled up to the center hall colonial I'd called home for nearly two decades. "Good on you, Miss Daisy."

After I fished my parents' keys from my bag, I let myself in. The grandfather clock in the hall chimed seven. Doris and Hugh wouldn't be up for an hour or so at least. I dragged my overnight bag up to my room and settled in for much needed horizontal sleep.

"Bronwen, honey. You need to get up." Fantasies of a hot night with Raphael blew away like smoke, as my mother pulled the summer blanket off me. I hated when she did that. But if I didn't respond, the torture would only get worse. Ice clinked. She had a drink in hand. That ice could graze my neck and shoulder any minute now.

"I'm up, Mom."

"There's some toast downstairs if you want it. Don't make too many crumbs. Mary did an extra cleaning yesterday, and the caterers need it to be spotless for set up."

Against my will, one gritty eye focused on my mother. "What time is the party?"

"Twelve-thirty."

I sat up when my mother opened my luggage.

"I can do that."

"No need. You had a long flight. I'll help." She put her Bloody Mary on the long white enamel dresser still crowded with my childhood treasures.

She pulled out a blue silk dress and my striped silk pants. Silk was big in late summer. Linen was more comfortable but always bagged on me.

"Raphael is in town," I said.

My mother hung my navy blue oxford and two camisoles carefully on padded satin hangers. She peered around the room. "Is he here?"

"I wouldn't spring a guest on you like that," I said. "He's flying into Olde Haven today. He has a show at Quinnipiac."

"I thought you said he worked on a TV show."

"He does, Mom. It's just a weekend gig. I think he's filling in for someone who couldn't show up."

"Does he want to come to the party?"

I could see the gears turning in her mind. But I wasn't sure if her invitation was genuine. I didn't know if I wanted him there, either. He might be uncomfortable among our crowd, so I made the decision for him.

"He lands too late. But he's invited us to his show if you want to go." That would put a few dozen feet and a couple hours between him and my parents.

"I'll ask Hugh. That could be fun."

I lurched out of bed to the bathroom. When I came back in my mother and her glass of spiked tomato juice had disappeared. The bed looked so crisp, it was hard to believe I'd only woken from a nap in it moments ago.

The party was typical Doris. A hundred people, ninety of whom I'd never met, spread out across the back lawn. White linen draped tables littered the flagstone patio. White candles floated in the saltwater pool. Black bow tied, white oxford clad wait staff circulated with smoked salmon and puff pastry.

No less than ten mothers of children I'd known since childhood cornered me on my 'prospects.' And no less than ten times I told them I was seeing someone. My mother materialized at my hip on more than one occasion to brag that Raphael was in town. And surely he'd come to the club for supper tomorrow. I could show off my new beau then. Three hours of rounded eyes and wagging tongues. I couldn't wait.

THIRTY

RAPHAEL

I WAS NEVER SO glad to be in the middle of nowhere. This gig would pay my debt to Joel once and for all. The first payment from CBT had gone to pay my rent for a year in advance. Then reimbursing Gabriel had chipped away at the rest. The unexpected bonus was that Daisy was coming. I'd thought I'd have a lonely weekend without her and nothing but my own hand. Instead, I'd be seeing my girl in less than two hours. She'd promised to come backstage after the show.

My girl. The idea of Daisy being my one and only made me laugh. Who would have thought it six months ago? Someone knocked on my dressing room door.

"Come in."

"You're on in ten," a student said.

Twelve minutes later, I waltzed out onstage to pounding bass and pulsating lights. "Thank you Quinnipiac! It's great to be in Connecticut. I have a very special guest tonight. Please give a warm welcome to Bronwen Fletcher." A spotlight searched the crowd. I saw a pale hand wave at me.

Suddenly I was on fire. I would crush it tonight. "Now that you're older, you ever think about fairy tales? Let me tell you a story. Once upon a time, there was a poor and lonely carpenter named Mister Geppetto. Even though he wasn't married, he really wanted a little boy all his own. So he carved him out of wood. And when the wooden boy came to life, his wooden nose grew and grew and grew. I gotta ask you. Was Mister Geppetto the founding member of the man-boy love association? Oh, NAMBLA's real. Look it up."

The laugh was long, ending in applause. I was killing.

Back in my dressing room, I had to close the door to keep the coeds from the room. They had accosted me in the hallway asking if I wanted alcohol or drugs. The school merely supplied soda and chips to the entertainment. I opened at the third knock, and Daisy stood there in a filmy mesh top and knee length skirt. I pulled her in and kissed her right on the mouth. No one would mistake my intention. The clearing of a throat behind me kept me from daring to go any further.

"Raphael, these are my parents Doris and Hugh Fletcher." Both were fit looking older white people. I shook their hands firmly.

"Hope you enjoyed the show," I said.

"We did," Hugh said. "How long have you been at this comedy thing?"

Daisy leaned against the makeup table, watching the inquisition.

"A little more than ten years," I said. "Started right out of college."

"Bronwen says you went to Pomona," Doris said. I knew that Daisy had gone to Owen, but I was surprised her parents still thought about those things. Outside of the USC versus UCLA rivalry, colleges weren't talked about much in L.A.

"I did," I said. "Can I take you all out for a drink? Dessert?"

Doris turned to Daisy, her movements a little unsteady. Was

she half lit? "Bronwen, honey, did you invite your friend to stay with us?"

"No, Mom. I'm sure the college has put him up."

Doris turned back toward me. "That's no way to spend the rest of the weekend. When are you going back to California?"

"I'd hoped to catch Daisy's flight."

"So you'll be here tonight and tomorrow?" She spied my overnight bag in the corner of the room. "I insist you come back with us tonight. I'm sure I can root out a little something to eat from the party today."

Hugh had taken his wife's cue and was fitting the strap on his shoulder. I looked at Daisy. She shrugged, and all four of us made our way to the parking lot.

Like pre-teens on a movie date, Daisy and I sat in the back of her dad's behemoth BMW. After a few attempts at conversation shouted over the hiss of the tires and roar of the engine, the car was quiet. Speeding along the freeway in near darkness drew out the anticipation of finally spending time with the woman next to me.

Without endless mini malls lit like Christmas, the bane of the California landscape, little distracted me. I inched over the console and grabbed Daisy's hand, running my thumb along the smooth skin of her palm. A single street light illuminated her face for a moment, and I could see the ghost of a smile on her lips.

Set far back from the street, Daisy's house was huge. And not in the gaudy McMansion way that I'd learned to associate with the well-off in California. It was a sprawling mass of old money.

Daisy's mom peeled off toward the kitchen. And Hugh hefted my bag up the stairs, ignoring my protests. "Let's go to the den. I'll start a fire," Daisy said, pulling me down the hall.

For such a rambling house, the rooms were surprisingly

small. Except for some fussy red flowered curtains, the den was a simple room. I sat on the sofa, avoiding the broken-in leather club chair and fussy wingback that looked like they belonged on the set of All in the Family, while Daisy lit the fire.

"I hope you're hungry for a little something," Doris said, heavy tray in hand. I stood up and grabbed it from her, easing the groaning tray onto a wood coffee table.

"Wow. This is quite the spread," I said as Hugh came in the room, drinks in hand. He handed a martini to Doris, keeping some amber colored drink for himself.

"It's a shame you couldn't come to the party this afternoon," Doris started. I looked at Daisy. Her back was to me. The swoosh of a match, and the smell of burning wood filled the air. The fire started to crackle. "Too bad your plane got in late. You could have met some of our friends."

Daisy had never mentioned that I was invited. I'd have jumped at the chance to spend the afternoon with her, meet some of the people she'd grown up with. My mind spun with reasons that she'd avoided having me at her parent's house. I waved away the alcohol that Doris offered, accepting coffee instead. Was Daisy ashamed to have me meet her people?

"No matter, Doris. You'll come to Sunday dinner at the club," Hugh said, ending the discussion.

Fire roaring, Daisy disappeared, coming back with what looked like a White Russian. I helped myself to some very good pastries while I patiently answered her parent's questions about my career and my upbringing. When the clock struck eleven, they excused themselves, claiming they had a tradition of watching the late movie on Saturdays.

"It was lovely meeting you," Doris said.

"Bronwen can show you to the guest room," Hugh said.

And with that, Daisy and I were alone. I'd survived the

inquisition. The minute they were out of the room, she was up, stoking the fire with some kind of iron poker.

I had no part of shame. "Why didn't you invite me?"

Daisy didn't pretend to misunderstand me. "I didn't want to answer dozens of questions."

"Like 'how is it to date an Asian guy?'"

She sat down, easing back into her dad's brown leather. "No Raphael, that's not it."

"Are you sure? Do you want me to come to dinner tomorrow? Will you have to answer too many questions, then?"

The skin around her blue eyes was smudged with tired. She waved her left hand at me. "It's not about that. I'm a thirty something woman who's single at an engagement party. I didn't want to answer a million questions about when am I going to 'set the date.' Didn't want to subject you to being grilled. That's all."

I stared at the flames licking at the weathered grey stones. I felt like a heel. "I'm sorry." Of course that kind of party would probably be crappy if she brought a date. "Come over here." Reluctantly, she moved from the chair to the couch.

"Have you ever been with anyone who wasn't white?" I asked.

Daisy turned slightly, her eyes meeting and holding mine for a long quiet moment. "No."

"Do you—"

"Do I what? Jesus, Raphael. I know that you're half Korean. I know a little something about Korean culture. My best friend is Korean, for Christ sake. I've met all her family. I love K-town. What do you think...?"

"Sorry. It's just that so many women have preconceived notions about sex, or what I should do for a living."

"We've already had sex. I've seen you naked. I work on your show. I saw you get arrested. I don't think there's much you could spring on me. Since we're playing 'true confessions,' have you dated anyone white before?"

I was thrown with that question. No one had ever asked me about my sex life before. So many people treated me like I was neutered. In late night drinking sessions, comics would go around a table talking about what they liked, blondes, or big tits, or big asses. No one ever sought or expected a response from me. Sometimes I wondered how people thought China got so populated.

That aside, my lengthy sexual history wasn't something I wanted to share with Daisy. "I think we've established that I haven't dated much."

"You know what I mean."

"I've been with other women, Bronwen. But no one who's ever been like you." I put a hand on her back, closing the gap between us. "Can I?" I asked, looking at her pale lips.

Her small nod was all I needed. I put my other hand on the back of her neck and held her steady. I kissed her slowly, warming her up to the idea of a little touching. She unwound the scarf from my neck. The chill was quickly replaced by her warm hand. I'm not sure how long we kissed, stroking each other outside our clothes. Twelve loud chimes announced midnight.

"I think we better go to bed," I said, rising not without discomfort.

While Daisy banked the fire, I pressed my hands against the cool glass of the French doors. Shoes in hand, Daisy led me down a long hall toward the guest bedroom. She kissed me briefly at the door, pulling away when her mother peeked out of another door, throwing a broad wink in our direction. Great, I'd just got caught kissing the Fletchers' only daughter.

THIRTY-ONE
DAISY

I MANAGED to keep Raphael out of my parent's clutches much of the day. In the morning, we walked the grounds. He saw my treehouse and the places I'd haunted as a child. At lunchtime, I borrowed Doris' SUV and drove down to the beach. We ate some chowder and walked and talked. Raphael was funny and sweet and charming. He was everything I could have hoped for when I'd met him that first night, minus the gay part.

We sat on a dune for a long time, silent. I watched the waves come and go along the sound.

"Do you want to ask me something?" He looked directly at me, not allowing any wiggle room.

Were we kidding ourselves was the question I wanted to ask. I lowered my chin to my chest. Everything was so good right now. We were having a great time, but I wanted to know if we would ever make love like two normal people. The pull I'd felt between my legs for the last twenty four hours was killing me. I wanted to ease that ache, but I didn't know how. I knew so much about sex and so little at the same time.

"Out with it."

"I...I want to be with you." Words stumbled from my mouth in fits and starts. "But I don't know how."

"Is this about Lexi?"

The name made my skin crawl. I hadn't thought about her once since I'd touched down in Connecticut. She wasn't me. I wasn't her. Heat crept up my neck, engulfing me in a cloud of shame.

Raphael grabbed both of my hands. "And I'm not that guy from five months ago. We need to start over. Can we try?"

I nodded, ready to find a room. I wanted to try, right now. To hell with dinner at the club. Those old geezers could drink without me.

As if sensing my urgency, he laid a palm against my beating heart, which did little to calm it. "Later, Bronwen. After dinner."

I was mentally packing my bag all the way back to my parent's house. The area along the Sound was filled with quaint inns. We only needed one room.

"WOULD YOU LIKE A COCKTAIL?" Doris asked Raphael. We were dressed, ready to slog through dinner at the club, but my mother wasn't quite ready to go. She liked her drinks cheap. And nothing cost less than drinking at home.

"No, thanks. I think I'll need my head for dinner."

My mother took the last sip from her highball glass and set it next to discarded flyers on the hall table. Finally. I straightened my dress, stood tall in my pumps, and walked out to the driveway. We all piled in once my father had pulled the car out.

Sometimes I wondered if someone had frozen the area along the Sound in amber. The clubhouse stood as it had all my life. The large wooden structure was imposing with its floor to ceiling arched windows interrupted only by clapboards weather beaten gray. As we made our way to the dining room, my parents angled for their usual table. It was next to a window, making for an uninterrupted view of the sixth hole and the water.

I pulled my starched white napkin into my lap. My parents hadn't even gotten their drink order in before the inundation started. Once two or three different couples came over, the floodgates opened. No question was off limits. Raphael answered questions about his show, his comedy. Whether his parents objected to him pursuing this line of work instead of math or science. Another asked him to give the son pushed forward reluctantly pointers on studying since Asians were the masters at it.

I closed my eyes during the salad course. I cringed my way through prime rib. I requested a box, ready to take the apple pie to go. Prejudice was an appetite killer. My mother apologized profusely on the way home. I wanted to do anything I could to stop her. But Doris continued speaking anyway, unaware brain and mouth had separated.

While Hugh helped Doris up to their room, Raphael and I sat at the kitchen counter, finishing up the dessert we'd skipped. One smile from him and all the social niceties and obligations fled from my mind. My thumb massaged the pulse beating in my wrist. "So, there's a bed and breakfast downtown. I could tell Hugh that we're going to leave early."

But before I could do precisely that, I was summoned from the dining room. "Bronwen, can I speak with you a moment?" To Raphael, he said, "Excuse us, please."

I followed my dad to his study. Maybe he wanted to talk about Doris. She was the worst I'd ever seen her. I hoped that he'd finally realized something needed to be done. I stood ready, poised to tell him that I'd heard residential treatment could be effective.

Hugh sat behind the antique wood desk, its spindly legs in sharp contrast to the substantial limbs of my father. I stood like I had so many times before, one hand holding the other wrist behind my back. There had never been another seat in the room. When I was three or four, I'd sat on the floor. After that, I was convinced Hugh had never gotten a chair to keep me on my toes, alert for his pronouncements.

"Dad, I have a guest. Do you want to talk about Mom? We can do this tomorrow morning. I can come back early."

"Where are you going?"

"Out...for a drive," I hedged.

"What are that man's intentions?"

"Are you serious? This is not the twentieth century." I placed both hands on the warm wood, leaning on the desk, asserting whatever adult authority I'd mustered over the years. "I'm thirty-one years old. I don't care what his intentions are. I'm not looking to get married."

"Why not?"

"I don't know. I've only known him for five months. I don't need a husband. I have a job, a house, a life."

"But men are dogs, honey. They're only after one thing. I've told you this time and again. Unless they put a ring on your finger, they'll...you know...then forget you." Hugh had been spouting that sentiment long before Beyoncé.

"Men want sex, Dad. I know that better than you."

"What are you saying? That you've been handing it out to every Tom, Dick, and Harry in Los Angeles?" Yup. I'd also been handing it out in Houston, and Miami, and even Connecticut as well. But I didn't say that. If I were to tell the truth about Lexi and Images of Harmony, he'd never believe me. I told my truth instead.

"I've hardly been handing anything out, Hugh. I have some sense of decorum. Men aren't all bad. Raphael isn't bad at all."

"I need to check on your mother. Help her to bed. So I won't go into detail. Remember who you are, Bronwen Margaret. You don't have to debase yourself for any man."

Arguing had no point. Unless I was married to some androgynous patrician banker, his suspicions wouldn't abate. "I hear you," I said. I leaned over and kissed his roughened cheek. "If I don't see you in the morning...."

"Thanks for coming all this way. It was very important to your mother."

So important that she needed to drink her way through it, I wanted to say in rejoinder. I held my tongue. "Is she going to be okay?"

"Doris is a Cliffie, a trooper. She'll be fine. We love you."

"I love you too." That was my cue. Hugh was rarely demonstrative and he would feel uncomfortable if I stayed any longer. I closed the door behind me gently. The sound of Glenn Miller's brass accompanied my exit. I stood there, trying to erase the lecture from my mind. My father was as precise as a guided missile. If a guy showed the least bit of interest in me, he would shoot him down with talk of men and their base needs. He was a more effective prophylactic than a condom.

A creaking floorboard made me turn around. Raphael was slouching a few feet from the door, grim expression on his face. "You heard all that?" I asked, pointing to the study door.

"Yeah."

I wanted to disappear. "Sorry."

"You still want to take that drive?"

Anywhere but my parent's house sounded good. "Let's go."

I drove to the Madison Manor. I parked in a visitor spot and stashed the keys in my bag. Raphael made no move to open the door either. "We don't have to do this. It was just an idea—"

Banishing my father from my thoughts, I got out of my mother's car and stood in the gravel. Raphael joined me and we rang the bell. The inn was full of chintz, flowers and quaint cuteness. After we checked in, acknowledging we had no luggage, the innkeeper showed us to our first floor suite.

"I've lit the fire for you," he said.

The room was dominated by a richly stained wood four-poster. The king bed was draped with soft looking white linens. The bathroom had thick terry robes and a four-person whirlpool tub.

"Thanks," I said, slipping fifty dollars into the man's hand. The money wasn't a tip. It was a bribe for discretion.

Then we were alone. All pretensions gone. I sat on a bench at the end of the bed easing off the heels I'd worn through dinner and dessert. I stretched my toes.

"You're wearing stockings. Never saw you do that in L.A."

"This is not a bare-legged state." When Raphael wandered away to the drink cart, I stood and peeled off my stockings, tossing them in my tote. Other than the TV and Raphael, the room didn't offer much in the way of entertainment. I climbed up on the bed and stretched out my legs. Lying back, I closed my eyes. This was the first I'd relaxed all weekend.

Two thuds were Raphael's heavy leather shoes hitting the floor. He sat opposite me, his feet on a pillow. "We can just sleep, Daisy."

"You didn't call me Bronwen," I pointed out.

"I'll leave that for your parents." I knew what he was trying to do. But I'd liked him calling me by my Christian name. It had taken the sting of derision away and replaced it with something very different.

I took a deep breath. "I don't want to sleep, Raphael." Suddenly my dress felt like a straitjacket. The plaid gabardine that had been a good idea this afternoon was strangling me. My heart, my breath wanted to explode from its confines. "Do you want a drink?" I asked, knowing that alcohol had gotten us into trouble before.

"I think we need to be stone cold sober." The timbre of his voice echoed off the walls.

I was going to try to be as honest in person as I was online. "I don't know what to do."

Raphael came closer, fiddling with my sweet sixteen locket. "What turns you on?"

"I don't know," I lied.

"You *do* know. Tell me." I bowed my head. This would be so much easier if I were really and truly Lexi. *She* had no problem asking for what she wanted. "Do you like it when I kiss you?"

"Yes," I whispered.

"Come here." At his command I moved. We were hip to hip. His hand cupped my head and tilted my face up. I blinked and looked him in the eye for the first time in an hour. The intensity in the chocolate brown eyes made my pulse beat a little harder. His full lips parted just the tiniest bit before they met mine.

I groaned, hoping this one kiss would relieve some of the pressure that had been building up over the last two days. And it did, if only for a moment. Then the spring wound tighter. Finally, finally we were getting somewhere. His tongue slipped past my lips, caressing my own and the spring wound tight again, tighter than it had been before.

I pulled away, needing a minute, a breath, a pause before what, I didn't know. I stretched out my hand against the black button down shirt Raphael wore. When he didn't protest, my left hand joined my right. "Can I?" I gestured toward the buttons. He nodded, and one by one, I loosened the tiny disks from their hold. I pulled the tail from his pants and spread the shirt wide.

The ribbed tank underneath kept me from him. His eyes at half-mast, I slipped first one hand then the other under the shirt.

His skin was so hot to the touch. He shrugged off his shirt, and I pushed the tank up and over his head. His broad smooth chest fascinated me. I'd rarely gotten to examine a real live man up close and personal like this before. I wanted to savor the feeling as long as I could. But before I could rub my hands and maybe more down his chest, he spoke.

"Turn around, Daisy."

I turned my back to him, and the zipper on the back of my dress came down with a whoosh. My nipples beaded as cool air met my skin. I turned, dangling my legs over the side of the bed, stepping down. With a single shrug, the dress pooled around my feet. I stepped out and draped it over a wingback chair. I turned out the incandescent lamp, allowing the firelight to bathe the room in flickering orange. I turned. Raphael hadn't moved, seemingly rooted to the bed.

He came to stand facing me. I looked down at the full coverage bra and briefs I was wearing. Nothing approaching sexy, merely foundation garments for dinner at the club where nothing was ever revealed. Despite the heat from the fire, I shivered.

"What do you like, Daisy?" Lexi liked a lot of foreplay. But most men thought a blow job was foreplay. "Come back here." Raphael's hand was on my shoulder, guiding me to the wingback. The midnight blue fabric was soft. He gently parted my legs, kneeling between them. Eye level with me, he implored. "Tell me."

Images from various porn sites flashed through my mind. Men squeezing tits and pinching nipples. Legs spread, shaved pussies wide. Journeymen going at it like it was a job, not pleasure. I didn't want any part of that. I wanted Raphael to be with me because he liked me, not because he liked sex.

"What are you thinking about?"

"The men in porn videos really hate sex, I think."

"But I don't," Raphael whispered. I leaned closer to hear him. "I very much want to make love to you, Daisy. But first, you have to tell me what you want."

"I want you to take off your pants, and belt, and socks," I pushed out. It was all I could ask for. I wanted to see him in his underwear. I needed to see if his erection was straining against the fabric. He stood. With a flick of his wrist, the belt was undone. Pants pooled at his feet. His hips were even with my eyes. No mistake, he was hard for me.

"Closer," I said.

He knelt again. Each of his large hands held a shoulder. "And now?"

Raphael was so close. His intense eyes were only for me. I sucked in air, trying to fill the vacuum in my lungs. "Can you kiss me again?"

"With pleasure," he said. He didn't hesitate this time. He didn't hold back. Each kiss was hotter, wetter than the last. His hands were on my butt, and then I was sitting on his lap, the chair abandoned. Raphael did nothing more than kiss me. His hands didn't stray anywhere. When I realized nothing was going to happen that I didn't initiate, I relaxed with every kiss. The more I relaxed, the more I wanted. I wanted that sexy mouth everywhere.

I hooked one hand in each bra strap and pulled them down my arms. "Take my bra off, please," I begged. With one deft movement, the cups loosened and the fabric slipped down my arms and chest. At his intake of breath, I looked down. My skin was flushed, and my nipples were hard, but it didn't compare to the buxom women offering themselves up online.

Raphael's nostrils flared, but he didn't move. I pulled at the scrap of lace, tossing it aside. He rocked back the tiniest bit, and I moved, my heat meeting his. I couldn't stop myself from rubbing my center against his cock. It felt so damned good, that friction.

"My nipples...please," I pleaded.

"Do you want me to rub them with my thumbs, kiss them, suck them, or bite them? What do you want, Daisy?"

I wanted him to stop talking and start doing. But one look at his eyes, and I knew it wasn't going to be that easy. "Any, all. Touch me, please."

"Damn, you're beautiful," he said. I didn't feel beautiful, I felt achy and needy. I laced my fingers behind his head and pulled that full lipped mouth forward. Raphael caught my eyes. Despite my embarrassment at his frank stare, I couldn't pull my eyes away. He sucked a thumb into his mouth and released it with a soft pop. I closed my eyes, not ready for what was coming next. His mouth closed on one nipple, sucking it deep. The thumb rubbed back and forth against the other. Jesus, fuck. I wouldn't survive this. I pushed against his erection.

I reached between us and pulled his penis free of his briefs, rubbing my own thumb against the tip. He took my whole boob in his mouth, before releasing it and starting on the other. From his mouth alone, I was close. I wanted him inside. I wanted to ride him like a stallion. "Can you? Can we?" I asked, gesturing toward his cock.

"Just...hold on." He felt around, locating his pants, pulling out a condom. I pulled off my briefs then his. I pushed him back on the braided rug. With shaking hands, he managed to get the rubber on, and I put one knee on either side of his hips. I propelled myself up, one hand on his chest, and with the other hand positioned him, enveloping him with one swift move. "Daisy," he said, a prolonged two syllable hiss leaving his lips.

I didn't move for what seemed like a long time. The obvious pleasure on Raphael's face, the crackling fire mesmerized me. Then a hand brushed my pubic hair aside. His finger, feather light, touched against my clit. Just one, and I thought I would die. "Again," I whispered.

His touch was more firm this time, more sure. I was so close, but I needed to move. Up and down, I went; one stroke, two. Raphael lost the rhythm with his fingers, but that was okay. A few more strokes, and I was there, coming. He moved with me, faster and faster. I could feel his hips jerking. Spineless, my noodle body collapsed on him.

"I have to—"

The normal tone of his voice brought me back to myself. I lifted myself very carefully so Raphael could get to the bathroom. I slipped into the large bed to the sounds of water turning on and off, waiting.

Would he find me wanting in some way? Not sexy enough? If the numerous videos I'd seen were anything to go by, a man had to know everything was on the menu, the minute he came to the table. Would he be upset that I was not as confident as Lexi, or as easy as my drunk self? But I brought up the more immediate humiliation.

"I'm sorry about Doris and Hugh," I said when he slipped into bed beside me.

Raphael pulled me to him, his front to my back. "Don't apologize for your parents, ever. I'm grateful. They made you into the woman you are today."

"But—" I wanted so badly to explain that Doris wasn't always sloshed, that Hugh only said what he did out of love.

His hand left my breast where they'd been brushing against my nipple and moved to my mouth. A single finger rested against my lips. "Shh. My own parents don't speak to us because my brother's gay. It doesn't get much worse than that."

THIRTY-TWO

RAPHAEL

HOW DID I become this guy? The guy holding my girl's hand, kissing countless times on two different airplanes across ten different states. Opening Joel's back door for her. I settled into the back of the seven series Beemer, glad to be headed home. Bronwen's place was out as she was going to try to stop into the network today. I didn't have it in me to go into work. Needed sleep and fortitude to deal with whatever hell the writers and the network had dreamt up for me while I'd been gone.

"Did you get the check?" Joel asked.

Unzipping the pocket of my carryall, I passed the paper forward. This was my last payment on the borrowed money. "Here."

From the mirror, I could see Joel's eyes survey us in the back seat as he tucked the check away. He didn't take too kindly to the role of chauffeur. But I didn't want to leave Daisy's side for a moment. I squeezed her hand, and she brought her gaze from the world outside back to me. She gave me a small smile and squeezed back. The mid-day traffic was light, and we were nearly at Daisy's building in less time than I would have liked.

"So we're done with this Cleveland business now." To

Daisy, he said, "I hope you can keep this dog on the straight and narrow."

"That's a mixed metaphor," she said off-handedly. Then Daisy's eyes swung back to me. "What *Cleveland* business?"

Fuck you, Joel. I was deciding if saying that would be going too far when Joel answered her. "Rafe here hasn't told you about Judith? Sweet Jude, the virgin he fucked in Cleveland, threatened to cry rape if we didn't pony up." The motherfucker.

With that little revelation, Joel stopped the car. Daisy had opened her door and was out before I could move a muscle. She stood in front of her building for a long second without her purse or luggage. I ran to her, wanting to stuff the words back in Joel's mouth, maybe punch him in the throat for good measure. She jabbed a finger toward Joel. "Is he serious?"

I grabbed at her hand, but she spun from my grip. "It was a misunderstanding, that's all."

"Well, I guess our investigators suck because this little gem wasn't in their report."

"She didn't know?" Joel asked, always slow on the uptake. I tried to look behind his dark-as-night sunglasses.

"Are you high?"

"She was there when you got arrested. She had to know you were a player."

"Daisy's right here, Joel. She can hear everything you say."

"Can you open the trunk?" Daisy asked stiffly.

Joel fumbled with the key fob, finally getting the big trunk open. Daisy grabbed her bags and stalked to her building.

I pulled open the lobby door then stood in front of her. "I can explain."

She looked over my shoulder. "I'm sure you can, but maybe you should catch your ride before he leaves you stranded in Los Feliz."

I looked at the brown Beemer. Joel had either let his foot off the brake by mistake, or was actually rolling away. Mother-fucker. "I'll call you," I yelled out feebly as I ran to my ride.

I jumped into the passenger seat, slamming the door. "Am I going to have to fire you?"

"She's just one girl. You've had more than Magic Johnson."

"Not true."

"You can't kid a kidder. I've known you for five years. You don't want me to do a rough count."

"Drop me off at CBT."

"I thought you needed a break from work. They're not expecting you today."

"I work. You get paid. Drive."

"How will you get home?"

"Now, you're worried about me?"

IT DIDN'T TAKE TOO much effort to find Daisy's office. It was darker and smaller than I'd imagined for a network execu-tive. But it had an excellent view of the parking lot. All the lights were out except an antique looking piano lamp. She was jabbing at a script with a blue felt-tip pen.

"Hey, there," I said, knocking on the hollow core wood.

"Close the door," she said. I took one of the chairs, flipped it around and straddled it. She wasn't throwing me out. "How many?"

I pretended ignorance. "How many what?"

"Girls, women. How many have you been with?"

"After that first time, I didn't think I'd ever see you again."

"I'm not asking for excuses. I'm not your girlfriend, or your wife. Answer my question."

Her tone of voice indicated she'd never be either. My first thought was that it wasn't fair. Then I wondered why single me gave a damn. Unbidden, dozens of faces scrolled before my eyes.

I didn't want to count. I wasn't Magic Johnson, but I wondered if I wasn't far behind.

"I don't know."

"Seriously?"

"I'd hate to see you at an AIDS counseling center."

We both laughed easing the tension. "Can I use that? It would make a great bit. Maybe I'd need a calling tree."

"Sure. No one here asks me for creative advice. I'm just the stern teacher bashing the naughty student on the knuckles with a ruler."

Images of Daisy with glasses, a short black skirt and a ruler invaded my mind. I tried to push them away. She tilted her head and looked at me in such a way that I felt like a bad kid.

"So..."

"So what, Raphael?

"Do you want to do something tonight?"

"On Monday? After I've already missed a half day of work?"

"Yeah."

"Um. No."

"Why not?"

"Your bedroom sounds like Grand Central Station. I'm not an indiscriminate train."

Bronwen Daisy Fletcher was slipping through my fingers. My mind raced. Did she want some kind of commitment? What was I supposed to do now? I studied her. The lamplight made her hair shine. Her lashes fluttered on her cheeks every few seconds. She'd gone back to scribbling on the script in front of her.

"I'm not seeing anyone else," I said.

"From what Joel said, that sounds like a good idea."

"Ouch."

Daisy looked around, though with the door closed, I don't

know what she was worried about. "Seriously? You won't tell me how many women you've been with. Not because you're shy or it's bad form, but because you don't know. And I swear to God, every time I turn around, you're getting arrested or sued because of your sex life. Excuse me if I want to get out of—"

A knock sounded, and her boss came in.

He thrust out his hand, a half-smile on his face. "Good to see you."

We engaged in small talk about the show for a minute. Daisy looked like she was holding her breath. "You wanted to see me, Connor?" she prompted.

"Nothing that won't keep. I'll let you finish up your meeting," he said. Connor left and pulled the door shut firmly behind him. I think the guy liked me. I'd figured I'd be persona non grata after that stunt at the house, but support was coming from the most unlikely place. I'd have to file that one away just in case.

Daisy pointedly looked the small watch on her dainty wrist. My mind flashed to those slim hands on my chest and her riding my cock, her face flushed with arousal. "I have to finish up this script in an hour and get it back to the producer," she said, interrupting my mini-daydream. Damn, Daisy was dismissing me like an elementary school student.

I sat for a long moment, waiting for something more. Nothing came. I picked myself up and let myself out. I'd lost this round, but I'd be back from the ropes.

"IT'S the seven thousand block of Melrose Avenue," I said before hanging up on Whiskey Bob. It was all set. Tomorrow, I'd be doing my second shoot. The photographer and director were the same. My subscribers would be getting what they asked for. One Asian girl, one black girl, some three way with a little bi-action. And my little Goth starlet would be back.

I tilted my chair back, propping my feet on the desk, letting the smug satisfaction wash over me. Hugh had always said, to make money, you have to spend money. Dad had always followed three rules when it came to business. He paid himself first, he treated his employees right, and he always reinvested ten percent of his profits back into the business.

I clicked over to my business account. Figuring off the top of my head, I knew I could take five thousand out of my account, do another shoot and make it back in one month. And if I redirected more of my sites to myself, and not to someone else's business, I could easily double that. My dad and his cronies would be proud that their advice on business had not gone to waste.

Banking a hundred grand or more would give me the flexibility I needed. After I doled out this content, I could sit back and earn passive income. It was the way my parents and most people I'd known most of my life lived. Sure, their money was from owning a building in New York City, or earnings from some long ago invention, but the theory was the same: let your money work for you, don't work for it. CBT was fun, but entertainment was fickle. I needed a sure thing.

"Hello," I said, leaning forward to answer the ringing phone. I swear Angelenos could be so provincial. Had these models not heard of GPS? If I had to give directions one more time on how to drive over 'the hill,' I was going to lose my mind. But models could be flaky and I didn't want to give them any reason to miss this shoot.

"It's Raphael." What was the point of caller ID if I never looked at it? If I'd had bill collectors after me, I'd know better.

"Come to dinner with me."

My brain wanted me to say no. But my hammering heart and the heavy pulse beating between my legs were in control. "If I get to pick the place."

"I'll pick you up in an hour."

The only words spoken on the way to Kenmore Avenue were me giving directions. For someone who'd asked for a date, he didn't looked thrilled. My mouth watered at the idea of Korean barbecue, though. I never gave up the opportunity to go.

"*An-yŏng-ha-se-yo*," I greeted the host, bowing slightly. Dressed in a pig-theme polo, he led us to a small table with a vent hood overhead and a small grill in the middle. I watched Raphael peruse the menu.

I was practically bouncing in my seat with excitement at the prospect of grilled spicy pig parts. Pork belly was the sole reason I'd never be as thin as my dear friend Nari. "I'll order," I said, relieving him of the responsibility. When the waiter came over, I started talking before he could address the man at the table. "We'll have the pork special." Without consulting Raphael, I opted for belly over ribs and *doenjang chigae* over *kimchi chigae*. The table quickly filled with *banchan*. I started to pull my metal chopsticks from their holder when Raphael's hand covered mine. My whole body zinged like I'd been electrocuted. Crap, I was going to lose my appetite. This was not doggy bag food.

"I want you to come home with me tonight."

"I don't want to be a notch in your bedpost," I heard myself say in a bang up imitation of Hugh.

"I'm not with anyone else right now," he said tracing lazy circles on my thigh. The thick fabric of my khakis did nothing to deaden the sensation.

The waitress came back, a platter stacked high with meat. Scissors cut through the flesh and each piece hit the oiled grill with a sizzle. The grilling, turning, and cooking took long, silent minutes.

"If I go, you're going to have to close the revolving door."

"What are you asking for, here?"

"I don't want to be your girlfriend or wife, Raphael. Calm down. We have a good time together, so maybe we can do that. But I can't be passing girls on their way in and out of your place."

There. I'd put it out on the table. I wanted to see what it was like to have sex with Raphael again. If I could step back and take a breath, it could be fun. Maybe I could have two regular dinner companions, not just Nari. Given our latest issues, I needed to diversify not only my cash flow, but my friends as well.

"I've never invited a girl to my place," he said.

"Except you invited me that night you got arrested, remember?"

"You're the only one."

"Oh, okay." Raphael was more confusing than an Escher drawing. "Let's eat." I piled meat, soybean sprouts, and various *banchan* on his plate.

. . .

"SHOW me the rest of the place," I said ninety minutes later. I didn't need to beat around the bush. I wanted this man, and the best way to get him was to get to his bedroom. He flipped on the light in his office for a minute. The desk, laptop, all of it looked unused. I briefly wondered where he did his work, writing jokes, or working on the show, or whatever, but I didn't want to know half as much as I wanted to know if we'd be good together again. I don't know what I thought his bedroom would be like, but it was meticulous. Damn, if I'd seen this first, I'd definitely have thought he was gay.

What I saw of his closet was a rainbow hue of neatly arranged clothes. He had more shoes and accessories than I would ever have. Everything had a place. The only break in the flow was a slightly rumpled bed. My knees nearly buckled with the visualization of him rising naked and warm smelling out of bed, aroused, ready to take on the day. My bottom hit the bed, hard.

He sat next to me. When I turned to say something, anything to break the silence, he pulled my chin toward his and kissed me. Damn, this alchemy was dynamite. I didn't want to think about Lexi or my job or anything. I wanted to get naked as the day I was born and have him fuck me right there and now. All of a sudden, the foreplay that I usually craved was meaningless.

Raphael never stopped kissing me while I unbuttoned first his shirt then mine. I pulled back to slide the black shirt from his arms then tugged the tank over his head. I was working my fingers through the leather in his buckle when the fingers against my nipples stopped me right in my tracks. I sucked in all the oxygen that I could into my starved lungs. I looked up into his eyes while his fingers teased me relentlessly. His stare was so intense, I almost came right there.

"Stop. I want to be naked. With. You," I pushed out between breaths. I slipped off my blue shirt, unhooking my own bra. No sound came from his side of the bed. I looked up to find him staring at me with what I hoped was appreciation. Once the rest of my clothes were off, I moved to get under the covers.

"Don't," he said. "I need to see you." He shucked his jeans and socks, coming to lay next to me. His penis looked so hard, I wondered if it hurt. I tentatively ran my thumb along the slit, gathering the moisture there. "Jesus, Daisy." He grabbed my hand, holding it in his. The hand gripping mine squeezed tight. "I'm going to take the lead tonight, okay?"

I looked at those melting brown eyes and they only held tenderness and passion. I nodded, trusting that he'd treat me right. We kissed again for a very long time. Each time his lips and tongue left mine, I guided him back, not quite sated. When I pulled him back this time, he shook his head, his mouth covering one nipple. His other hand slipped between my legs, sliding back and forth, in and out, torturing me by slow degrees. I couldn't help myself, my hips moved in response to his hand. And before I knew it was coming, an orgasm hit me like a freight train.

"I'm sorry," I said immediately. Was it bad form to come when the guy hadn't gotten his turn?

"Shh," he said, drawing a finger to my lips. "There's nothing to be sorry for." He reached back into a drawer next to the bed and pulled out a condom. "Can you do this for me?" he asked.

Like a conscientious health student, I pulled the foil open and did my best to smooth it over his erection. The surge into my hand when I got to the root was unexpected. "I'm sorry," I said again.

"Don't be. I just couldn't... Ah Daisy," he said then kissed me again, his hand sliding through my hair, along my scalp, down my neck, across the sensitive tips of my breasts, and through my curls. I dragged a grateful breath of air into my lungs. Even after earlier, his touch overwhelmed me. "Can I? Can you?" he asked.

"Yes, please yes," I whispered. He faced me, lifting my leg over his hip, and then he surged into me, again and again. His eyes never left mine. The twisting in my lower belly started again. Then he was filling me, stroke after stroke, until I couldn't hold back anymore, my release inevitable. His hoarse shout joined mine.

When he came back from the bathroom, I'd tucked myself under the covers. He joined me, sliding his still heated body next to mine.

For the first time in a long time, the silence was awkward between us. I lay back, closing my eyes against his scrutiny. The look in his eyes, the goose bumps stealing the heat from my skin, and the prickle at the back of my neck told me that it was time to go in order to avoid whatever Raphael was about to ask of me. I wasn't ready to talk about Doris, Hugh, or Lexi.

"What is it you like about Korean culture?" he asked.

That one was out of left field. Saw something coming, but not that. Thoughts tumbled through my mind as I sought out an appropriate answer that didn't make me sound like some silly Korean wave, k-pop fan girl. "I've always found the legacy of the Chosun dynasty fascinating," I answered like it was the first line on an essay test.

"The Chosun dynasty ended—"

"In nineteen ten, I know with the beginning of the Japanese annexation and occupation. South Korea, at least, didn't really become independent until nineteen forty-eight."

"I know the history of Korea. You're not answering my question."

I closed my eyes again, this time adding the barrier of my forearm. "The food is good. I love Korean dramas even though they're campy and melodramatic. Nari's family has always been this warm, chaotic swarm that has always welcomed me," I said truthfully.

He pulled my arm away from my eyes. "More welcoming than your family?"

Heat suffused my face. "I guess," I said. My eyes mapped the microscopic cracks in the plaster ceiling.

"Look at me, Daisy." My eyes snapped to his, commanded by his no nonsense tone.

"I'm not some fantasy K-drama hero," he said, his voice slightly hoarse.

I rolled to my side again, using my free hand to trace the fold of his eyelid, the nearly black brow that swept above it. Sifting through the coarse mop of hair that fell across his forehead, I leaned in, kissing the bridge of his nose. "I know who you are, Raphael." I kissed him this time, slowly, lingering. "I'm not all *Leave it to Beaver*, either," I said, grateful he didn't pretend to misunderstand. "More like *Mad Men*. All day martinis and bloody Marys, lead to less-than-perfect evenings." It was the closest I'd ever come to talking about my less-than-ideal home life. But he'd already seen my family laid bare.

"My mother didn't want to leave Busan, you know. When her family found out she was pregnant, by an American serviceman, no less, they pressured her to leave when his time was up. I don't think she ever loved him, but she knew that acceptance of her half-Korean children was more likely in American than Korea. And even if she'd stayed, her family wasn't rich. It's not like TV where everyone's father is the Chairman and their mom some matchmaking socialite. Much of her family fished. She'd have grown up stringing pollock along the beach, or maybe even working in some factory."

"I'm not like one of those *otaku*, obsessed with Korean culture. I enjoy it, that's all." I took a deep breath, letting the truth hang out there. "But I'd be lying if I didn't tell you that you being half Korean and very cute wasn't a major turn on." The cloud of heat that engulfed me would suffocate me for sure. He looked at me, a slow smile spreading across his face. His hand reached back for a fresh condom and we stopped talking for a while.

I peeked over at the glowing numbers of the clock. Midnight, damn it.

"You have to go somewhere?" he asked, not taking a break from sweeping lazy circles across my body with his fingers.

"I have to work tomorrow," I said, rising reluctantly from the bed.

"At CBT? Is there some live show that you need to do?" He looked tired, sated, and now confused. I didn't want to hide my life from the man I was sleeping with. I slipped on my underwear and bra. Even though I'd done it for myself thousands of times, I turned, loving the feel of his hands joining the hooks and sliding the straps on my shoulders. He pulled me down to the bed and I acquiesced. I leaned forward, even the sweep of my own hair a sensual brush against my collarbone, a strong counterpoint to the lips kissing my neck, the hand counting each bump of my spine.

"I have a shoot tomorrow," I answered. "For Images of Harmony."

All movement stilled in the dark room. Raphael snapped on the bedside light. I blinked at the glare of incandescent light, stark against the black and white duvet.

"What are you doing? I thought—"

"Securing my future. I've done the math. This shoot will more than double my income."

"You have a job."

"I have no one to count on but me."

"If things got that bad, wouldn't your parents help you out?"

"I don't want to ever have to ask. Money comes with obligations."

"What obligations? Weddings, dinners at the club? Hardly seems like work. Plus it doesn't fuck up your world view. Look at me, Daisy," he said, putting his hand on my bare shoulders, turning me to him. "Did you think about Lexi or any of the videos you've seen tonight?" I dipped my head, examining the geometric splashes of white against the black of the cover. "Did you?"

I shook my head.

"That's good. Really good. I liked having sex with the genuine Daisy. It felt so good to see the real you enjoying every kiss, every touch."

"That won't change. I've got it all compartmentalized...up here," I said, tapping my skull.

Raphael turned away, sinking under the covers. I quickly pulled on the rest of my clothes. "Good luck tomorrow."

THIRTY-FOUR

DAISY

WHAT IN THE hell was that supposed to mean? I dropped the dirty paper towel I'd been using to rub down the furniture, into the trash bin. I looked around the space I'd rented on Melrose. Bright morning light flooded the former factory floor. Velvet couches and tall linen covered screens made the loft feel almost cozy.

Two bathrooms and a kitchen made the space habitable. I should have done it this way the first time around. I had no idea space could be so cheap. Five hundred for the whole day was far less than losing Nari's trust and her family's acceptance. I shook my head. Woulda-coulda-shoulda would not wind back the clock.

Whiskey Bob was on time. He'd claimed to be busy until I upped his fee. Then he and his crew got unbusy in a hurry. I only had one repeat cast member, Jinx. I was half toying with asking her to start a separate site for me. Maybe I'd see how popular she was the second time around before giving her a hint about what she could do on her own.

The guys were generic Midwestern looking white guys. I imagined that's what my average customer looked like and was more interested in putting themselves in their shoes rather than seeing great looking guys get great looking girls. At 9:30, I tapped my watch, pissed off. Of course the Asian girl had flaked. After Jinx, Asian was the most popular request. I'd sent out a call time of nine o'clock and everyone else had made it. I decided to get started and work my way around that little dilemma.

I gave Whiskey Bob my shooting script. It wasn't much different than before, the players were merely switched around. He did the 2257 shot, had them sign releases, and they were off.

For ten minutes, I watched two men stick their dicks in every hole the black girl had. Then I needed air.

Sex wasn't like that. I couldn't believe I'd ever thought it was. Sure, tab A fit into slots B, C, and D, but it was only an imitation of sex. The guys were only aroused because testosterone patches and Viagra kept their penises hard. The girls all needed buckets of lube to make it through the day.

I stood on the roof, looking around Los Angeles. The streets choked with traffic. Smog turned the sky brown. I looked south and spotted CBT, less than a mile from my post on Melrose. No doubt that building was half full with people scurrying about, worried about what their boss might think. I raised my arms to the heavens, liberated from all of that.

When I got back downstairs, one of the models pointed. Relieved that I wouldn't have to find a last minute back-up, I watched the swinging dark hair and back of the Asian girl walk to the changing area in the back. Whiskey Bob had another release, everything under control, so I slipped to the office. I pulled a script from my bag and worked through a couple of Saturday morning cartoons.

Doing this first pass without storyboards was the hardest. Animators were clever, and you never knew what craziness they'd slip in there when you weren't looking. What looked like a plain vanilla script could blow up in your face in storyboards. I thanked the heavens that *The Simpsons* was on Fox. A show like that would cause way too much stress.

I heard more moans and fake climaxing from the main room then the sound of movement—of equipment, people, furniture. Only a few more hours to go. I got up and opened the fridge, ready to pull out lunch. The guys would eat everything, the girls nothing, but I had to make nice either way.

One of Whiskey Bob's lackeys knocked on the open door frame. I jammed the script in my bag. It was a small town and I never wanted this to get back to Broadcast City.

"What's up?"

"The Asian girl did one straight scene, but she's not keen on doing the other guy."

I sighed. Swear to God, I just wanted everyone to do what they were asked. This was always the risk with the young ones. The older pros knew the score and came prepared. But the viewers wanted them young, young, young, and barely legal at that.

"Hi, I'm Lexi," I said to the girl's bathrobe clad back.

She turned around to face me. "Eunji!" What in God's name was Nari's cousin doing on a porn set? I grabbed her arm in my best imitation of a bullying K-drama hero and pulled her to the roof.

"Daisy?" Bewilderment creased her young face. "I thought I was working for some woman named 'Lexi.'"

"I am Lexi. It's my name in this business. I've been doing this for ten years. You haven't. Did you have sex with one of the guys?"

Tears started leaking from Eunji's eyes, taking the bulk of her mascara with it. Someone should have told her about waterproof. Makeup melting, the girl I knew to be nineteen looked more like herself, not made up like a modern day *kisaeng*. Eventually a small nod came my way.

"What are you doing here?"

"My parents are mad that I didn't go to Cornell. USC is nice, but it's not Ivy League."

"What does that have to do with selling your body for sex?"

"I saw the ad online and thought it would be a good way to make money. They've cut my allowance and Nari won't give me anything." I looked at a girl who'd probably never rebelled. She'd come to a porn shoot to have public sex at her parents, not for the money. That was the excuse she was using to justify her actions. I didn't have time for teen rebellion and I still didn't have an Asian girl.

"How'd you get here?"

"Bus. That's why I was late. L.A. is nothing like Seoul. You can't get around without a car."

"You'll sit in my office until we're done." She nodded, not willing to rebel against me. "You brought something to read."

"I have to review my notes from Biology Lab." Of course she did because this little rebellion was all she had. At the end of the day, she'd go on and become the doctor they all wanted her to be. I left her studying from a three inch thick book and checked on the actors who knew what in the hell was up.

Three hours later, I cut the shoot short. Without the third girl, the number of combinations decreased exponentially.

Tiny steps took us from the elevator, down the corridor, to Nari's. This was the walk of shame. I'd take walking across campus in the previous night's clothes over this, anytime. I pressed the doorbell next to the smooth wood labeled 10 C.

Nari pulled it open, a deep divot between her brows. She was in the oddest state of undress, like she'd been in the middle of trying clothes on. One tall boot graced one foot, a pump on the other.

"Eunji? Daisy?" She pulled open the door further, hopping on uneven legs.

With an unceremonious shove, I pushed the teenager into the room. "She showed up at a shoot today."

"At CBT, on a Saturday?" Nari pulled off the pump and sank into the couch, working the boot off. The suede cuff was at least ten inches long. Why didn't it have a zipper? "Your parents would kill me if you showed up on some stupid, ditzy coed reality show. Please tell me you were in the audience and not on the stage."

"I wasn't at CBT today. She came to a shoot for my website."

I could see Nari working through all of it in her head. I pushed the half made up cousin into a kitchen chair, where she sprawled like a rag doll. Exhaustion etched lines across her young face. Today had probably been the greatest education of her young life. USC would never match up to this.

Nari fished through the heap of clothes on the carpet, found her slippers and pushed them on her feet. "So the way you pay your parents back is to become a sex worker?"

"It's not like that, *sachon-eonni*. When I gave up my spot at Cornell and decided to come down here, they cut my allowance in half and made me come live with you."

"Well, I'm not thrilled with it either, Eunji."

"I don't want a chaperone," she said.

"And I don't want a child invading my apartment," Nari said.

"Stalemate," I threw in.

They both looked at me like I was a car's fifth wheel. I stood, ready to leave them to work out their family problems. "Sit down, Daisy. You need to explain to this girl why porn is *not* a good idea."

I sat for a moment trying to think of all the reasons a nineteen-year-old girl should work at a yogurt shop instead of having sex on camera for money. "It'll make it harder to get a job after school. This kind of job may not show up on a background check, but I could just see a man interviewing you and realizing he recognized you. It would kind of be like taking a selfie while smoking pot and posting it on the internet."

Nari squinted in my direction. "That's the best you could do?" She shook her head in disdain. "I shouldn't have trusted this to someone whose judgment has gone out the window."

"How am *I* a bad influence? I've had this job for years and you never judged me."

"I wasn't talking about this job. I was talking about Raphael. You're seeing him again, aren't you?"

"So what if I am? He's turned out to be a nice guy. I really like him."

"You mean you like the sex."

"Is that so bad? I thought you wanted me to get out more, meet a nice guy and all that."

"He got arrested."

Eunji's gasp of surprise rose above all ambient sound.

"He got off. It was a bogus charge." I looked away, hurt all over again about the girl in Cleveland.

"What else?" Despite our recent estrangement, Nari could still read me like an open book.

"He, um, deflowered a virgin on the road and she threatened to sue unless he paid up."

"This is not what I meant when I urged you to get out more."

"But Raphael is more than that. He's patient, sweet, funny. Kind of perfect." I knew I sounded like a dreamy teenager, but couldn't help myself.

"For a man whore," she finished.

"Not objectively perfect. Perfect for me. We're both a mess

and it kind of cancels out." Eunji's head ping-ponged between us. This was not the kind of supervision her parents had envisioned, I bet. "Slut shaming isn't nice." I looked at Nari's cousin. "Eunji, you're an adult, and you can make your own decisions. If I were you, I probably wouldn't get into sex work. It doesn't pay well. You will constantly be asked to do things beyond your comfort zone. And it's a thankless job."

"What would I have been asked to do today?" I blinked, remembering we'd agreed to keep her one transgression a secret. I sighed. Another scene I'd have to delete. Today was going to be a bust.

"Oral, vaginal, anal, DP. Maybe a cream pie or having a guy come in your mouth." Her face screwed up in distaste.

"I thought it would just be sex."

"That *is* sex." When she and Nari blanched, I hedged. "Or that's sex as the Internet defines it."

"Would I have to do all that? I thought I'd do some kissing, and then, you know." She had only done kissing, and the 'you know.' I quelled my urge to rush home and post the footage. Amateurs who showed their naiveté were gold. Porn connoisseurs had seen enough thirty-year-olds in pigtails. They loved new, fresh, and green. I turned back to the girl.

"Have you checked out any porn sites?"

Tiny head shake. When would she have done it? "Yes, you'd be expected to do all of that and more. And if you didn't, there are hundreds if not thousands of girls behind you ready and willing."

"Why?"

"Who knows? That's an age-old question that I don't have to answer. I only need willing bodies. I don't need to know why the body is willing."

"Are you gonna keep seeing that guy?" Eunji asked.

"I don't know," I replied without thinking. Maybe Nari had

a point. Maybe he *was* unsuitable and I was being easily swayed by the sex.

"Are you going to marry him?" the girl pressed further.

"It's not nineteen fifty nine. I have one life. He has another. We're having a good time. That's all." I left Nari and Eunji to their family imposed prison. Jean-Paul Sartre had nothing on their collective parents.

With one eye open, I watched the footage from the day. It wasn't half bad. In fact, it was pretty good. The girls were into it, the guys were into it. That Jinx could light up a screen. I went to my bar and downed two martinis.

Then I looked at the Eunji footage. It was money. She was innocent, but not too. She was sexier than I'd have ever thought watching her grow up with braces and acne. I shook my head, empty drink in hand. It was the best original footage I'd seen in a long time, and I couldn't use a single frame of it. I checked in on the e-mail from the site. It took me an hour, but I made it through the two hundred plus e-mails.

For years, Lexi Quinn had been nothing more than a fictional curator of paysites and content for my customers. But with the explosive growth of *sultrynewcummers.com*, they wanted to see Lexi in action. I felt like a whorehouse madam being pulled from retirement. A trickle had turned into a flood. E-mails asked for one of two things, Jinx or Lexi.

What would it take to give it to them? Sex with Raphael had been liberating. No longer did I feel like the loose woman my father harped on. And I knew not all men were bad. The sex business was no more exploitive than apparel. At least the men and women who did it were volunteers. I wasn't some sweatshop owner locking underage victims in a factory, making them sew until their fingers bled.

My videos weren't awful by any stretch of the imagination. They had no spanking or speculums. It was good, clean fun. No one had left either of my shoots looking any worse for wear. Not even Eunji who kept texting me on the sly, wondering when I was going to put up her footage.

As much as I knew it would satisfy the subscribers, I couldn't do that to Nari's family. Secrets never stayed that way. And I planned to work my way back into their good graces one day. Showing their little girl taking it doggy style probably wasn't the way to go.

Ideas spun through my head. Me tutoring Jinx on the art of love. I could wear a blond wig and green contacts or something. I could do it on the cheap, something like behind the scenes or deleted scenes or something. Maybe I could even get an Asian guy.

This was good. Bank my career on it, good. I picked up the phone. I needed to line up Jinx and Whiskey Bob. This would be the last shoot for a while, I promised myself. Once my bank account was at a safe one hundred thousand, I'd feel secure enough to focus on just the one job, and the one guy, and my future.

THIRTY-FIVE

RAPHAEL

"WE WERE TAPING the pilot episode tonight. I stood, pacing the dressing room, to the mirror and back, to the couch and back. I flipped through the script I'd memorized backward, forward and upside down. The back of the silly director's chair they'd made had the name of the show in a pseudo Asian-looking font, "Brothers Kim."

When a PA called my name, I made my way backstage. Ellis Armstrong was doing audience warm-up. I don't even know if Armstrong remembered the drunken half-assed advice he'd given me that night at the Comedy Store, but his friendship was appreciated. This was my way of returning the favor. The audience was clapping and smiling. I couldn't tell if it was because they thought he was funny, or because he was shooting free *Brothers Kim* t-shirts from a cannon. Either way, they looked primed for a good time.

The premise of this first show was kind of silly, but the script turned out both funny and sweet. The writers swore to me that my being sweet the first couple shows would take the edge off if later episodes went raunchy.

The director called action, and we started the show.

Fake Gabriel and I are surprised when our mom loses her house to foreclosure. Of course, in a coincidence only found on television, the apartment manager's place is empty and Mom moves in. In the first Jack Tripper-like game of musical chairs, both my brother and I try to get our dates out before Mom turns up.

An hour and a few retakes later, it was done. The adrenaline pumped through my veins, making me feel as hepped up as the one time I'd tried coke.

Daisy coming up to me with a big hug and even bigger kiss made the whole night worth it. She'd promised to come to the cast party with me. I was thrilled to have my girl on my arm tonight. I had some business to get through first, but I didn't want to let her go.

She'd been the perfect companion, reminding me who everyone was, giving me a little fact to make a connection with every well-wisher. I had Daisy's hand firmly wrapped in mine, when she whispered in my ear.

"Your brother's here," she said. I turned and gave my brother a big hug. If it weren't for him, I'd never be standing where I was. I tried not to get teary eyed. I even had a swift hug for Ted, who managed not to say anything snarky.

"I brought someone," Gabriel said. I was only half listening. Daisy was talking up some executive, and the din of the crowd had only grown louder after the audience left.

I turned, prepared to meet yet another friend of Gabriel. His social circle was legendary. He made friends everywhere and never lost touch with anyone. "*Young-soo,*" a voice said. My Korean name? No one called me that except....

"*Oma?*" I turned around, losing Daisy's hand. My little mom, her now graying hair tightly permed, robed in a hot pink cardigan, reached out to touch my face. The bitterness I'd held in for so long left and love flooded through my veins. I swooped my mom into a hug. She smelled the same as always like the baby oil she'd used on her skin for as long as I could remember. "I'm so glad you came." I looked behind her.

Small head shake. "Your dad not here," she said.

"*Oma*? I want you to meet my girlfriend." I turned, scanning the room. Without excusing myself, I pulled Daisy from her conversation and brought her to stand before my mother. When had my mom gotten so little? Even Daisy at five foot five seemed to tower over her. "This is my girlfriend, Daisy Fletcher."

"So nice to meet you, Mrs. Augustine. I've heard so much about you," Daisy said. Her manners were perfect.

"How long have you been dating?"

Daisy looked thoughtful. "Maybe four or five months. He's made me your *samgyetang*."

"How many roots did you eat?"

"I was sure to count," Daisy said. "Three."

"You'll live that much longer," Oma pronounced.

"That's great. It was so lovely to meet you." Daisy fingered her badge. "I work here at CBT and have to go talk to some other people. I hope to see you later at the party. Okay?"

Oma nodded, a little unsure. My mom had never been social outside her circle of Korean friends. She'd always been unsure of her language skills. Despite her reticence, I wanted her to get to know Daisy and vice versa.

Gabriel stepped in. "Maybe later, bro. I promised to get her home before it got too late."

Before Dad found out she wasn't with her friends, he meant. Disappointment poured through my veins like molasses. I'd been given a gift, only to have it snatched away moments later.

"I gotta catch up with Daisy," I said, turning my back, the familiar anger burned like an ulcer in by gut. Everything had changed and nothing had changed. Everyone was moving on to the restaurant on Melrose we'd booked for the party, so I let the crowd sweep me in its wake, putting my real parents out of my head.

Three hours later, Daisy whispered in my ear. "You ready to go?"

The scent of her sophisticated perfume enveloped me, shielding me from beer, sweat, and Mediterranean food. The post-show gathering had been like a birthday party and Christmas all wrapped up in one. I'd started out the center of attention. As the night wore on, though, everybody was having their own good time. They'd never miss me now.

I kissed the pulse point beating right below the tiny sapphire stud in her ear. "I'm more than ready."

One of the writers I'd clashed with was a little bit tipsy as he waved us out the door. "Same time next week?"

I nodded and gave him a handshake and half hug. I had to get out of there before I got maudlin.

We gossiped about the show and the cast and crew as I drove her home. I tried to follow the thread of the conversation, but thinking about the night that lay ahead had me hard. Blood was flooding away from the conversational part of my brain.

Daisy kicked off her shoes and was at the bar before I could even close her door behind me.

"You want a drink?" she said, waving her Manhattan in my direction.

"No thanks." I'd really made an effort to stay sober when I was with Daisy. Drinking on the road and when I first met Daisy was at the root of a lot of the shit I'd gone through. With Rose, with Jude, even with Daisy. She'd been pretty good about not drinking too. But when I came back from the kitchen with a glass of water, she was well into a second.

"Hey there," I said, pulling her down next to me and setting the drink aside. "Slow down. I want you to be—"

"What? Your girlfriend? I can't believe you said that to your mom and every person who saw you holding my hand."

Maybe I should have gotten drunk. Five seconds ago, I thought I was getting laid. I could feel my dick deflating. "What do you want me to call you?"

"Daisy," she said, retrieving and finishing her second drink.

I took the glass from her hands. "Why are you picking a fight?"

"We're not those people."

"What kind of people?" I took her hand in mine. She shook free. Whoa.

"Not the kind of people who hold hands, who kiss in public, who chat about their day."

Something was off. I thought we were those people, or at least becoming them. I'd never been, but I wanted to be that guy for Daisy. She deserved that kind of man. God knows I'd never tell her, especially in this mood, but I was falling in love for the first time ever. I took a deep breath.

"I'll have that drink after all."

"What—"

"Whatever you're having." I downed the bittersweet liquor in one swallow, allowing the whiskey to burn my throat.

"Can we keep it light?" Daisy asked.

"Light?"

"Dinner, hook-ups, you know. I mean neither of us wants to move in together or get married or anything like that, right? So let's keep this cool so no one gets hurt. That seems fair."

I closed my eyes for a moment, watching the best night of my life quickly devolve into the worst. Damn. I'd thought she was different. But here I was, trying to figure out if she wanted me to push harder or pull away. I looked at her red-rimmed eyes.

"I'm outta here," I said as casually as I could muster, standing to go. For my own sanity, I needed to leave her to work out whatever was bothering her tonight. I leaned down and kissed the top of her head, my lips meeting warm scalp and cool hair. Once in the car, I looked at my watch. I'd give her six hours. A smile I couldn't suppress played around my lips. I'd see my girl in the morning whether she was ready or not.

HAPPY BIRTHDAY TO ME. Dressed only in underwear and a robe, I sorted through the stuff I'd gotten from the drugstore. A lubricant promised me a good time in a very heterosexist, 'stick with your own kind' way. No couples like Gabriel and Ted, or even Raphael and me graced the full color instruction booklet.

Why was he acting like we were a couple? Two months ago, he couldn't wait to jump out of my bed and into someone else's. And now he wanted to hold my hand in public and play nice with his mom. Whatever. I needed to psych myself up for this performance. I'd watched thousands of women give it their best shot. I couldn't be any worse than them. Ironically, the more awkward I was, the more popular the video would be.

I didn't want to blow any more money on an expensive set, so it was just going to be Whiskey Bob's crew, Jinx, me, and a new guy today. I hoped the guy was at least half as attractive as Raphael. I couldn't take a Ron Jeremy type. My skills at pretending weren't that great.

"Who lives here? This is nice," Jinx said when she came in. She hadn't varied from her usual get up of black everything and Doc Martens. My customers loved those boots.

"It's a friend's," I lied. I didn't want them to know where I lived.

"She's not going to come home mad, is she?"

"Nope," was all I said.

When the phone rang, I hoped it was Nari, at least wishing me a happy birthday. She'd always taken me for a few drinks and Korean bar food. I know she was still mad about the apartment, but I wondered if we were drifting apart. She hadn't invited me to Hawaii and now no birthday dinner.

"You gonna get that?" Bob said, pointing to the phone.

I picked it up, but instead of Nari, it was Zach, our last model. When he got to the door, I had to admit, he wasn't half bad. Looked like the head shot he'd e-mailed: blond hair, brown eyes, nice smile, if not a little bit high.

"Lexi," I said, extending my hand.

"Cool."

Well, I wasn't paying him to talk.

Beating around the bush wasn't going to get a damned thing done. I got Zach on tape, scanned his ID, and directed Bob to set up in the bedroom. I locked myself in the bathroom with a bloody Mary, heavy on the vodka, light on the tomato. I pulled out makeup I hadn't used in years and carefully applied a mask of foundation, mascara, eye shadow, blush and lip gloss. I pulled open my robe and examined my body. It would be fine. I wasn't stick thin, but that didn't play well on screen. I turned up a tube of red lipstick I'd never once used and dabbed at it with my index finger.

Slowly, I rubbed it on my nipples, making them look like they'd been aroused by an eager man. I took the sable brush and did the same for my chest and neck. When I pouted my lips, I looked like a woman who was having a good time. I closed my robe and padded to the bedroom. I needed to get my scene over with first because I didn't want to take sloppy seconds after Jinx.

I pulled three-inch pumps from the closet and pointed to Bob to take it from there.

"Okay, Lexi. Kneel on the bed, facing the windows. Untie your robe and let it fall open. That's it. Zach? Walk back out the door. When I call action, you're going to come in, kneel behind Lexi and slide the robe off. You'll kiss her neck, back, then push her forward on the bed and do her pussy. Got it?"

I shivered in anticipation. This wasn't going to be bad. It might even be good. I could feel my heart speed up and my stomach tighten in anticipation. Then Zach was there. His hand was cool as it slid the silk from my shoulders. Zach reached around to squeeze my nipples.

He squeezed hard, and I had to make myself smile instead of flinching. The camera missed nothing. He bit the side of my neck then sucked hard. His other hand slid through my curls, finding me. The breath I was holding hissed out. I could do this.

I landed on my elbows when I hit the bed. Nothing happened. I heard the lighting guy say, "Oh shit," before commotion started.

"Do me, Zach," I urged in the huskiest voice I could muster. I wouldn't get the balls to do this twice.

"Zach will not be doing you, honey. That's something only I get to do."

Raphael? My brain turned to mush. How in the hell? I turned around. Raphael and Nari and more voices in the living room. I wished I collected weapons. A self-inflicted wound was in order.

As fast as I could, I scrambled from the bed and locked myself in the bathroom. With all the water I could drink and toothpaste for breakfast, lunch and dinner, I figured I could survive there for a week at least. By that time, they'd have to leave me alone. But I shouldn't have worried because not a single soul knocked on the door. The apartment got quieter and quieter. I assumed Whiskey Bob and crew left first, Jinx and Zach next. Then finally Nari and Raphael.

No doubt they'd be on me about payment. And now they knew where I lived. With a little investigation, they'd have my name too. I peeled myself off the floor, sure I was alone in my little den of misery. I went into my bedroom and changed the sheets, then duvet cover. Digging deep in my closet, I pulled out baby blue sweats; the hideous kind I used to wear on snow days in Connecticut when I stayed home from school and no one could see me.

I carried the laundry bundle into the living room, wondering if I'd have to do this in two trips. A scream tore from my lungs before I could stop it. Nari and Raphael were sitting on my couch.

I closed my eyes for long seconds, willing them to be an illusion. I reluctantly lifted my lids. They weren't. "What are you guys doing here?" My voice animated them, shaking them from stillness.

"I don't even know what to say to you," Nari said.

"Is this going to be an intervention?"

"Maybe you need one," Nari answered. After a long pause, she said, "What would your parents say?"

I held out my hand, palm up. "Well, let's see." I ticked my index finger. "My dad would say you're only doing what men expect from you." I ticked my middle finger. "My mom would wonder aloud in between drinks whether it was suitable behavior for a girl who graduated from Olde Haven." I tapped my ring finger. "Then when Hugh'd left the room, Doris would pester me on details on what it was like being a porn star, no matter how short my career." I tilted my head, smiled and did an elaborate bow like I was curtseying to the Queen of England.

I looked back and forth between them. "How long have you been here?"

"Two hours." Geez, had I been moping that long?

"How did you do it? You guys don't even like each other."

"But we love you," Raphael said, speaking for the first time.

The protective layer I'd wrapped around myself crumpled like a paper bag. "What?" I shook my head.

"I love you, Daisy. I certainly hadn't planned to tell you this *after* your entry into the porn world as an entertainer, while your best friend sat next to me on the couch."

"Oh." I didn't know what to say. I didn't know if I wanted them to come or go. I wanted to rewind one day or ten. Maybe even ten years.

"I brought you *mujigae ddeok*," Nari said.

Rainbow rice cake was one of my favorite Korean desserts. Once Nari's mom had discovered that, she made it every year on my birthday. Some years we drove out to get it. Sometimes her dad would drop it off when he was doing other things in town.

"Where did you get it?"

"*Oma.*"

"I thought—"

"They've known you for years and are trying to understand and forgive what happened."

"I'll cut the cake," Raphael said.

"DAD'S AN ASSHOLE," Gabriel said. He was sitting on the steps outside my apartment. I fit the key in the lock and we both went in. "What's that?" he asked, pointing to the small pink striped bag in my hand. "You into women's underwear or something?"

"It's rice cake."

"What kind?"

My mouth reluctantly formed the shapes learned in youth. "*Mujigae ddeok.*"

My brother rubbed his hands together like a 1980s cartoon villain. "I'll get plates."

I'd used this table more in the last few months than I'd ever used it the entire time I'd lived in this apartment. Pulling back the straight-backed wood chair, I sat opposite Gabriel. He came back with two plates and utensils. He reached into the bag and split the fluffy concoction into two mammoth slices.

"It's Daisy's birthday cake."

"Why aren't you eating it with her?" I shoved back from the table. Maybe I needed milk. I slammed around the kitchen. No milk. Looked in the pantry for tea. Nothing. *Oma* would have given us that pine nut tea or green tea in a pinch. Never kept shit like that there. The only drinks in the fridge were beer and bottled water.

I paced between the kitchen and dining room. "She's having..."

"Having what?"

"I went over there to...talk to her about something. Met her best friend in the elevator with the cake."

"Oh, man. You didn't know it was her birthday."

"It hadn't come up."

"So she was pissed that you'd missed it? Did you get the best friend to cover for you? Pretend you'd gone in on the cake together or something?"

"Her birthday wasn't the problem."

"What was?"

"She was filming herself having sex." Gabriel's fork fell to the floor with a clatter. I picked it up. Got a sponge for the crumbs. Ants were the last thing I needed in my apartment. "Put your eyes back in your head."

"Nothing I've ever heard of even comes close to this." My brother sat back, cake forgotten. Silence stretched between us. "Would you date a sex worker?"

"She's not a prostitute or adult...actress."

"You didn't answer the question. I've known guys who dated go-go dancers. But maybe sex and monogamy is a little looser with us."

I stood and paced through the apartment. How come it was so damned hot in there? I threw my scarf into the closet. It floated gracefully to the floor. Anger unabated, I threw my shoes. Far more satisfying. Cooler, I went back to the dining room. Gabriel had resumed eating his cake. I tried shaking the adrenaline loose from my limbs.

"Are you going to break up with her?" His eyes pierced me.

"I think—" I could barely say it out loud. It made me nervous just thinking about the idea.

"What? You think what?"

"I'm in love with her."

"Ted thought that might happen."

"Fucking Ted," I said, shaking my head.

"He was right."

"Ted wins!" I held up my hands like a football referee signaling a touchdown.

"Life's not a game, Raphael. Can you accept her if she becomes the star of her own show?"

"No."

"So your love isn't unconditional?"

"It's conditioned on her not having sex with other people."

"Have you been faithful?"

I thought about Judith, the Cleveland girl. That was a blip. They weren't really together. "More or less." I rushed to head off any questions. "I haven't slept with anyone else in three months."

"That's a record."

"Why did you say Dad's an asshole?"

"I talked to *Oma*."

"And?"

"She loves me—us unconditionally. She's really proud of you. She liked Ted. Gave us a belated wedding gift and everything."

"How much?"

"Three million won."

"Seriously?" I had to laugh at my mother going to the bank, exchanging dollars for the more familiar currency they couldn't spend in the U.S.

"She's wanted to see us for years."

"Did she just discover the telephone yesterday?"

"Dad wouldn't let her. He threatened to leave her without any support."

"She could divorce him. Get alimony. Get Social Security. We could help. It's all an excuse."

"Dad hid her passport. Her naturalization papers. She was really scared, Raphael."

Fucking drama. I was skeptical, but I'd play. "What changed? Did my sudden stardom win out over her fear?"

"Dad had a stroke."

Guilt twisted my gut. I knew dear old Dad wouldn't live forever. I may have even dreamt of dancing on his grave. But I set years of animosity aside for a moment. For better or worse, he was my father. "Is he okay?"

"Yes and no. He's doing some outpatient rehab. But he's walking with a cane and his talking is slow.

"I think *Oma* figured out his leverage was gone. When she was in the hospital, she got the lock to his shed picked. Her papers were in there. They're now in a bank safe deposit box. He begged her not to leave him, when he was laying there half-paralyzed on the hospital bed. She made a deal. Us back in her life, back in their lives and she'd stay."

"Deal with the devil, if you ask me."

"She didn't ask you. I, for one, am proud of her. She wants to get to know your Daisy as well."

I got up and paced again, knowing I was going to wear a path in my floor if I didn't stop. Usually when I had this kind of pent up energy I expended it on a willing woman. For the first time in years, that idea held no appeal. Damn. Went to my room and rooted around the closet. Gabriel had cleaned up the food and was brooding on the couch when I came back.

He looked me up and down. "Where are you going?" His tone held suspicion.

"Gonna stay out of trouble. I'll see if I can get some stage time. This TV gig's gonna make me rusty."

"That's all?"

"I don't have the energy to do something I'm going to regret."

"While you're out there, can you think on something?"

I was bouncing on the balls of my feet. I needed to get out of my own head for a while. Get the juice of talking to a live audience. "Yeah. What?"

"Please think about your capacity to forgive."

"Who do I need to forgive?"

"Yourself, first. *Oma*, second. Daisy, third."

"Daisy and Mom, I get. What do I need to forgive myself for?" I had my jacket on, keys in hand, door open. I was done with this for now.

"You'll have to answer that yourself," Gabriel said, following me out the door.

THIRTY-EIGHT

DAISY

"COME TO DINNER WITH ME?" Raphael had pulled me aside off set. It was Friday and time to tape the second episode of *Brothers Kim*.

"You're still speaking to me?" I'd studiously avoided Raphael as much as possible. Every time I thought of him and Nari walking in on my short-lived porn career, mortification spread throughout my limbs like molten lead.

"You didn't stop being my girlfriend," he said matter-of-factly. My legs turned wobbly. I'd thought for sure last weekend had been the end of us. Whatever 'it' was. Especially when he didn't call or e-mail or text to break it off. "So, can you come?"

I nodded, speechless.

Three hours later, after watching an audience get tired of clapping, retakes, and the t-shirt cannon, Raphael approached me. "Ready?"

I shrugged then pulled a sweater from my purse. I followed him out of the studio. After we drove east on Beverly, I thought maybe we'd eat in Larchmont or Hollywood. Then on Silver Lake Boulevard, I thought we'd eat there or near my place. I was skating on thin ice and didn't want to rock the boat, but finally asked, "Where are we going?"

"La Crescenta."

"You grew up there, right?"

Raphael nodded then turned his attention back to the speeding freeway traffic. Twenty minutes later, we pulled up to one of those postwar tract homes that must have dotted the entire southern California landscape before mini mansions reigned. This neighborhood hadn't seen one iota of McMansionization.

"Your parent's house?"

"My mom's cooking." Hunger and trepidation warred within me as we ascended the three front steps.

"I thought your dad had disowned you."

"Mom and Gabriel talked last week, after she came to the show." And with only that as an explanation, he held open a white security door for me. "Open the door. They're expecting us."

I walked into a living room dominated by a piano. A man sat in a wheelchair, facing a large screen television.

"You're here," a woman trilled from somewhere. "*Young-soo*," his mother said, wrapping him in a bear hug which was difficult for her, given her diminutive size. "So long..." She touched his face as if memorizing the features. Though her accent was heavy, I didn't need a translator to understand what was happening. The man in the chair never broke his gaze from the documentary exploding on screen. For long moments, no one acknowledged me.

"*Oma*, you already met Daisy at the show," Raphael said. I reached out to shake her hand. Instead, she tilted in a little bow.

"Young-soo?" I asked.

"My Korean name." Raphael turned to the man in the living room. "Daisy, this is my dad, Clayton Augustine."

Only then did his dad pull his eyes away from a show featuring World War II home movies. Even with one side of his face slack, his disdain was palpable. "How'd you get a girl like this when you still dress like a sissy?" The large red-faced man slurred his S's. Unconsciously, Raphael fingered the scarf he wore.

"Nice to meet you," I said, extending my hand.

His right shoulder shook with effort then stopped its tremor. "Can't shake. Right side not working these days."

Raphael's mother brought out a tray. Without ceremony, she plopped it on the tray table. A little chicken soup sloshed on the saltine crackers lined up neatly alongside the bowl. She laid a napkin on her husband's lap. "Our dinner's this way," she said.

The small dining room table was set in typical Korean fashion with communal soup, meat and fish bowls. Each of the three settings had its own *banchan*. I sat where she pointed me.

"Mrs. Augustine, thanks for doing this for us," I said, waiting for her or Raphael to start.

"Call me Mrs. Park, "she said.

"I'm sorry." It was the custom was for Korean women to keep their name, but I'd assumed from her devotion to her husband she'd followed that American custom. I picked up the chopsticks. At least I was capable of handling those. "Is that *maeuntang*?" I pointed to the soup, careful not to gesture with my chopsticks.

Mrs. Park beamed. "Young-soo, have you been cooking for Daisy?" He didn't answer. "I'm so happy. I was worried you were ashamed of where I came from."

As his mom spooned soup into my bowl and laid the best cuts of fish, shrimp, and clams on my rice, I let the small deception stand. I jumped when what sounded like cutlery hit the living room floor.

"Damn it!" Mr. Augustine yelled. He didn't slur his swear.

"Minnie, get in here. God damn it!" Her own chopsticks clattering on the table, Mrs. Park scurried from the room like the hounds of hell were on her heels.

"Do you judge me for this?"

"What do you mean?"

"My parents. My father's being a colossal ass. Despite that, my mother ran in there to do his bidding. Thirty-five fucking years of this, and she still dropped everything to serve him."

"It must work for them on some level, I guess." Diplomacy was going to replace Margaret as my middle name.

The remainder of the dinner was uneventful. The praise I heaped on the food was genuine. Home cooking put my favorite Korean restaurants to shame. I also probed his mom on the boys' escapades. There didn't seem to be many that she knew about. But from the mischievous look in Raphael's eye, I imagined she wasn't privy to what really went on.

"Who plays the piano?" I asked about the huge instrument that fought with the television for domination of the living room.

"Both boys took lessons."

I looked at Raphael. "You play?" I knew so little about this man, but I wanted to know so much more. I really wanted him, but didn't know if we'd be close again. I'd messed up so badly.

"Serviceable," he answered. "Gabriel was Oma's little virtuoso."

"That's not right, Young-soo. You were more talented than your brother. He tried a little harder, though."

"In piano?" He sounded dubious.

"In everything. Your progress reports always said you didn't apply yourself. But maybe you were only looking for your focus. This comedy fits you."

"Did you like the show?"

"I enjoyed it. You were very funny. I think it'll be popular on television."

Except for Mr. Augustine's interruptions, it was a very pleasant dinner. The food was good, and on the drive home, I realized I was falling a little bit in love with Raphael.

We continued the discussion about his parents in my apartment. I think their behavior really disturbed him. "That's just it, Daisy. It works for them. What we're doing here, works for us."

"What are we doing here?"

"What I'm doing here is loving you," he said.

When I would have looked away, Raphael bracketed my face with his hands. "Look at me."

"What do you want from me?"

"Just you."

"But I..."Wasn't worthy.

"There are no buts here."

"So what are we supposed to do now? Ride off into the sunset?" That would be so L.A.

"We try a relationship. We do stuff together, go to sleep together, wake up together."

"What's the catch?" But because this wasn't a Hollywood movie, there had to be a catch.

"Why—"

"What's the catch, Raphael?"

"You give up Images of Harmony."

"DO YOU LOVE HIM?" Nari cut to the chase.

"Not enough to give up my job."

"You have a job. At CBT, remember?"

"And who is going to take care of me in my old age? I'm putting money away for the rest of my life. There is *no* social safety net in America. I do not want to dine on Fancy Feast."

"What are you worried about? This place is paid for. In full. You have no loans. No debt. Nothing."

"What if my car dies? Or another assessment comes down the pike?"

"Then you do what normal people do, Daisy. You take out a car loan, or take out some equity."

My head was going to explode. Good sex and a potential boyfriend were not an even trade for giving up my livelihood. In the days since Raphael had given me his ultimatum, I'd done a portfolio assessment. I had about four hundred dot coms in my name. I'd designed four thousand websites in the last decade. Even with dwindling sales, I could sock a five figure income into my mutual fund for years to come.

"How much money do you have?"

I didn't answer because I knew I hadn't heard her right. If Nari and I never talked about sex, and we definitely never talked about money. Why was it suddenly okay to break all social taboos?

"Well?"

"How much do *you* have?" Deflection was my friend. She'd never answer.

"I have about two hundred thousand in my retirement account. Twenty thousand in my savings. A few thousand in my checking. And I owe maybe fifteen thousand on the Land Rover."

Cue me. "Oh. Okay. Not enough to buy your parents out of the condo, huh?"

"This is not about me. I'll deal with that when the time comes. Spill it."

"I think my net worth is seven hundred fifty thousand."

"Including the condo?"

Unless it was a rental property with income, my dad had taught me never to count the place you live among your assets. What was real was what could be liquidated in a week. "No. But I bought the condo for three hundred thirty in two thousand six."

"With none of the crazy California real estate appreciation factored in, you're easily a millionaire, Daisy."

"A million dollars doesn't go as far as it used to." Repeating the words Hugh had said so many times made me sound like an asshole. Nari's look confirmed it.

"If you keep your job, I don't see any scenario where you'll be panhandling on a freeway exit ramp. So if money's not the reason, why do you hold on to this porn webmaster thing?"

"I'm in control of men," I said without thinking.

Nari's brows furrowed. A perfect crease marred her otherwise smooth forehead. "How?"

"It's a perfect relationship. They think they're using women for their pleasure, for their amusement. But in reality, I'm the puppet master pulling the strings. Their sexuality comes at a price. I control that."

"That makes you happy."

"It's made me rich."

"So what about Raphael?"

"What about him? You don't even like him."

"But he loves you."

I got a little shiver in my belly. "I'm not sure what he loves. The idea of doing a WASP from Connecticut. Dominating a woman who's in charge of her sexuality. I mean, he had sex with someone after we slept together that first time."

"Did you expect him to be faithful to the idea of you? I saw you push him out the door that morning. Even I thought I'd never see him again." Nari paused, her look critical. "You're an adult, Daisy. People have sex with other people. If you commit to each other, that stops."

"But he's had sex with like a thousand people."

"You're exaggerating. No one's had sex with that many people."

"Basketball players."

"Daisy."

"He won't tell me the number. But from listening to his manager, it sounds like he's had a girl in every city he's ever worked in. I've only slept with three people, Nari." Like a small child, I held up my index, middle, and ring fingers for emphasis. "Three. Jeremy Hewitt, Brett Lynch, and Raphael. That's it.

"Do you really need his number? What's that going to tell you?

"Whether he's always going to be cruising for the next barely legal girl." I paused. "How do I know that I'll ever be enough for him?"

She considered that for a long time, looked like she was going to say something, then paused again. "Maybe you need to ask him that," Nari said, finally.

I didn't want to ask him that. Maybe the answer would be no. Then where would I be? After Nari left my apartment, I called Hugh. He was a big help. In only two hours, I had a business valuation and prospectus. Since I didn't have much inventory beyond licenses to use content and the content I created, it wasn't too hard. Before I could change my mind, I uploaded my sale sheet to a few webmaster sites. Raphael or not, maybe it was time to move on.

FORTY

RAPHAEL

I KNEW she was going to dump me. Daisy had asked me out on a bona fide date. This wasn't a date type girl. If I'd learned nothing over the last few months, I'd learned that. I looked in the mirror one last time, adjusting the collar of my white shirt, straightening my blazer. I paced to the living room then back to the bedroom.

Time for a change. If Daisy wanted me, then it was me she was going to get. Gone were the leather shoes and pressed pants. In their place I put on my comfortable jeans and my Vans. Gay as my father thought it might be, I carefully tied a scarf around my neck anyway. I waxed my hair the way I liked it. Staring back at me was the me I'd become. A me I liked.

A knock sounded at the door. Daisy? But she couldn't have gotten in the gate. Maybe it was Gabriel, or God forbid, Ted.

Daisy stood there, looking the most unsure I'd ever seen her. She was wearing some blue dress that skimmed perfectly along her body. The headband and conservative shoes were back.

"I'm sorry," she said.

"For what?" I backed away from the door so she could come in.

"You know what. Please don't make me say it." She stood awkwardly, leaning against the door, purse swinging by her knees. She dropped the bag to the floor then took off her shoes.

"Why do you take off your shoes every time you come to my house? I've seen you wear shoes at yours."

"Because I always take off my shoes when...I'm at an Asian person's home. Okay. That's why. Do you want me to put them on?"

I wasn't sure what was going on anymore. Was she there for a date? To apologize? To break up? This was her show, but she didn't look ready to come out on stage.

Took a deep breath, laid it out there. "I love you, Daisy. Can we try for a future together?" This was the second time I'd told her how I felt. What did she think of me? How did I convince her that I wasn't the same guy she'd met those long months ago?

Getting every women I could didn't hold appeal anymore. If Rose had injured that drive, Jude had killed it dead. I wanted only one woman in my bed night after night. The one who'd met my mother and charmed her. Who'd met my father and not been scared by him. Who'd accepted my brother and his husband without batting an eye. The woman who'd accepted me after my arrest for making a mistake with one girl, and who didn't blink an eye at the extortion from another.

She looked down, wiggled her toes. "I'm sorry for thinking I could do the shoot. I didn't want to sleep with anyone other than you."

"Why did you do it?"

"You seem to take sex so cavalierly. I thought I could too."

I pulled her close. My hand rested where her waist met the swell of her ass. With my other hand, I cupped her cheek. I ran my thumb along her plump bottom lip. "I take sex with you very seriously." She looked down. I titled her chin back up. "What do you need from me?"

"To know that you can be faithful. I can't be with someone who wants to be with someone else."

"I don't want to be with anyone else, Daisy. I love you and want to be with you. *You* only."

Without asking, I pulled the dress up over her head and from her arms. She shivered before me in white cotton bra and panties. Though everything was hidden from view, I could imagine the pucker of her nipples, the dark triangle of hair that concealed her sex.

"Raphael?" Her voice was a question.

I answered her with a kiss. She hesitated only a moment before her lips parted for mine. Our tongues mated in the same way I wanted our bodies to come together. I pulled her to me, her heated flesh warming mine. I hoped she wasn't hungry. We weren't going to make it to dinner.

I propelled us to the bedroom. Pushing her down on the bed, I snapped open her bra and eased down her panties. She lay naked before me like a feast. I sucked each nipple, pulling them into peaks in my mouth. They hardened. She moaned. Jesus. I wanted this today, tomorrow. Whenever we could. I couldn't imagine ever getting tired of this woman.

"Daisy. Come for me." I licked my way down her body. I tasted her below like I had her mouth not minutes ago. Both were hot, sweet, wet for me. I resisted the urge to rise up and plunge into her. I loved it when she came first.

The flush of her skin, hard nipples pointing toward the sky, belly rippling in pleasure, red tipped toenails curling, made me harder than I'd ever been. Teasing her with my tongue, I was relentless. I could feel her at the very edge. A sole index finger was the difference. Daisy came with a series of cries that nearly sent me over the edge.

I pulled open the bedside table, sheathed myself, and with a single nod from her, buried myself up to the root. We lay face to face and I watched her eyelids flutter open then shut. Long steadying breaths later, I moved. Daisy's breath quickened again with the friction. I fused our mouths, tickling her tongue with mine. A single finger pressed against her clit and she was clenching my penis. The pleasure was too much to bear and I drove into her without pause.

"Are you hungry?" she asked after I'd reluctantly separated from her.

"Yeah," I said, trying to stay awake for the dinner we were supposed to have.

"Can I tell you something?"

"Sure," I said.

"I love you too," she whispered into my ear.

It was the best news I'd gotten in years. But one niggle of doubt. In the same way she didn't want to compete with the women I'd sought out, I didn't want to continue to battle the demons on screen.

"I QUIT," I said to no one in particular. Elation and fear warred for supremacy. Selling Images of Harmony had been easier than I thought. I got four strong offers from serious buyers. Two of them wanted me to stay on and teach them the business. So I picked the guy who already had a thriving portfolio and was willing to put cash on the table.

I'd flown to meet with him in Minnesota. We could have done the deal through FedEx and lawyers, but I needed to sign my name on the dotted line in person.

When I'd first walked into the office, the buyer had thought I was the lawyer. It was probably the gray silk suit.

"You sell sex?" he said when I introduced myself. I looked at him, a middle aged white guy who could be a friend's dad, some girl's uncle—and probably was both.

"Not anymore," I said, gesturing to the documents spread out on the desk. Domain transfers, licensing agreements and a thick contract nestled among other papers.

"It's just that you don't look the type. You look like you come from money."

I ignored him and sat down. The whole thing took no more

than a half hour. I left the room three hundred thousand dollars richer. I cast one last glance at the buyer. I wanted to tell him, he didn't look like the type who had that kind of cash laying around, but there was no reason to be rude.

Once I was back in Los Angeles, shredding the decade of files and notes I had took a day. Organizing a decades' worth of tax documents, another. Purging my hard drive took a few hours. I sat in my clean workspace at loose ends. What in hell did people do with their time?

Nari shopped, but I wasn't interested in picking up that habit. I tapped my fingers on the newly polished wood. I had a good twelve hours before I left for work in the morning. I texted Raphael. He was there within the hour.

"What's up?" he asked casually as he strode in my door.

"I quit."

"What did you quit?" I could see him trying to tamp down hope.

"Images of Harmony. I signed the papers on Friday. I'm out of business."

"Congratulations?" he said, a question in his voice. "Are you happy?"

"I don't think I'm going to miss it." And I wouldn't miss looking at new content, with one eye closed in case it upset my carefully drawn boundaries. I wouldn't miss looking for ever younger girls doing even more adventurous things just to keep my numbers where they'd started. I surely wouldn't miss being the star of my own show. Mortification swept through me each time I thought about what I'd nearly done, even what Eunji had done.

"So why the long face?"

I threw up my empty hands. "I don't have any idea what I'm going to do with my free time."

Raphael pulled me into his arms, kissing me soundly. I

couldn't imagine ever getting tired of being in the arms of this man. He pulled me toward my bedroom.

"I think I might have a few ideas."

♥

THANK you for reading **TAMING THE BAD BOY**. I really loved writing about the crazy beautiful love between Daisy and Raphael.

READY FOR A TRILOGY that will take you on an emotional roller coaster ride? Check out **What Was Perfect**.

Like my mother, I belong to a billionaire.

Unlike my mother, I'd do anything to be free...

If you enjoyed this book, you should sign up for my regular newsletter Moore Confidential. Not only will I give you first dibs at new releases and preorders. You can also follow my own search for crazy beautiful love called **#50firstdates**. I'm keeping a journal of my quest for love just for newsletter subscribers.

Finally, if you haven't picked up my full-length freebie, **Her Secret Crush**, download it here.

It's the crazy beautiful love story of Sabrina and Henry. Oh and Spencer the dog. I wouldn't want you to forget that Sabrina's dog Spencer is the one who brings them together.

JOLIE MOORE IS the author of crazy beautiful love stories. You can find my online chronicle of #50firstdates at:
www.joliemoore.com
facebook.com/xojoliemoore
instagram.com/xojoliemoore

Have more crazy beautiful love delivered to your inbox:
ebooks.buzz/jolienews

ABOUT THE AUTHOR

I write crazy, beautiful love stories because I believe storytelling is magic. I love complicated heroines with secrets, strong heroes who fall hard, and a long winding road to happily ever after. When I'm not writing, I love to travel to witness the diverse tapestry of humanity, photograph the beauty of the world, visit museums, and watch live theater. I live in West Hollywood, California ten miles from the nearest airport.

♥

I haven't found my own happily ever after, but I'm not done trying. This year I'm going to go on fifty first dates. Join me as I try to find my Mr. Right or maybe Mr. Right Now. #50firstdates #joliemoore #crazybeautifullove

Sign up here to get weekly date updates as well as new release notifications.

joliemoore.com/50firstdates